A Pride & Prejudice Reimagining

# Hope & Hopelessness

Pride, Prejudice, & New Adventures
Volume VI

# NEY MITCH

*Hello all. As it often is my custom, the last book was left on quite the cliffhanger, and I hope the response will be to your satisfaction.*

*Once again, I am very thankful for those who made this book release possible and helped all my dreams come true. And no one will ever tell me that it is not about the reader. On the contrary, when it comes to the dedication, it will always be about you all, and how splendid you are for continuing.*

*Now you shall find out Georgiana's answer to Jason Whitfield. We begin this tale with her response.*

## ❧ I ❧
# THE ANSWER

I t is a hidden feeling, generally experienced by the recipient of whomever undergoes it, that when asking a question and not receiving an answer, one begins to worry—to fear.

And therefore, as Georgiana stood there, looking on Jason Whitfield after he just asked for her hand in marriage, every moment she did not respond stung.

The lot of us stood there in wonderment. It was certain that we knew Georgiana adored Jason, however it counted for little if she did not respond in the affirmative.

Looking around at the rest of those in our party, I only wondered at their internal thoughts and considerations.

I knew that Kitty would be wondering at Georgiana's hesitancy.

Colonel Fitzwilliam and my husband would be angry that Jason had proposed without getting their consent, for they were her legal guardians.

Henry and Lydia would look on it in curiosity and little more. Henry had very publicly spoken of his proposal to Jane; thus, he was no stranger to not-so-private matters when it came to an engagement.

Jane would be apprehensive as well at Jason's very public proposal, and very well could have been remembering her own past experiences.

And I...well, to be in earnest, I did not know what to feel.

Yet, at last, the silence broke, and Georgiana smiled.

"Of course, Jason. I love you without reserve, and I consent to being your wife."

෬෯ඹ

"You do?" he asked eagerly.

"Yes, of course I do," she said with a smile. "Oh Jason, I have been resolved to being bound to you for so long now, how could you have ever doubted it?"

"I just... I cannot believe I found you!" He turned to Darcy and Colonel Fitzwilliam, his expression resolute. "I do not ask for your forgiveness, future brother and cousin, for it is not your happiness that I consider in this case."

Jason closed the space between him and Georgiana and kissed her passionately.

"Oh, dear lord, I am going to be sick," Mr. Darcy moaned under his breath.

"Fitzwilliam," I hissed, "be quiet."

"She's my little sister. Have you not the slightest idea how repulsive this is to me?"

"And I said quiet yourself. Do not make me count to three."

"You wouldn't..."

"One. Two. Three."

"Oh, very well."

All became quiet as we all left them alone in the yard and entered the house. It was prohibited to give them any privacy, yet the rules felt as if they were of little consequence and while the rest went to the sitting room, Darcy and I watched the newly engaged couple from the glass of the windows.

"I suppose I should be happy," Darcy said with a sigh.

"Of course, you should be," I replied archly. "Are you not?"

"I cannot be truly. You know what I have confessed. A part of me did deeply desire to have her just be with us at Pemberley for the rest of our days, with nothing changing—you know I hate change—even though it be a natural thing."

"No one likes change, even if it is for the better sometimes. It is in our nature to easily allow ourselves to get stuck in our ways."

He nodded. "And I do. It should have been us at Pemberley, along with Jane teaching students in our east wing, and Georgiana looking after the tenants and our sons having two of their aunts under the same roof as their mother. Three mothers they could have had, and who would want more?"

The mention of our twins brought an ache to my heart. How I missed them! And how easy I thought it would be to leave them. I was a fool. "You wanted our sons to be spoiled?"

"I wanted them to never feel as if they are alone. And I always have and always will want family near me—as long as it is the good kind. However, every time a sister of yours comes to visit, I feel as if that is when another chooses to leave us. Will it ever stop?"

"Jane shall remain, I promise," I said, brushing my lips across his knuckles.

"Then that is comfort enough. I have lost one sister now, and I do not wish to lose the in-law one any time soon."

"You are such a contradiction, Fitzwilliam. For one who does not often possess the talent of conversing easily with strangers or making new friends, you are so bound by loyalty to those to whom become close."

He smiled down at me. "It is not so strange. I simply am different and therefore believe it easiest for me to keep my friends close and my enemies far away from me."

I chuckled gently, then looked out the window at Jason as he lifted Georgiana up and spun her around.

"She looks happy, though."

"She is," I confirmed. "Be happy for her, my love. Georgiana has found not only a love, yet she has also found herself along the way."

Upon our friends' return from town, Mr. Bingley, Miriam, and Caroline Bingley entered and we immediately availed them with the news. Miriam was overjoyed, Mr. Bingley was highly amused, and Caroline Bingley attempted a smile to hide her disgust.

However, disgusted, she clearly was.

Though coming from a good family, Mr. Whitfield was still a man of a profession from a long line of men who had professions, and though the occupation of an attorney was respectable enough, it still was not fully respectable enough for her tastes. It was apparent that she believed it below Georgiana to have engaged herself to a man who was anything less than a gentleman of no profession. And the addition that Jason was not only a civil servant, but also a street preacher and the younger son whose brother inherited the Whitfield Estate and lion-share of the wealth also did not escape her notice and keen observation. Thus, it could be said that she could not detach the man from the myth of what he should have been, and therefore thought him too far below our notice. As a result, she did not see that he was still on our level.

And yet, as I every now and again spied her as we all sat there and listened to the happy couple express their joy, I believed that it was more than that. She may have been a very judgmental and offensive woman sometimes, yet she was never a stupid one. She had to have noticed that in every other circumstance, we were all finding ourselves, whereas she went from day to day still not knowing who she was and therefore filling herself with the words and standards of others. She was a woman who appeared happy and yet was not so. Therefore, it left me to conclude that another part of her might be jealous.

Jealous that Georgiana was the one who came to New York and found love and purpose as well.

Jealous that Lydia had come to Philadelphia and won Mr. Henry Darcy, when he was Caroline's second plan after her first one failed.

Jealous of Jane for being at Pemberley indefinitely and always in the company of high society who must admire her for her benevolence.

Jealous of me for stealing her dream—even though it was never hers to have.

Maybe it was not only spite that ruled Caroline Bingley's life, but envy.

Therefore, as the evening wore on, Caroline offered her congratulations, yet had grown quieter as the night progressed, allowing everyone else to speak without her interruptions.

Yet I was not blind to it.

Georgiana's happiness ate away at her self-assurance and pride. Although both were two traits that I was not sure Caroline Bingley ever earned the right to have.

❦

"If I may," Jason said as his carriage rolled up to the house, "might I come tomorrow and join your company for the day?"

"I have no choice of course," Henry Darcy said, "for if my honeymoon was meant to bring out the joy in another quarter, then who am I to get in the way of it?"

"Then I thank you, Mr. Darcy, for allowing me the right to fall in love with your cousin while you and Mrs. Darcy here are on your honeymoon...and thank you as well, for letting me propose to her!"

We all laughed at that, then Georgiana and Jason held hands briefly before he entered his carriage and it rolled down the lane and onto the road.

"I am getting married," Georgiana said, turning to us. "It is just...yes, I knew it, yet now that I say it to myself, only now does it feel real." Georgiana then turned to Jane. "I did not even think that I would marry. I began to just wish to be like you—content with my purpose and no more."

"Oh, dear Georgiana," Jane said with a sigh.

"And yet now I have another...now I..." Georgiana's arms began to shake, and then she fell on the ground, holding herself. All the women in our company rushed to her to help her up as she laughed giddily, excited beyond words.

She stopped laughing to say, "He actually was worried that I would say no? The fool! What would possess him to believe that I would deny him? What could he have thought otherwise? He said that he practically fainted when I gave him my answer. For it was the most important answer he would ever receive. Yes...the most important answer that I have ever given. The most important."

## 2

# ONE BENNET ON THE SIDE OF AMERICA AND THE REST ON THE ENGLISH

The next day came, and it was the beginning of our preparations to depart. Mrs. Hale spent much time going to and fro', making sure much of our items were packed away. When Jason arrived, before he would spend most of his time with Georgiana in Arruin's gardens, Mr. Darcy decided that was the best and only time to inform him of our soon departure back for England.

"I feel badly for leaving Lydia and Henry Darcy alone like this to travel back to Philadelphia without us," I said as I began to give Lucy orders of what she should pack first.

"You need not worry," Mr. Darcy said as he sat in the rocking chair in the corner. "When we all finally leave, they shall have a week here by themselves, which I am certain they are looking forward to. Let us be true to ourselves, my dear, we have quite intruded on their honeymoon enough. And they shall not travel to Philadelphia alone. Samantha and Mr. Eastbourne are planning on traveling with them as well, so that they may see their family again at Canterbury."

"Oh, Canterbury!" I exclaimed. "We shall not see Cousin Thomas or Emilia for years now. I shall miss them. And their other children as well."

"Yes, so will I," he added. "Yes, I daresay that they have quite grown on me."

"As they would. Yet what of Jason? Did you tell him everything?"

"I did indeed, and it is no trouble to him whatsoever."

"Fitzwilliam, dear, you must expand on what you mean."

"Oh, sorry. Georgiana had made him aware of our departure day a fortnight before now at the very least. This has given him time enough. He did not own a house but rented lodgings from a landlord in the heart of the city. Jason informed the landlord that he would no longer rent in a few weeks' time. He can pack away his things swiftly and has already made plans to book passage with us."

"So, he is going back to England with us?"

"Yes, he is. In hopes of being by Georgiana all the while, rather than allowing them to be separated for weeks."

"That could not have been better planned."

"Indeed, it could not. I must confess myself excited with how convenient it all has come about, with no strain on us at all. Peace is something I ask for much yet receive all too little."

"Oh, cease complaining," I said, teasingly. "Our conflicts always lead to good and fruitful ends."

"I just wish there were others in our circle to fight them sometimes."

"You and me both, my dear."

"Oh, and I sent word to Pemberley and Mrs. Reynolds, at special request of Mr. Bingley."

"What could he need from Pemberley?"

"I would like her to send out inquiries if there are any estates in the counties of Kent that are on the market and available for purchase. Bingley's time here in America with us has influenced him to quite make up his mind about giving up Aginfield."

"Oh, really?" I gasped. "He is really planning to do it."

"Yes, and he has already sent out notifications and posts in the newspapers that he wishes to release it. When he returns to London, he is hoping to have been met with a favorable offer."

"Then Mr. Bingley and Miriam will be close to us!"

"Yes, they will."

"That will be wonderful, as long as Miss Bingley decides to often spend time with her sister Mrs. Hurst instead."

"One can only hope. However, I still wonder why she even requested to come to New York with us. There was no happiness for her here. What could she have meant by it?"

"Oh," I replied lightly, "she was hoping to make one of you fall in love with her."

"What?"

"Yes," I said evenly, "she was hoping that one of you would fall in love with her and take her on as a mistress."

۞

"Lizzy, you cannot be serious," Darcy answered, frowning.

"Well, I have no real proof that she wanted to be your mistress, yet I would not be surprised if so. For what else would be her desirable outcome for all her intentions? Yes, the Hursts had to away, yet she still could have returned to England and done any number of things. Oh, indeed I am quite serious on the matter. I watched her every now and again, my dear. It was quite clear that she stayed to make you in some way regret choosing me over her, or to make Henry Darcy regret Lydia. I believe she might have even felt satisfaction of making Colonel Fitzwilliam drawn in by her."

"You think so?"

"Yes, call it vanity or pride, but to have seduced one of you would really have put a feather in her turban. Good lord, why does she wear those turbans? They look hideous."

"Why does any woman wear those turbans? They always look hideous."

"Fair point."

"And again, I could be in error on this subject, for I once believed myself to always see matters clearly, yet now I see that was hubris on my side. However, I do not believe so. She would look on you all with a desire to please you, charm you and therefore what could it all result in? Either she came to at least entice you and obtain an emotional victory, or to have one of you fall in love with her despite that you were unavailable, thus gaining a physical one."

"She would go so far as to come for that?"

"My dear, I wish I did not see it as so, yet that is what it was."

"How revolting."

"I could not agree more."

⚜

The brief number of days before our leaving went quickly, and once more, we found ourselves traveling to the port with Jane, Kitty, Georgiana, Miriam, Caroline, Mr. Bingley, Colonel Fitzwilliam, and Jason making our departure, and Mr. and Mrs. Henry Darcy, along with Samantha and Mr. Eastbourne along the way.

Our ship was called The Olivia, and while we stood in the crowd, our bags were next to us.

Their laments at seeing us leave were most heartfelt, especially since our family was now split down the half because it was no longer something that we could easily maintain. Yet the hardest of all appeared to be Lydia who would remain in America while we went back home.

"I was happy to see you adjust so well to living here, Lydia," I said, complimenting her. "And, you are content now, and that is wonderful."

"I know, it is more in my habit than anything else. Yet I am still surprised by it. However, I do not know when we shall leave, yet I shall find happiness in being in Philadelphia. Cousin Thomas and Emilia will do everything in their power to make sure that I do."

"'Tis all too true."

"And it is an amazing thing. If someone were to tell me that a time would come when a nation would separate me from my family, then I would say that it was a good joke. Yet now I live it. Now I am here. And it is all so strange. For there will be one Bennet girl on the side of America and the rest on the side of the English. And that one sister shall be me."

"Don't worry, no matter where you live, you shall always be a Bennet of Longbourn. Though it is a puzzlement that for the present, we are on two opposing sides."

The sounding of the ship went off, we all boarded, and like many of

9

the other occupants on the Olivia, we waved goodbye to those who had come to see us off. In the crowd, it was very easy to see Samantha, Mr. Eastbourne, Henry, and Lydia again. We waved to each other as the ship's anchor was raised and began to sail off down the river.

# 3

## HOME SWEET HOME

As the Olivia sailed on, Lydia and Henry Darcy grew smaller in the distance and were just two dots in a multitude of faces.

When I looked beside me, Kitty was by my shoulder, and she was crying.

"It is frightening."

"Why so?"

"Because now we are not only separated by an ocean, but also by a conflict. I am afraid that we shall never see her again."

I moved behind Kitty and hugged her around the waist, resting my chin on her shoulder.

"We may yet, Kitty. We may see them yet again."

"I hope so. For it would be quite tragic if the road of us five would end here."

"Oh Kitty, do not fear...this is a road that will never end."

The Olivia sailed so far that now we no longer saw the port of New York City, and we were far away from Lydia and Henry Darcy—and them from us.

But on a happier note, we were on our way home...to see our boys.

After we ate supper on the vessel, Fitzwilliam and I went onto the deck, and though it was extremely cold, we looked up at the stars.

"Do they ever make you feel small, Elizabeth?" Darcy began. "The stars, I refer to."

"Not them only," I confessed, "yet also the moon as well. Sometimes I wished that I could reach out and touch it. Just like that," I said, raising out my arm, and acting as if I was closing my hand over the moon. "Yes, when I was a child, I did sometimes wish that there was magic and that I could capture the moon in the palm of my hand."

"Why not the sun?"

"I do not know. Yet the sun seemed less romantic of a notion."

Sitting on the bench, I rested my head on his shoulder.

"You are so much taller than I am, Fitzwilliam."

"All the more reason it makes it easier for me to put you on my lap so easily. Quite a convenience."

I looked up at him and saw that his brow was furrowed.

"What do you think of now?" I asked.

"Of our sons."

"They are always in my thoughts. I often wonder how I let myself leave them."

"I know, and sometimes you never cease talking about it."

I nudged his shoulder. "Oh, quiet you."

"It is merely a fact. I just...you were right."

"Was I?"

"Though I would have loved to have had the memory of celebrating our first Christmas with them, we have given them so much more in this way."

"Yes, for now you return, and you are a hero. And one day, we shall let them know it."

"I am no more a hero than you."

"Then we both can hold to some form of courage. And courage is as much learned as it is naturally possessed. If we are to be so lucky to possess it, then we can teach them to."

"Ah, courage!"

"Yes, that trait that every Darcy male shall have. Yet Fitzwilliam, I must warn you."

"Warn me? Against what?"

"This is not a negative that I offer, but merely an observation."

"And what do you speak of?"

"I speak of Georgiana. Fitzwilliam, part of the reason that she fell in love with Jason is because they were frank with each other and shared many of the same social awareness. He has a cause, and she has found one, and he has encouraged her to have one. In other words, when we return to England, you must prepare for the fact that Georgiana may wish to get involved with female committees and begin to help campaign for women's involvement in politics."

He glanced at her. "You believe so?"

"Of course, she shall. How could you not think it after her actions in New York?"

"I thought it was her love for Jason that fueled her social commentary. And once she married, her passion would be drawn there as opposed to elsewhere."

"It might, yet I find it more likely that they both shall partake in political endeavors together. Jason did not listen to her just to indulge her; he did it because he cared. He did it because he supported her. I am just warning you that when we return, Georgiana will not be the same. And only time will show us the extent."

"Well, we shall have time," he responded. "For once we return to London, not only will we retrieve William and Caiden, yet we shall also meet the Whitfield family, who still is not aware of their own family member's good fortune, as of yet. And we shall also have to get to know them."

"And all the etcetera, etcetera and so forth."

"Pardon?"

"I mean that whenever we go to London, sometimes something else always manages to come upon us while we are there. I confess to being at that stage of life where very little would surprise me."

"You predict being met with rocky shores upon our return?"

"I simply predict being met with what we are always being met with, which is the unexpected."

"I hope, for our sakes, that peace will last a little longer this time."

"I do not know, Fitzwilliam, for with only peace, what chance is there to be more to our story?"

"We have a story to our lives now?" He smiled, kissing my hand.

"Oh, my dear, everyone has a story. Some are simply more compelling than others. And some have the intelligence to write it all down. However, before I choose to put pen to paper, I must ask for clarification. When we first met, why did you tell me that Wickham tried to elope with Georgiana after your father died? For now, that I recall, Mrs. Reynolds told me something different when she told me the truth about her nephew."

"Oh, forgive me, my love, you must understand that I had only just become acquainted with you at the time. I did not want you to know all of that had occurred during my father's life and of the connection Mrs. Reynolds had to everything. It was not my secret to tell."

"Oh, I see, you were keeping your promise to her."

"Precisely. And then, when she told you herself, I knew that she was ready."

"Your devotion runs deep."

"But from now on I shall be honest and never conceal anything."

"I am not mad, Fitzwilliam. Now I simply know which explanation to write down."

❧

As we journeyed on, we acknowledged that it would be wise to go to Longbourn after we remained in London, for it was my parents' right to see their grandsons. Though they were not related to Georgiana by blood, it would do well for them to meet Jason Whitfield.

Yet the rest of our adventure on the Olivia was met with boredom and no events of any kind, really. There was one night where there was a heavy storm and we worried, yet never was the ship in any danger as a result, therefore never was there an ultimate threat.

Also, at that point Jane and Miriam had completely got their sea legs and never suffered from seasickness evermore.

Therefore, our sea voyage felt like an intermission from any woes or cares that the outside world enforced on one. To be out on the open sea, with nothing but water around you can be daunting, yes, but also liberating. The world is far away from you, and one can merely enjoy the company without caring for decorum or impressing the ton. I found peace on the Olivia, as did the rest of us.

Yet all good things inevitably arrive at their natural conclusion, and sooner than I had anticipated, we were sailing up the Thames and arrived at London.

The Olivia made berth, the anchor was lowered, the walkway descended, and we all were commanded to walk on to land. When we did so, the solid ground beneath my feet was reassuring, yet it felt strange for reasons I did not understand. It would take me a series of minutes, yet I would learn that it was because we had reached the end of our journey, and I was ambivalent about our adventure ending. I could only assume that I had been undergoing them so often that I had forgotten how it felt to not have one.

Even if I were always on the move, but going nowhere very fast, I would still welcome the activity. However, then I reminded myself that our destination was retrieving our sons and since motherhood is a never-ending adventure, I allowed one to substitute the other very easily in my mind.

As our luggage was being unloaded, I secretly took Darcy's hand in my own.

"What are you feeling, my love?"

"I feel as if it was only yesterday that we left, yet also a lifetime ago"

"As do I."

However, as was his way, Mr. Bingley came forward, looked out at London, and smiled broadly.

"Well, here we are once more. Home sweet home."

## ❧ 4 ❧

# THE EVOLUTION OF MR. DARCY'S CHARACTER

J efferson arranged for our transport, and this was the first time that Jason and Georgiana departed.

"I must away to Downing Street," he said, calling for another carriage.

"But why?" Georgiana asked, worried.

"For that is where my family's townhouse is. I must go there so that we may make preparations to meet as soon as may be."

"Oh, that does make some sense."

"Only some sense, my dear?" He smiled at her mischievously. "If I did not know any better, I would say that you are overly protective of me."

"I am."

"Good. Continue to be so." He embraced her hand but dared not kiss her cheek before he was off to another part of London affluent life.

"I do not like being away from him just now," Georgiana confessed to Jane. "No, I do not like it one bit."

"Oh, you shall see him soon."

"I know. Yet I still feel irrationally inclined to worry for nothing."

"Then revel in it, for that is what it means to be truly in love."

"Love hurts then."

"Oh," Jane answered with a chuckle, "indeed it does."

※

The Bingleys parted with eager promises to partake in dinner parties or nights out at the theater with us. It was implied that upon their return, Caroline would immediately return to staying with her sister Louisa and her husband, Mr. Hurst. For the good of all, I would say. And though I must confess to sounding cold-hearted in my speech, I will allow myself to be ridiculed and criticized for my callousness of temper in this regard. Caroline Bingley was the sort of woman who needed someone to give her a proper set down. However, I believed no one had the nerve to do so.

Yet one thing was true: Caroline Bingley was the sort of woman who in some way had harmed all around her, whether it was through her words or her intentions. Her crimes were not those of the physical realm of the offensive, yet sometimes words hurt her fellow women worse. Out of all in the company, all wished that justice would be done upon her, and we wished to be the one to do so. Yet therein was the irony; honesty is often said to be the best policy. Yet there is a fine line between the quest for honesty remaining so, and the quest for honesty becoming a quest for vengeance. We all start out being frank to rectify an injustice, yet eventually it continues to be so, and we then always rail against people: all under the name of veracity.

That was the reason I assumed that very few people oppose those who are bullies. For if you stand up, not only does it cost a great deal of courage, but it also requires a person to run the risk of becoming the sort who always opposes those they disagree with because they cannot determine when it is best to speak up or when it is best to remain quiet. Passivity therefore is not the product of indifference always, but the product of indecision.

※

As anxious as I was to see my babies, I had a message from my Aunt Gardiner, asking that we delay our arrival for a bit, something to do with schedules. With our company now split fully, Mr. Bingley and Miriam left for their townhouse and Jane, Kitty, Colonel Fitzwilliam, Georgiana,

Darcy, and I traveled to Grosvenor Street. Darcy's townhouse was a comfort to see, for now we were home—or very near to it. For Grosvenor would always be second in our eyes and hearts, while Pemberley would always be the first.

After our arrival, I wanted to run through the halls, shouting with glee and mirth, for we were returned to our domicile, and it was the first signs that our lives would continue on—always continue on in hopefully a continuous and rhythmic fashion and there would be a sameness. A chance for steadiness to take hold and become a part of our routine. Yet we were still not full in number.

When alone with Darcy after we were met by our servants and saw to the meal that would be prepared for dinner, I looked to him and nodded.

"We are not complete. Prepare the carriage immediately, for it is time that we brought our sons back home."

✺

Once we arrived at Gracechurch Street in Cheapside, we did not even have time to ring the bell, for the door opened and our Aunt Gardiner emerged with her oldest daughters, Isabella, and Harriet. Harriet was the oldest at eighteen years old while Isabella followed her at seventeen. However, both had a similarity of beauty that also was different. Harriet was a little taller and had a more handsome form and face, yet Isabella was shorter, rounder, and her figure was nothing short of womanly. Her plumper figure was actually very well proportioned, and it therefore made her more pleasing on the eye, as well as her face. While Harriet was the lovelier one objectively, Isabella was the true beauty, for there was a marked difference to her features that could not be described, but only felt, even though most would disagree with me.

"We could see you from the window!" Isabella cried. "We were waiting for someone else, yet you have arrived first."

"Who were you waiting for?" I asked, happy at their eagerness.

"We shall tell you in a moment," Harriet said, "yet first thing is first."

"We must all greet you properly," Aunt Gardiner uttered. "Elizabeth,

Mr. Darcy, and Jane, you have returned safely from your journey, and we are so glad!"

"Thank you, Aunt Gardiner," Darcy said. "It is nice to be back in England and nice to see you again as well."

"And a delight to see you."

"Kitty, Miss Darcy and the Colonel wished to come as well," Jane said, kissing Aunt Gardiner on the cheek. "Yet we needed room in the carriage for little William and Caiden."

"And how are my sons?" I asked eagerly.

"You need not worry," Isabella said, "we did not cook and eat them. Though I cannot deny that we have fattened them up to possibly be ripe for a Christmas Feast."

"Your comedy has turned cannibal, Issy." I smiled at her choice of words.

"You know me, Elizabeth. I have always chosen the worst joke in the world and called them the most tasteful."

"Oh," I said, turning to Fitzwilliam, "forgive me, Fitzwilliam, you have not met my cousins here. They were always away elsewhere when you visited."

"Oh, really?" Aunt Gardiner realized. "I can scarce believe it, yet you are correct. My goodness Mr. Darcy, you haven't met my two oldest daughters. These are my treasures Harriet and Isabella Gardiner."

"Though when you grow comfortable," Isabella added, "you shall see that I mostly go by Issy. And the 'ss' part is pronounced like a 'z'. Issy."

"That is a rare nickname."

"Yes, I have always enjoyed it for some strange reason, and not any other name that could come of it."

"Either way, ladies," Darcy said, bowing, "it is a great pleasure to make your acquaintance, and while I wish it were sooner, I trust that you will hopefully forgive my taciturn ways." Darcy leaned in and lowered his voice fetchingly. "I can be quite the bear to meet upon first introductions."

"As long as you are not a bear itself," Isabella said, "I can survive anything you thrust upon me."

"I see that you and my wife both believe in having the same sort of wit."

"Where do you think I learned it from?" Isabella grinned, looking at me.

"It is nice to see that my personality was good for something," I remarked.

"And I must say," Jane added, "that you both seem to have blossomed overnight into two very handsome young ladies. I am not used to looking at you two as young women, but you are so."

"Thank you," Harriet said. "Yet we shall never become as lovely as you, for it has seemed impossible for the rest of us."

"Do not think of me now," Jane whispered. "Let me look upon my nephews."

"I second that notion," Darcy said.

"Of course, come inside, you three, and I hope you shall see your uncle when he returns. He remains at the factory, at present, and he shall not return for another hour's time."

"Well," Darcy said as we entered the home, "even if not so, it should not be a tragedy, for we shall remain in London for over a fortnight and would like to have you over for dinner a couple of times."

"Oh, of course we would like to join you," Isabella cried. "Oh, sorry Mother."

"Issy, you must cease to anticipate me," Aunt Gardiner said with a smile.

"Yes, I do make that a habit." She turned to Fitzwilliam by way of explanation. "There is something very much wrong with me, Mr. Darcy."

"Is there?"

"Yes, I have this habit of my mind moving so quickly that I sometimes finish people's sentences before they even do so. Or I say what they shall say before they even say it. I wish that I did not have that flaw, but I have it nonetheless."

"There are worse flaws, such as my own. And I have nothing like your excuse in having them, Miss Isabella."

"What my husband means, Issy," I said, "is that you are not forsaken, for our families are stricken with these habits. So never fear, and only laugh."

"And, so, I may run mad as often as I choose, but I refuse to faint."

"Oh, so you still run mad?" I asked lightly.

"Of course, I do, Lizzy. Every Sunday after church, I run like the wind."

Darcy burst out laughing, and then quieted himself.

"I made him roll his head and laugh without shame," Isabella said, clapping her hands. "I believe this must be some form of accomplishment."

"It is," Darcy said, "and it is rare. Enjoy it while you may."

When we entered the sitting room, Aunt Gardiner ordered Isabella and Harriet to bring in Caiden and William. As they were leaving, I leaned into my 'taciturn husband'.

"You are being particularly charming today," I whispered.

"I know. I'm really coming into my own now."

"Is that what is happening? The evolution of Mr. Darcy's character. Yes, I dare say that will be a marvel to watch."

"And drudgery as well," he replied, smiling. "For you know me, Lizzy, whatever move I make, it is as slow and methodical as a tortoise. Therefore, watching me evolve shall be like watching a flower grow. You will barely notice the progression until it has reached its pinnacle and blooms in full."

"You are too hard upon yourself."

"Am I?"

"Yes," I smiled fetchingly at him. "Very much so."

◈❧◈

Shortly Isabella and Harriet returned, each one carrying one of our sons in their arms. I bought my hand to my heart, for my delight was so great I thought it might burst from my chest. The love I had for my babies welled up inside me like an overflowing fountain.

"They are as lovely as I remembered them."

"And as loud probably," Harriet exclaimed. "Well, that is not fully fair, for William is as quiet as a mouse often, but Caiden, well, he loves to talk."

"He's talking already?" Darcy replied, startled.

"Oh, no," Aunt Gardiner said. "Words do not form yet. When one says a baby speaks, it means they move their mouths and try to make sounds often. They want to talk, but do not know how yet."

"And Caiden has become the talker?" I asked giddily, taking him in my arms. "That he must get from me. Oh, hello Caiden, it's me, your mumsies."

Harriet held William and she looked at my husband with uncertainty, not knowing if he was the sort to like holding his children or not.

"Oh, do not fear," I spoke for him, "Fitzwilliam is affectionate with infants."

"Yes, I am," he confirmed. Harriet acquiesced and handed over William.

"If I am not mistaken," Darcy said, taking William into his arms while still looking at Harriet. "You favor William, don't you?"

"I cannot help it. He smiles the best."

"Oh, did you hear that, William?" Darcy said to our son, looking down at him with affection. "You have the best smile and are the quiet one. Suffice it to say, you have much going for you in nature as well as nurture and you are Miss Gardiner's favorite!"

"I believe," I said, looking down at Caiden, "that you shall have many fine qualities of your own, won't you?" I placed my finger on his tiny hand, and he wrapped his stubby fingers around it. He laughed boldly, his small face growing wider. Then, as we were informed of, he began to talk! The ramblings of being brought into the world and trying to reach out to it, understand it and want to communicate that it knew it was alive. Caiden wanted me to know something, and I in turn wanted him to know that I was his mother. Only then did I regret all the time we spent away from home, for did he know me? Did he remember me? The bond I tried to forge between us had been severed for a time, and I no longer wished it to be. For a moment, I despised myself, for what mother would leave her children for four months? Especially when they were infants?

Then I turned my gaze to Darcy and my heart lifted. I do not believe that he knew how his face looked. He smiled down at William with immense satisfaction and paternal affection. When I looked on them, I felt as if he was moving in slow motion, for watching him seemed to be the perfect dream. Then he raised William up over his head so that William could look down on his father's face. His eyes widened as little William stretched out his little arms and ran them over Darcy's features. When William grabbed his father's nose, my husband laughed and then turned to me, his eyes bright with amazement.

"He remembers me. He remembers his father."

All in good time, I easily saw that my self-loathing as a parent had been ill-founded and had abated most readily. We were away, tis true, yet we left our boys in the care of the best of families: the Gardiners. And our leaving was not abandonment but simply our migration from one family to the other. My sister was getting married, and while we could not be there for Lydia when she made her first marriage, we could be there for her second one.

Now we were home, and now we would remain, keeping William and Caiden close to us for as long as ever. And we had brought stories of heroism in our wake, giving them something to admire in their parents. If we had left sooner, then we would not have been model guardians that they deserved. Therefore, how could we ever have believed ourselves the right sort of parents if we did not show our children how sometimes sacrifice must be required for the good of all? It had been often said that a person follows their parents' actions over their words, and as a result, our words of love would have meant nothing if we did not display our conviction through our behavior.

I looked back down at Caiden as he continued to talk to me and wondered at him. He was beautiful; a marvel to behold. And I would do everything to let him know that I saw that within him.

"Oh!" Aunt Gardiner announced. "And you shall be happy to know that they are crawling now."

"What?" I gasped.

"Yes, they can crawl. Would you like to see?"

"You must lie on the ground like this," Isabella said, lying down on the carpet. "Lizzy and Jane, do it with me."

At that point, the rest of the Gardiner children had entered from an outing in the park with their nanny and they joined us for my sons' spectacle.

I gave Caiden to Aunt Gardiner as we lay down beside Issy on the floor of the sitting room.

"Oh, do not mind us, Mr. Darcy," Aunt Gardiner said, "this is just the beauty of being around only family."

"There is nothing wild or improper in it," Darcy assured her. "Believe me, I regard it as quite the opposite."

"Brilliant," Harriet cried, taking the baby from him. "Because this will be a wonderful sight for you to witness." Next Aunt Gardiner and Harriet placed Caiden and William down on the floor on their stomachs. Then they came to the other side of the room and lay down beside us.

"Now tell them to come forward to us, everyone," Aunt Gardiner instructed, "and also Elizabeth and Jane, gesture for him to come forward to you in particular. And Mr. Darcy just stand back and watch."

Together we all told William and Caiden to come to us. At first, they lay there and did nothing, and then slowly they began to place their tiny hands on the ground, raised themselves up and began to crawl towards us with surprising speed. William began to laugh, and Caiden tried to talk all while he made his way to us.

Eventually they reached us. Yet to my internal disquiet, it hurt me that William and Caiden reached just as much to the Gardiners as well as Jane and me. Yes, I was very much heartbroken over the matter, although I knew it was my heart talking, not my head.

When they reached us and we embraced them, I turned and looked up at Mr. Darcy.

"Well, my love," I said archly, hiding my inner guilt and dismay, "what say you to that?"

Darcy's lips turned into a fine line, and he began to clap.

"Wonderful. It felt as if that was a miracle to see."

Upon our departure, we invited the Gardiners to our dinner at Grosvenor Square the next evening, extending it to Isabella and Harriet as well. Aunt Gardiner spoke in our uncle's absence, stating that they would all love to join us, and the plans were then set.

On the way home, I held William while Jane held Caiden, who took great delight in playing with her hair all the way back.

At first William cried when I had taken him, and I worried that he did not like me. Yet Aunt Gardiner assured me that he always cried when someone first took him, and soon he would settle down. The noise at first clearly annoyed Darcy, yet he bore it stoically. William quieted down soon upon our journey and began to fall into a beautiful slumber. After I looked up from his sleeping form, amazed by him, I looked on Jane as she held Caiden.

"Harriet was correct. He is a lively one. I hope it will not change. Too many children grow up and lose their spark."

"Very true," I agreed.

"You may not remember, but that was the way with me." Jane smiled sweetly, then turned to Darcy. "Mr. Darcy, tales of my serenity are recent and have been greatly exaggerated. When I was a child, I loved to run wild, jump high and hated attending to my studies."

"Really?" He smiled, surprised.

"Oh, very much so. Why do you think I can neither sing, play the pianoforte, nor paint tables? Yes, in truth my nature was not of the studious sort that would commit or aspire to true excellence. It is fitting and honest of me to admit that I was one of the notorious few who were perfectly content to be mediocre in life."

"You are not mediocre, Jane," I said.

"Oh yes I am. And I am very happy with myself, interestingly enough. For I know what I am. And yet now, I am a little worried." Jane looked down at Caiden as he pulled at her curls. "And it is a funny thing. I am worried that he will not like me. Isn't that odd? I assist in helping children learn, I teach often, and I am never nervous or worried there. Yet I am apprehensive now. I am terrified that my nephew will not like me."

"Jane," Mr. Darcy said, "I am certain that he shall think you the very best of aunts."

Jane smiled.

"If so, then that will be the best of comforts."

I turned to Mr. Darcy and looked at him in wonder.

"Has fatherhood changed you so very greatly? For you were always a good man, yet now you are the best of them it seems."

"Many things have led to an alteration of my nature which I cannot deny were hard to experience, yet all for the better. I was not always as I am now, and I wish that I had been. Oh, Lizzy, I am comfortable in my own skin now!" he exclaimed with glee, to which Jane and I laughed at this.

"And sadly enough, it feels as if it only took a lifetime for me to arrive at this place."

"The evolution of Mr. Darcy's character," I said. "You were wrong, Fitzwilliam. It is not as slow as you think. I daresay it was faster than most."

## 5

# THERE IS A THIN LINE BETWEEN FORESHADOW & PREDICTIONS

After we returned, Caiden and William were taken to the nursery, and I followed. While Lucy prepared everything for them, I sat with William still in my arms and I placed Caiden in the crib and rocked him with my foot. The reason that I held William was to overcome my growing fear that I might favor Caiden in the end, because I liked how he was born with the instinct to be heard. Therefore, I figured that if I displayed affection with William, I would be able to conquer this natural preference due to my own will. My mother originally had favorites, as well as my father, and while such a preference could offer comfort to the object of their affection, it also left the rest to feel slighted and greatly forgotten. I had suffered the efforts of it yes, however Mary's situation had been the worst. Never did I want either of my boys to suffer under such a fate.

Darcy came in and sat with me while Kitty, Georgiana and the Colonel entered to behold our fine boys. Yet eventually they all left one by one to tend to other matters, and I was left alone to feed them. With Lucy's help, they both took to their feeding quickly and eagerly.

"How did the boys do with the wet nurse we hired before we left?" I asked her, still feeling a bit of betrayal at leaving them at all.

"They both gained weight rapidly." Quickly she added, "You look well thus, Mrs. Darcy."

"Thank you for the compliment, Lucy. I still am amazed by my luck."

"Luck?"

I smiled and nodded. "Two healthy boys on the first attempt. Not only is it a miracle to have produced two male heirs, yet for them to be so strong. Many a time have babies not survived long past infancy and yet they both have done so. Is it the Darcy strength, do you think?"

"Perhaps it is the Bennet strength instead."

I turned to Lucy and chuckled.

"Well played, Lucy."

"Thank you. I have my moments."

We were startled when the door opened, yet there was no need for alarm, for it had only turned out to be Jane.

"I was told you and Lucy were in here alone."

"Come to see your nephews so soon again?"

"Of course, I have, yet I also wished to speak with you."

"Oh, well then..." I brought William to my shoulder where he emitted a healthy burp, and Lucy did the same with his brother whereupon Jane took him and held him close.

After Lucy left, Jane continued to study Caiden.

"He is your favorite, is he not? I could tell."

"A mother should not even be having favorites."

"You are right, they should not, however it is wise to admit this to yourself now so that you can overcome it and not let it weigh you down."

"You think so?"

"Yes, very much so."

Jane continued to hold him as he played with her hair.

"I think he might have my eyes."

I glanced at her. "Would you like him to?"

"Indeed, I would like him to have some part of me."

"Spoken like a woman who wants to be a mother," I said with firmness. Jane looked at me briefly and then looked back down at Caiden, avoiding the discussion I had just raised.

"Jane...are you now having any feelings of guilt of not having a child, for it is not necessary to feel."

"On the contrary," Jane said, "while the idea of having a child is bewitching, I have a truth to tell you...not all women wish to become mothers. Some of us do not have it in us to do so."

"Are you in earnest?" I gasped. "Other women I understand, however, you? You of all people are going to sit here and tell me that you are of the sort who does not want children?"

"You look upon me with disbelief." Jane simply smiled.

"I do, and I should. Jane, you of all of us had the best relationship with children and are now teaching them without receiving any pay."

"Yes, I can teach them and love them...yet now that it comes down to it, I do not know if I wish to have any of my own. I also do not believe I have the constitution to raise one successfully. When I teach my students, at the end of the day, their mothers take them home."

I laughed at that observation.

"And when I shall tire of looking after my beautiful nephews here, I shall hand them back to you. And just as when we had to look after our Gardiner cousins, I reveled in them, yet I also knew that eventually Aunt and Uncle Gardiner would return to take them away. I can look after a child, I can help and assist that child and think of them fondly, yet I could never keep to one."

"Strange indeed," I said, eying her with wonder. "Our paths seem so different than what I expected. I thought the journeys we took would be quite the reverse."

"And now motherhood has suited you while chastity and singularity have embraced me," Jane smiled, looking down at Caiden. "However, that is not why I have come. I have come for the real problem that has arisen."

"What problem is this?"

"The problem that is within you," she said, her eyes resting upon me narrowly. "The problem I have begun to suspect...which is that you are angry at yourself for missing all these months with your sons."

"I..."

"Oh, you must not blame yourself, Lizzy," Jane said reassuringly, "it is just that we have been sisters for our entire lives. I believe that I know how you look when you are feeling heartily ashamed of yourself. You hid it very well, but I was looking on, keenly. So, Elizabeth, am I wrong?"

"Well, you are—"

"And if you say that I am wrong, I know that you are lying. Just thought that I would warn you."

I smiled sheepishly, and then continued.

"You are correct," I said. "I am heartily ashamed of myself."

"Let us begin with the *'why'*. Now begin and use words sparingly."

"Are you treating me as one of your students?"

"Yes, I am. Oh, my poor students! I have been away for so long! We must return soon so that I may make it up to them."

"We shall return in due time, Jane; however, we must see others first and foremost. Yet I promise, upon our return, we shall also have a large feast for them, and you can make inquires of what their favorite toys are and we shall buy them one each."

"Oh, thank you, Lizzy."

"You are welcome. Now back to what you were saying before."

"Yes, well, why are you ashamed of yourself?"

I breathed out evenly and though I did not wish to speak on the matter, I knew Jane to be right; speaking would help me.

"I am ashamed of the choices I have made. Our time in America could have shortened if I had not been insistent in joining Henry and Lydia on their honeymoon. If I had been firm and made us leave after the wedding, then I might have been here to see my sons' first beginnings of crawling."

"And if you had left, then we would not have gone to New York, and all of those poor captured people would still not be free."

I looked at her, beginning to feel a sense of hope.

"I try to tell myself so," I said, "yet that voice is growing more and more faint by the minute."

"Do you turn from the memory of you saving all those people so easily? Are you hard on yourself for being a hero?"

"I just do not want to be the sort who excuses ever being a negligent mother by being absent because I wish to save the world in some way."

"Sometimes the world needs saving."

"Sometimes it does. And a son needs his mother *all of the time*."

"Until he grows up and realizes that he needs the world as much as he needs you. Until the day that he wishes to become a hero in his own right, which will happen inevitably, Elizabeth."

Considering her words, I did my best to tunnel my attention and look to the future. What was youth but a time for one to feel as if they at one point could change the world? Or at least wish to change it? My son did need me as well, however Jane was correct in that he also would inevitably need his own time to choose global obligations over domestic joy.

"Lizzy," Jane continued, "it matters not if you were not there for so short a time in his life because of such deeds being done, as long as you have returned and will be there for him now. And sometimes you will miss great things in their lives, as long as you do your best to be there for as much as you can and love them terribly while you are there. The quality of the time you spend with them is just as beneficial as the quantity of days. A woman who spends every day with her children, but not only pays little heed to them and does not stand up for the liberty of a race of people, is not a mother. You are. You also left them with your family who has grown to love them. And whatever preference your babies might feel toward the Gardiners will veritably come to an end once they are with you every day. Look where you are now. See that you are here now, with them, holding them and loving them."

"Then I ought to be proud of myself?"

"Most decidedly. And if you ever feel remorse and guilt over this again, then tell yourself that you were not there to see them crawl for the first time because you were busy helping to free women who now, if they ever have children, can see their sons and daughters crawl for the first time and not worry that they will be taken from them and sold elsewhere in the end. You, Darcy, and Georgiana gave all those children a mother who will not be torn from them. There. Do you feel better now?"

Deep within my soul I felt a burden lighten. How could I, I who thought I saw matters so clearly, been so harsh upon my own nature that I would judge myself by an improper scale? It should not be endured, nor should I carry the weight of missed opportunities rather than focusing on producing whole new ones.

"You are correct, Jane," I said, "that was wonderful to hear."

"Yes, so stop fretting, and enjoy them while they are this size. For as you know, they do not remain this way."

"Have you always been so great is wisdom, Jane?"

"Of course not. It is the product of not being married and with child! For when you are removed from a situation, you are at liberty to see everything with clear distinction." Jane then placed Caiden in his crib and looked down upon him and smiled.

"Love your Aunt Jane, Caiden, and the irony that rules her life."

Jane smiled at me once more and stood up, preparing to leave.

"And for goodness sakes, Elizabeth. You only missed them crawl. Honestly! Just be there to witness their first steps and you shall still be the greatest mother of the moment."

She patted my shoulder and then left me to the peace of my two boys.

Our dinner party night came quite soon and the Gardiners, consisting of my aunt and uncle, Isabella and Harriet attended. The Bingleys also were to attend, yet Caroline Bingley was not in the party, and we were able to enjoy the evening with just Mr. and Mrs. Bingley from that quarter. Jason Whitfield also attended, yet his family did not, for one brother was not in town. The other brother did not wish to leave his wife, who had fallen ill at the moment and he wished to remain with her for a little longer.

"So," Uncle Gardiner said, "Miss Darcy, I must congratulate you on your happiness, and Mr. Whitfield, I hope you are made of a noble constitution, for Miss Darcy here is a splendid creature to have obtained."

"Oh, you need not worry, Mr. Gardiner," Mr. Whitfield said. "I know that my fortune is great indeed."

"Here! Here!" Fitzwilliam said, raising his glass at that.

"Now," Aunt Gardiner said, "you must tell me all about America, and New York in particular. How was your time spent there?"

"Yes," Harriet added, "we are starved of news of the States is all, and it would be nice to know of what has occurred."

"And the wedding that shocked all," Isabella said. "For Lydia to marry an American Darcy is still a wonder to me."

"Our news is great," Kitty said, "on many levels."

One by one, we all began to tell them of our time in Philadelphia and New York, beginning with Lydia's wedding and ending on the topic of the Trekenna Trial. Jason Whitfield took over most of the discussion on that score and as he gave his narration of the events, the Gardiners were enthralled.

"My dear heavens," Aunt Gardiner gasped. "So, it is all a miracle. And the part you all played in it, well, that is positively courageous and humane. I am proud of you all."

"Yes, well done," Uncle Gardiner added. "I am truly...amazed."

"Thank you," Georgiana said, "yet still the most credit ought to go to Jason and Fitzwilliam, for one fought continuously to liberate the oppressed, while the other found the evidence to save the people. Therefore, you were both too great boulders of strength."

"And what are such natural monuments if there is no bridge to link them?" Jason said. "And that bridge was Mrs. Darcy and yourself, my dear Georgiana."

"Oh, remember Mr. Whitfield," Darcy warned, "before you are wed, she is still Miss Darcy to you."

Everyone chuckled.

"Very well." Jason bowed his head, chuckling also. "Miss Darcy."

"Very good, sir."

"And yet, does it follow that this liberation will be rare?" Isabella asked. "Slavery is gradually being abolished here, due to the 1807 Abolition of the Slave Trade Act and the West Africa Platoon that patrols the coast of the continent to prevent any Slave Ships from attempting to load cargo. But it still does remain here nevertheless, and still thrives. I cannot help but wonder how long it will be before the abolition makes inroads in the States, do you think?"

"It already has begun," Jason said. "And we thought it would have made more progress since the United States also made international slave trade a felony in that same year, however the injustice is still going strong. Yet we still have the Trade here, therefore, it makes sense that they do. Sadly, it is a hard practice to release. Needless to say, however long it takes for freedom to be granted for everyone, well, that time cannot come soon enough."

We all grew silent, thinking on this matter with great diligence, for Jason was correct. It would take a long time. Suddenly he perked up and smiled at Isabella.

"Yet you are very well-informed on these historical matters and facts."

"Oh," Our Uncle Gardiner said, straightening in his seat, "yes, I followed the progress of the abolition over the years, and I have been rattling about it ever since, giving my children no choice but to know all the dates to when certain Acts were passed in the House of Commons and the House of Lords."

Jason nodded his approval. "That is very wise, sir, for it is nice that all women should be so well-informed and fathers keen to allow their minds to be astute and filled with the best of knowledge."

"Precisely my sentiments, sir."

There was a little more discussion on the matter and then the subject eventually changed to talk of housing and when we would all return to Pemberley.

"Speaking of Pemberley," Darcy said, "Charles, I have some delightful news."

"Is it about what I hope it is about?" Mr. Bingley smiled.

"Yes, it is. I have received word from Mr. Arthur Pennington who owns Allenwell Estate in Kent, not more than seven miles from Pemberley, and since he has no children to inherit his legacy and is looking to retire to Bath, he is willing to sell Allenwell."

"Why does he have no children?"

"It is unknown; however, it is heavily implied that he has been proven infertile."

"He cannot have children?"

"Yes, there is even a great rumor that he accused his wife of being the infertile one, and that he attempted to have children by other means, and they all did not work, showing him the painful truth that he was the *problem*."

"Poor man."

"And poor woman," Miriam said. "For his wife must've been devastated."

"Yes, it is a hard fate to have."

"Yet he still fully desires to sell?" Mr. Bingley asked eagerly. "For I already have a couple who wish to take Aginfield from off my hands, since they desire a country seat."

"Oh, do you?"

"Yes, the husband is a navy man who has found his fortune in the war against Napoleon and now wishes to settle until he is called away to serve."

"And what is the man's name?"

"Admiral Croft is his name. His wife, Mrs. Croft, and he are excellent naval people, for she has lived with him on some of his ships."

"Has she?" Miriam said. "That sounds most exciting."

"It does indeed. Therefore, once I have seen this Allenwell Estate, then I shall like to meet with them at Aginfield to discover if they shall enjoy the place."

"Then it might very well come to pass," I said, "that Aginfield will not belong to you. Though I am overjoyed to have you so close to us if all comes to a good end, I still will be shocked to see anyone else at Aginfield but you both."

"It shall hurt, like a paper-cut I daresay," Mr. Bingley smiled. "Yet if Allenwell suits me fine, I shall never look back. And if I push you all to be easily persuaded, then perhaps I can coerce you into doing the correct deed."

"The correct deed?"

"Is there a chance that I can persuade you all not to go to Hampshire after you leave London, but return immediately to Pemberley so that we may join you and I can see Allenwell all the sooner? Then if it is or is not to my liking, we can then travel to Hampshire where you may see your parents and remain with me at Aginfield while I show the estate to Admiral Croft. And before you object, think of it first, I beg you. This way, you shall get the chance to return to Pemberley."

"And that is what I fear," I confessed. "If we go to Pemberley, then we may wish to never leave."

"While that is true," Darcy added, "Lizzy, I must confess to liking the plan. We only were to travel to Hampshire for your parents to see their grandchildren Yet what shall a couple of months be regarding slighting them? Their grandchildren will still be this small, no doubt, just as much then as now, and I can check to see the maintenance of my home."

"And I wish to see my students again," Jane added. "If we remain for a month, I shall be able to further their studies before I am whisked away again. Perfection comes from much practice, and I worry that they have not been practicing in my absence."

"While I still worry over the idea of returning home for a while to only be whisked away again," I said, "I do see the logic of your schemes. And Mr. Bingley should see Allenwell as soon as may be so that it does not remain on the market for too long."

"Then I have persuaded you all?" Mr. Bingley smiled.

"Yes, you have," I said with a chuckle. "Enjoy your present triumph, Mr. Bingley, for I plan to win the next row."

"Will do, Mrs. Darcy. Then, it may be as good as settled?"

"Yes Charles, after London, to Pemberley we go."

"I hope nothing impedes our progress."

"I see no need to worry."

"Oh, dear then," Isabella sighed theatrically, "whatever shall we Gardiners do again, while you are all to be happy and away in Kent!"

We all smiled and continued eating.

◈

After all our guests left for the evening and it was time to retire to bed, Darcy and I reflected on the dinner.

"I have noticed something." I smiled at him.

"What, my love?"

"It is a small thing."

"Were you about to comment on my handsome features?"

"No Fitzwilliam."

"Oh pity, or my strong countenance?"

"No Fitzwilliam."

"Oh pity, or of my intelligence?"

"Definitely not Fitzwilliam."

"Oh pity, then what of?"

"I believe that you liked Isabella Gardiner."

"Oh, I confess that most readily. Harriet is a lovely sort of girl, but Isabella is the more remarkable in my eyes."

"And for that you deserve a pinch." I leaned forward and pinched him on his stomach, and he cried out, over-dramatic.

"Ouch! And what was that for?"

"That was for being a hypocrite. You get angry when I offer a man any form of a compliment, yet you flatter my cousins? Mr. Darcy, am I to be jealous of my own kin?"

"It is nothing of the sort, my dear. And if you please, you should take it as a compliment to yourself."

"And how do you figure that one, sir?"

"She reminds me of you."

"Oh, does she?" I replied, surprised.

"Yes, very much so. She is similar to Kitty as well, which is only natural, for you and Kitty are very much alike in many ways. Yes, that is the only reason I find myself comfortable with offering her a compliment. Isabella is lovely because she is like you. Though she is not as beautiful."

"Now you flatter me."

"Is it working?"

"A mere little. I have not fully decided whether I shall let you sleep in the same bed with me or not."

"Oh, so it is that sort of punishment?"

"Yes, it is."

"Well, my dear, I do actually like when you punish me, therefore I am not so disturbed."

"You like when I punish you?" I scoffed. "Yet that then leaves me no ways of ever exacting revenge."

He gave me a wicked grin. "I know."

I leaned forward and challenged him.

"If that is the case, I promise Mr. Darcy, I will find something within my power to still make you squirm."

"Oh, you can try. You are about to kiss me, aren't you?"

"With great enthusiasm."

I sat on his lap, and we kissed passionately. Tearing off my nightgown while rolling me over in the process, Darcy lowered his body onto me and ran his lips down my neck, along my breasts and at last he teased my nipples with his teeth. Then he separated my legs with his hands and pressed his fingers deep within my softness, eliciting a moan of pleasure from me.

"Mrs. Darcy?"

"Yes," I gasped, still enjoying the act of lovemaking as much as the first day we had done so.

"Is there anything special you would like?"

"Can you not guess?"

"Oh, very well, let us be traditional about it."

"Oh, you shall not!" I cried, rolling on top of him, then I crawled up his chest and with my thighs parted, I rested my knees on each side of his head. "Same act," I said, "yet with a different position."

"Interesting," he said quickly before he raised his head and I felt his lips and tongue work their magic upon my person, sparking a desire and sensations that I never wished to end. He pressed his hands desperately over my bottom, driving his lips further within me while I rocked up and down, lost in all the passion that eclipses one during such a state.

I did not know what impulse drove me to act so boldly and uniquely, however I always wished to know what it would be like for me to be tasted in such a manner by him—and now it had come to pass.

I was lost into oblivion.

Overwhelmed by desire.

Desire that I never wished to end.

Sitting completely upon his face, for my strength had left me, the urgency of his kisses showed me that he did not mind, and he only contin-ued. Up and down my body, and I grabbed at the headboard for dear life, for I felt that if I didn't, I would fly away into the stars.

Then with one final thrust of his lips and tongue, my body stiffened, and I was overwhelmed when I had reached my peak. When he had finished, I moved my thighs down his back and our middles touched and

I rested my thighs at his hips. Immediately acting upon impulse, we entered one another and thrust back and forth with overwhelming urgency.

As we did so, Darcy raised himself up and held my back and neck to keep us moving deeper within each other. Then he roared as his body and desire was utterly spent within me. We lay together after our energy had been exhausted and we were one.

I expelled a deep sigh. "Thank you, that was perfect."

"You still feel wonderful to the touch and taste, my love. And you are growing bolder the longer we wed."

"I am not afraid of not knowing how to please you anymore."

"Very good, for you always please me."

As we lay there, with him on top of me as I held him, I ran my hands gently down his back.

"Elizabeth..."

"Yes, my love?"

"You shall hate me."

"Shall I? What sin have you committed of late?"

"I am about to ask you to do something you might not wish to do."

"Such as?"

"When William and Caiden become two years old, I wish for us to have another child?"

"Fitz! Are you serious?"

"Yes. I was hoping for a daughter. I want a girl as well."

I closed my eyes and wished that I could pinch him, for his confession was well played. Yes, pregnancy hurt me, however Darcy's desire to also have a daughter was the most vulnerable and beautiful of confessions. And while pregnancy did hurt, I knew I had the strength to easily survive it again. Therefore, he was not putting my life in danger, but asking me to undergo physical agony that was normal for a wife to do.

"Oh, Fitzwilliam." I gave him a tender swat. "I hate you. You absolutely made it impossible for me to be upset by your adorable and sensitive reply, and that was really not fair."

"No," he replied wickedly, "it was not. I am a scoundrel. Yet I am a scoundrel who has quite won, have I not?"

That was when I kicked him in his kneecap, but the proud man was so solidly built he hardly felt it!

The next day, I prepared our staff for the eventual arrival of Jason Whitfield's family members. Jason informed us it would be one of his two brothers, for the third resided in Somersetshire. After that had been done, I went to my desk and looked through all the letters and invitations that had accumulated over our time spent away. Most I threw into the dustbin once I read the third sentence of the invitation, however there was one that seemed of great import. It was the invitation of Lady Henrietta Russell, who was hosting a party for her son's engagement to a baroness, and the invitation was in Lyme. The party however would take place in four months' time, and I did not understand why in god's name an engagement party would take place so late, when smart engagements never lasted more than a month? Confused about it, I rose and sought out the assistance of the only man that I knew might have any knowledge on the matter.

I went to the servant quarters, and I found Jefferson once again with a servant woman holding hands with him.

"Oh, forgive me, mistress!" she said, moving away from Jefferson. "I did not mean to—"

"I am not upset," I rushed out, "though I wish for you to consider discretion and restraint, I know that Jefferson here is very persuasive."

"Oh, yes, I mean..." The servant woman looked from me to Jefferson, who only looked wickedly innocent, which I was not buying for a moment. "You are dismissed," I said, "and do not worry, you have not lost your situation here in the household. Yet in the future, try your best not to give in to him."

"Thank 'ee missus." Taking one last look at Jefferson, she left us alone.

"Mrs. Darcy," he said, "I know you think me a scoundrel."

I gave him a gentle smile. "I do not think it, Jefferson. You *are a* scoundrel."

"I do not understand myself," he said. "Why do women enjoy me so? You look upon me—you see how ugly I am."

"You have a certain way about you, and you are confident. That means a lot to some women."

"Yes, well, does Mr. Darcy need me?"

"No, but I do."

"Oh, what secret do you need extracted from me?"

"I have received an invitation from a Lady Russell to—"

"Oh, she invited you for her son's engagement party that is so long away as well?"

"Yes—yes," I stuttered. "You knew about this already."

"I have a never-ending supply of sources as you see, and I find servant girls to be the best. They hear much and speak to each other; therefore, it can easily be said that the fastest thing in London is not a horse and carriage, but rumor."

"Well, I was wondering if you knew why it is so long away. Is there some foul work at play?"

"Oh, you need not worry. There is no more foul work at play in this situation than there usually is in the cases of marriage. Her son, Mr. Edward Russell, is away in India, for he has taken an interest in some of their markets and culture. He is quite anthropological in his ways and does have a harmless curiosity for other cultures, which is his main virtue."

"And what did you mean when you said there is no *more* foul work at play in this situation than there usually is in the case of marriage?"

"Oh, what I meant by that is that Mr. Edward Russell is known amongst the servants for his many dalliances with the hired help."

"He has had flirtations with servant girls?"

"Many great men do, but he is the most flagrant about it, and he is also marrying his fiancée, Miss Clay, because she is wealthy."

"It is a monetary match, rather than one of affection?"

"She is said to be a very plain looking woman. Not that I am a selective man myself, and many a man has fallen madly in love with women that society would call plain. Yet he is said to not be of that sort."

"Therefore, it shall be a loveless marriage."

"Possibly." Jefferson sat down, feeling comfortable. "So, what do you come for in regard to advice?"

"I... I am not sure if I should accept the offer or decline it."

"Which do you wish to do more?"

"I wish to simply return to Pemberley and except for our journey to Hampshire, I wish to stay at Pemberley only."

"And you have a right to. For you have been jumping from here to there with much ease and you owe it to yourself to have a rest."

"Thank you. However, Lady Russell is the sort of woman to have much influence amongst the circles of the ton, and should it follow that I retire to Pemberley and think of no one but my own happiness?"

"Master Darcy would love to return as well."

"Yes, we all would, however with Georgiana's marriage as a probable landmark in our future, she needs to be amid many of her peers now. If it became known that we were attending, I would begin to be a proper mistress of Pemberley by making myself social, while also encouraging Georgiana's match amongst the ton, and integrating Mr. Whitfield into the social circles as well. With his profession, he needs connections here. And if Georgiana wishes to pursue a more active role in committees, she will need the support of the women of London."

"And once again, you find yourself needed to be the Great Link." Jefferson smiled. "Mrs. Darcy, it does begin and end with you quite often, doesn't it?"

"I suppose so."

"It does and you are correct. Mrs. Darcy, I know why you came to me first rather than Mr. Darcy, and I cannot make the decision for you before you speak to him on the matter. Yet if you require me to give my advice, then I would suggest that you accept the offer. You are right. A woman in your place, with so many others under her supervision, needs friends. This is your chance."

I rolled my eyes. "That is what I am afraid of."

"I know it is hard. I always said that there was always one thing that was more daunting to me than being utterly poor."

"And what is that?"

"Being utterly rich."

"Thank you, Jefferson." Before I left fully, I turned back to him. "And Jefferson, please make it a habit to be careful with the women here. Some of them may not see that you are not sincere in your attentions, and they might fall in love with you by accident—and she would not be to blame for your rakish behavior."

"What is it with women falling in love with me? Again, as you can see, I am hideous."

"There is more to attraction than beauty, you fool, and I do not want the maids thinking I will not protect them."

"Very well," he answered with a bit of a smile, "I solemnly swear that I shall not do anything to make you disappointed in me—unless I have no other choice in the matter."

"There is always another choice one could make."

"Very well...oh, and Mrs. Darcy."

"Yes?"

"You might wish to go to Mr. Darcy's study, for he shall need you very soon."

"Need me, for what?"

"Well, I am not sure myself. Yet I have the suspicion to believe that he is about to get some unsettling news."

"What is it you are not telling me?" I urged.

"I do not know what I am not telling you, for it is just an assumption."

I looked at him in confusion. Yet, I did not remain, but left immediately and went to Darcy's study. Upon going to the door, I knocked.

"Who is there?"

"Fitzwilliam, it is me. May I come in?"

"Of course, enter for I need to tell you something."

That admission gave me a slight ominous feel, yet I entered and closed the door all the same. When I did so, I turned to Darcy who was reading a letter.

"Fitzwilliam," I began, "what is it?"

He closed the letter and looked up at me.

"Remember when you spoke of how we should prepare, for whenever we expect peace, instead something always presents itself."

"Yes, dear lord, what has happened?"

Darcy opened the letter once more and held it out for me to take.

"There is a thin line between foreshadow and predictions, it appears. And my dear, you saw that line with perfect clarity."

# 6

# WHEN DUTY CALLS BEFORE DESIRE

"Is this news good or bad?" I asked, indifferent, for as is the nature with all things, time and experience had worn me down and I felt desensitized to any surprise that could have presented itself to me.

"It has only taken me off my guard is all. It is from our dear friend, the Prince Regent."

"The prince?" I gasped, taking the letter. "What more could be needed on either side?"

"Read it, my love, it is most amusing." Opening the paper, I read through the letter quickly and then lowered it upon being finished. "Can it be true?"

"Yes."

"The prince really wishes us all to join his royal banquet at the end of the week to learn particularities of the Trekenna Trial."

"Yes, he does," Darcy responded on a sigh. "And it makes perfect sense when one thinks on it. Naturally, he has not learned of the outcome of the trial and wishes to know of it."

"Well then," I said with finality, "we must write back to confirm our coming, for we cannot slight him, I believe."

"No, there is nothing for that. It is all too alarming," Darcy said firmly, "that he and I are to be thrown so often into the same set of circumstances."

"Is there any way that you can write back with not only a favorable reply, but also request our invitation to include Mr. Jason Whitfield, and the Gardiners."

"Why the Gardiners as well?"

"Because," I began shyly, "they have done so much for me by way of opportunities that I feel as if I owe them, which we both do."

"Do we?"

"If they had not taken Kitty and me on a holiday from Longbourn over a year ago, then you and I never would have met again, and we would not be married now. And if they had not obtained tickets for Jane and me for Almacks, then I would never have met you in the first place."

"Oh," Darcy said. "Yes, I do see your point, my dear."

"And all too often when we journey to do something magnanimous or are asked to a grand event, we very rarely ever include them. I know that my Uncle Gardiner's involvement in trade makes him below the notice of the ton that revolves around the prince. Yet if we ask his highness nicely, then there is a chance that if he accepts them, no one else shall look down upon them. I know that I might bring humiliation upon you, but my dear, please try and do this, for me."

"While I should be frightened by the potential repercussions of it, that is not what worries me, for I am at the place in my life where I feel that society can go and hang for all that I care. I am simply worried about asking the prince for anything else."

"Ah, that is a natural fear. However, as far as depths go, I believe you are both at the age of your lives when you can count yourself even. Even if you both still do have a couple more requests up your sleeves each."

Darcy leaned forward, placed his chin on his hands and pondered.

"I was in fact hoping to return immediately to Pemberley with all speed and allow us to fall away from the rest of man that was outside of Kent. I wished to be so remote in nature that we were free of all restraint. Yet I fear, if we do attend, then there might be something else to stop us from retiring so soon."

"There is already something that deters us from remaining there all the rest of the year, without interruption."

"And what is that?"

"We have been invited by Lady Russell of Somersetshire. And she has invited us to her son's engagement party in four months' time at Lyme."

"Lyme!"

❧

After I had told Darcy of the invitation, he sighed, acknowledging that there might be nothing for it but for us to attend, especially if we did not wish to slight anyone around the time of Georgiana's engagement.

"Is the world so determined to pull us in each direction, Lizzy?" he asked me, resigned.

"Yes, I believe that it does." I kissed him and then I stood up. "I am going to check on the babies and I leave it up to you to tell everyone in the household of our change of events. And will you write back to his royal highness, assuming he reads his own letters."

"Oh, he always reads mine."

"Why so?"

"Because he worries about any clerk reading what I might potentially write to him."

"All this secrecy, to the point where it makes me wonder if he is in love with you."

"Elizabeth, ill!"

"Sorry darling, I did not mean it that way. I meant that he has a strong link to you that even he does not like to acknowledge, and he relies on you, for he looks up to you."

"Looks up to me?"

"It is the nature of men to admire stronger men. The prince has strong influence of course, but you have strength in your person, and he cannot deny that to himself."

"I do not want his admiration just now, however. I want only to be left alone."

"Alone...you cannot be left to."

I walked out of the room and to the nursery to sit with William and Caiden, enjoying the peace and chaos that went hand in hand with motherhood.

☯

After an hour of being in the nursery with my babies, for I held William and Kitty sat opposite me, holding Caiden, there was a knock on the door. Jefferson leaned his head in, his eyes relaxing from being happy to have found me.

"Mrs. Darcy and Mrs. Fitzwilliam," he began, "Master Darcy just wished to inform you that he has sent his acceptance letter to the Palace."

"Very good, thank you, Jefferson."

"Ma'am."

"Oh, and Jefferson?"

"Yes Mrs. Darcy?"

"How did you know about the contents of the prince's letter?"

"I didn't actually."

"Well then how did you know that Mr. Darcy would need me?"

"Because the prince wrote. When the prince writes, it is never an easy matter that does not affect all around Master Darcy, and more than likely it is some form of demand that shakes the very foundations of the household. Was I wrong?"

"No, you were not. I wished for you to be, yet you were not."

"I know. I know. Whatever it is that he requires, however, I shall join you in your carriage and remain sentinel in the adjoining rooms where the banquet shall take place."

"You think it necessary to protect us?" Kitty asked. "I did not know we were in any danger."

"You are not," Jefferson said, "I am simply paranoid. However, I have learned something important."

"And what is that?"

"That in my line of work, paranoia is simply reality viewed threw a spyglass; close and every detail fine-tuned."

Jefferson bowed to us, and he left.

"He worries too much," Kitty said when he was gone.

"Yes, he does. Yet in his line of work, it is best that he worries too much as opposed to worrying too little."

"And yet, it is a little frightening that he knows so much. At first, he amused me greatly, yet now I wonder if it is proper for a man to specialize in information to that special a degree."

"You need never worry, Kitty. Jefferson has a large heart and worries because he has seen conflict in battle. That changes anyone."

"You know his past, finally?"

"No, I simply know that he has served in action. However as for the rest of him, he is a man who defines his life by protecting others. It is best to always have such a man around."

"Then it has all come to this," Kitty said. "We are to meet the Prince Regent again."

"Yes, we are."

"I may not always like royalty, yet I can say that they do amuse."

"Yes, when they are not being boring."

"Actually, I find them most entertaining when they are being at their most boring."

"Why so?"

"Because they have absolutely no idea that they are being so—they honestly think they look smart."

We both laughed merrily at Kitty's observation.

"Yet we must be wary to keep any demeaning feelings from being expressed toward Aunt and Uncle," Kitty continued. "I think the gesture you made was a great one, however I still worry about how they shall be received."

"That is where I place trust in them. They may not be a gentleman or gentleman's daughter, but they are so refined and elegant a couple that they are sure to make everyone feel at ease. Yet we shall make sure to help them if ever a bad word is said."

"Yet one thing is certain. Without Caroline Bingley there, at least our burdens shall be lessened."

"Yes, that is true. And in matters where duty calls before desire, then this is one more thing that has to be undertaken."

"Well, then...royalty, once more we descend upon you. And we hope that you are prepared."

## ❧ 7 ❧

# A TALE TOLD BY AN IDIOT

That night, we awaited the arrival of the Whitfields and they arrived precisely when expected. Lined up outside of the house, the carriage rolled up. The footman opened the door and then a man stepped down who was of a medium height, taller than Jason Whitfield. Yet there was a similarity in the facial features that made it clear he was one of Jason's older brothers. The man then held out his hand, a woman's arm emerged, and his wife descended. Next came another man who we could only assume was Jason's younger brother, yet I could not tell, for there was no similarity of facial features.

"Jason!" the tallest one said, "we have made good time, I presume."

"Oh, for goodness sakes, Jeffrey," Jason said, coming forward, "you always think yourself late and never are."

"It is better to fear the event of being late rather than to actually be consistently undergoing the event of it," Jeffrey said.

"Jeffrey, Nicholas and Josephine," Jason said going up to them. "It is wonderful to see you all again."

"And you as well," said Nicholas. "It's been years since we last saw you and here you are, still looking the same."

"It is the New York air that I have been breathing," Jason said. "It is so dirty and sordid to smell that it strengthens one's immune system, I suppose."

"You always did prefer things the hard way."

"Well, not in the manner of love. It found me quite easily, and now, enough dawdling, for it is time to meet your future in-laws." Jason then turned to us and began the introductions.

"Darcy household, it is my great pleasure to introduce you to my family. These are my brothers, Nicholas Whitfield, who is the second oldest."

"As you can see, I got the best height out of all of us," Nicholas said, to which we all chuckled.

"And next," Jason continued, "is Mrs. Amelia Whitfield, his wife, and my youngest brother, who is the baby of the family, Jeffrey."

Jeffrey and Nicholas bowed while Mrs. Whitfield curtsied demurely, and then smiled at us. Mrs. Whitfield was not really a great beauty, however Mr. Nicholas Whitfield seemed to be very considerate of her, for he looked down at her often, and took her arm in his immediately.

"And now, for this side of the introductions," Jason continued. "We have the master of Pemberley Mr. Fitzwilliam Darcy with his wife Mrs. Darcy, then there is Mrs. and Mr. Fitzwilliam, Miss Jane Bennet, Mr. and Mrs. Bingley, and this," Jason said, standing next to Georgiana, "is my fiancée and the woman who has made me the happiest of men, Miss Georgiana Darcy."

"Welcome to our home," I said, and we all bowed or curtsied in turn.

"Thank you for your warm greeting," Mrs. Whitfield said, "and we are pleased to make your acquaintance."

"Now then," Darcy declared, "let us all get out of the cold, for I fear it may begin to snow any minute."

We all entered, our coats were taken, and we showed them into the sitting room where tea was served all around.

"Apologies for our oldest brother not being here," Jeffrey said first and foremost. "Yet he lives away from London on our home, Errodin Abbey Estate, and therefore cannot make his way to London so easily. We have sent him a letter informing him of Jason's returning to England and of his engagement to your lovely sister here, Mr. Darcy."

"That is very well."

"As long as he plans to make his best effort to attend the wedding," Georgiana said, "I shall have no problems on making his acquaintance before I walk down the aisle."

"Oh, hopefully it shall not have to come to that."

"I do not know, Nicholas," Jeffrey said, "for when it comes to Victor, that is always possible."

"Victor is his name then?" Colonel Fitzwilliam asked.

"Yes, he is, Victor Whitfield, the constant bachelor."

"Oh, so he is not married."

"No, he is not, and so far, for a man who is the sole inheritor of Errodin, he has no qualms in being so."

"I do not begrudge him for it," Nicholas admitted, "for if he never wishes to have children, then my own can suffice for his heirs."

"Oh, don't talk of such things at the dinner party of your brother's engagement, Mr. Whitfield," Mrs. Whitfield scolded. "Talk of the happy event already."

"You are very correct, forgive me," Nicholas apologized, and then he turned to Georgiana. "We owe you much, Miss Darcy. For we thought we had lost Jason to America completely, thinking he would never wish to return home. He even wrote us of such a couple of times."

"Did you?" Georgiana asked Jason.

"Yes, I did. It was a large problem for me, yet my heart was torn. England was my home, but America was where my feet seemed to like to rest. And I cannot begrudge the impulse, for my wandering feet led me to you."

"And you were his guiding light it appears," Nicholas continued. "For in finding you, he wished to find his way back home again."

"It is true," Mrs. Whitfield said. "When Mr. Whitfield here told me that his brother had returned from New York, I could scarce believe it. Yet here he is. And now that you see the three of them together, Miss Darcy, do you not enjoy the look of the three cousins re-united?"

"They do make a memorable trio."

"Yes, they do. However, whenever Victor decides to grace anyone with his presence, which is rare, they make the most curious quartet that you have ever seen."

"And who is the tallest one?" Jane asked.

"Victor, without a doubt."

"Which makes me the shortest," Jason said, resigned to the fact.

"Darling, what you lack in height, you make up for in confidence and charm," Georgiana smiled.

"You are trying to butter me up, my love," Jason said. "I do so like it when you are doing that."

"And we are the poor fools who must watch you both do so," Jeffrey said. "Be careful, Jason, some of us are not bachelors by choice, therefore you make us quite jealous."

"Oh, dear lord, Jeffrey and Nicholas," Jason cried. "You both are still too much inclined to confess your inner feelings in the presence of others. If I did not know any better, I would say that you were not raised to be English gentlemen. Forgive my brothers, Mr. Darcy, and all. They lack formality."

"It is quite all right, Mr. Whitfield," Georgiana said to Jason. "As long as they mean no offense ever, we can most readily forgive your comfort with each other, for it puts us more at ease in our own manner."

"You see," Jeffrey says, "your lady insists us to be ourselves."

I looked toward Darcy, whose jaw was set, and I could tell that he did not like the looseness with which the Whitfields spoke. I therefore decided to take advantage of it.

"So then," I began, to Jeffrey. "You are not a bachelor by choice, yet by disappointment then?"

"Aye and I do not deny it. I have not been able to find myself eligible for domestic joy as my brothers here. I often wonder if I should take matters into my own hands."

"Or you may try to repeat your older brother's method," Miriam said.

"Precisely," I agreed. "Your brother was preaching morality and justice on a street corner when his eyes happened to fall on our dear Georgiana. They met by sheer accident that was not forced into happening and their intrigue over one another occurred organically."

"So, you are saying that I should simply stop walking to my fate and let it come to me? That is not too passive an approach?"

"With love, letting it approach through passivity is always the best policy," Miriam concluded. "True attraction cannot be forced but made to arrive organically. I promise you, if you one day stop looking for love, then by a month's time, it might find you."

◈

"Well, let us see," Nicholas began as we started the first course of our meal in the dining hall. "Miss Darcy, are you the sort to enjoy hearing about the mischief your fiancé used to get into when he was a child?"

"No, she does not!" Jason cried.

"Of course, she does!" Georgiana squealed. "And Jason do not speak for me in matters such as this."

"Nicholas shall do his best to paint me in a negative light."

"I will still remain engaged to you afterward, so do not worry."

"Precisely," Jeffrey said. "Now, Miss Darcy, my brother Jason here always used to hide my clothes from me, and sometimes our mother would blame me for it."

Georgiana turned toward him. "Did you, really?"

"Yes," Jason sighed looking red in the face. "Yes, I did."

"You naughty bully," she said with a smile.

"Well, it is the way with brothers," Jason replied, defending himself, "and Jeffrey, it's not nearly as bad as what Nicholas and Victor did with me!"

"I admit to being a tyrannical older brother," Nicholas said, "there is no denying it."

"You still can be," Mrs. Whitfield said to her husband. "Honestly, Mr. Whitfield, your brother has not been back to England for more than two weeks and you are already thinking of a way to sabotage his stockings in some way."

"You were planning on putting jelly in the bottom of my stockings again, Nicholas?" Jason cried, "Are you in earnest?"

"I was simply thinking of doing it to offer you a welcome home gesture. It was meant to make you feel like you were back with the family again."

"A simple 'Jason, it is wonderful to see you, here are a handful of pounds!' would have sufficed."

Jane stifled her laughter, but Kitty had no qualms on chuckling openly, and Colonel Fitzwilliam joined her as well.

"That reminds me of myself, actually," the Colonel said, "and I did not simply do it to my youngest brother, but I had no problems with my older brother, Henry, for boxing my ears because of a prank I would pull. My favorite was stealing their breeches, stuffing then with straw, and making them appear as if they were scarecrows on the edge of our estate."

"Wait…then that was you?" My husband blurted out. "One day when we had gone to stay at Matlock, I found my favorite breeches and jacket missing. Then I found that they were placed around a stuffed scarecrow on one of the farms. I thought Georgiana had done it."

"It was not me," Georgiana said primly.

"Of course, it was not her," Colonel Fitzwilliam said. "Because it was me."

"You devil," Darcy responded, but without rancor.

"Yes, I know, I am." Colonel Fitzwilliam grinned. "I very much am."

"All these wonderful anecdotes," Mr. Bingley noted. "And it makes me quite sad."

"Why is that?"

"Because when I was growing up, I was too afraid of my sisters to ever pull any prank on them. Yet those of you who know my family cannot deny that it is not my fault—my sisters are positively terrifying."

And we all laughed at that confession.

"Yes," Mr. Bingley said wiping his eye, "they…they are very much terrifying."

The rest of the evening went as such, with us exchanging stories about our histories, and therefore, by the time that the evening had come to a close, Jason's brother made certain that we knew everything of him, from vice to virtue and from good deed done to bad deed forgiven.

"I had no idea they would be so vulgar," Darcy murmured as we prepared for bed. The dinner had been long ended and the Whitfields had left hours ago.

"Too crass for you, I gather," I said, pulling on my nightgown.

"Elizabeth, you know they were."

"Their manners were very pleasing and proper. Therefore, I could not help but find them amusing."

"They spoke as if we were not there, as if they were merely in the presence of family."

"Because they were, and I do believe that maybe that was their objective. They wished to make us all feel comfortable as family, in hopes of strengthening Jason's bond to Georgiana. If both families get along, then the couples both shall do so in turn. Family easily destroys tranquility if it so decides to. They were perhaps speaking often to the point of desperation in hopes that silence would not reign, because awkwardness sometimes can be its own sin in the eyes of some. And I admit, Fitzwilliam, that I did appreciate that gesture."

"I just thought that being a family of attorneys would train them to be more refined and—"

"Stiff?"

"Well, yes actually. It is a very prim and strict profession that one becomes distinguished through rhetoric."

"And the human spirit cannot spend its life in straight lines, I think. Fitzwilliam, imagine if you were an attorney. Such dreary work, and even drearier in the courtroom I would imagine, therefore, if one were to be such a way all the time, even when one is not working, where is their outlet? Where is their search for joy? There would be none. I do not know what they are feeling, yet it could very well be possible that they use family as their source for amusement and relinquish strict decorum as soon as they are able, to just remain sane. Or I could be completely wrong—or it could be one other aspect."

"And what is that?"

"They could just be a family of brothers who were close growing up and who had not seen one of them for years. And now they are together and are reverting back into their old ways of being filial."

"It very well may be, however, my dear, is it me, or do you always object to everything that I say?"

"It is you," I exclaimed.

"No, it is not."

"Oh, yes, it is."

"It is very much not."

"It very much is. I agree with you often, however you seem to choose to only remember the moments that I disagree with you. Fitzwilliam, though we are each other's match, we cannot always be in perfect accord with each other."

"You lie, temptress," he said, grinning at me, and insistent. "You never agree with me. When I look at you, do you know what I see?"

"What?"

"The Goddess of Discord."

"Oh really?"

"Yes."

"Well do you know what I see when I look at you, Fitzwilliam?"

"What?" he challenged.

"I see the man I married."

❦

Fitzwilliam blinked, surprised at my comment, and taken so much aback by sincerity of my compliment, that he burst out laughing, content. Following suit, I laughed as well and we both sat there, on opposite sides of the room, filling the air with our guffaws.

"Lizzy," he said, giving me a warm smile, "that was very well played."

"Yes, I know my dear. I am a genius."

"Oh, is that why I married you?"

"Yes, that is why you married me. Why, did you think you married me for any other reason?"

"Personally, I thought I did so because I was very bored."

"You forget that you like being bored."

"Do I?"

"Yes, you are very strange for it."

"But I hate being confined, however. Therefore, I am still interesting, in that way."

"My dear..."

"Yes?"

"I climb trees."

"What?"

"I... I climb trees," I repeated, not knowing why I chose that moment to confess it, yet I could only assume that it was time. "I have been doing it ever since I was a child, and sometimes I still do it."

"Elizabeth, that is dangerous."

"I never do it with high trees, and only climb them when I know that I am safe."

"Why do you confess this now?"

I frowned. "I do not know. I just figured that we were finally ready."

"Ready for what?"

"For you to know all about me and still think I am the perfect woman."

"Elizabeth, I..." Darcy trailed off and looked at his hands. "Of course, I think of you as—"

"I know that you do."

"Right. And you must not forget that I do."

"I will not."

Darcy stood up and began to pace around the room.

"Amazing, is it not?" I asked.

"What is?"

"What are we humans so afraid of? But ourselves. We fear others, we fear what is within us. It seems as if fear rules our lives. But is there much to be afraid of? We fear true feelings, absolute integrity, we fear having amusement in our lives even. Why when we grow older that we are told we can no longer run mad in the rain? Why when someone says anything with conviction, it seems as if we all would die of fright? Why when soldiers return from war, they are forbidden from speaking of the tragedies they witnessed when they integrate back into good society? Why do we fear the poor? And why do we fear those who must work? It is all so puzzling. Yet now that I look back upon it, there are so many foolish things that we choose to allow us to hold one another back."

Darcy sat down and remained silent. I continued to look upon him but did not know if he wanted me to say anything. He indeed seemed to be within his own thoughts, attempting to understand something. Thoughts seemed to rise to the surface of his being, doubt and curiosity filled his eyes, yet his body remained still, except for his fingers. Only those moved. However, the way that they did so was more a twitch, moving back and forwards sporadically.

After a moment, I gathered my courage and leaned forward.

"Have you realized something?"

"Yes. I realized that there is nothing to fear."

"No, there never was." I smiled.

"Elizabeth, if you like, and as long as it is safe, you may climb trees."

"Oh, thank you for accepting me in full."

"Of course."

And that was the moment that Mr. Darcy fully began to rise to the height that would rule his life. After that moment, his character never would shorten, and he would walk as tall as he was, and never fear what the world had to offer him ever—or how it would reprimand him if he wished to be different.

Life was very strange in many ways, for it was a constant paradox.

It always seemed to come slowly.

It came in images at first.

Then came the words.

Then came the theories.

Revelations.

Then came our courage.

And that word: courage, was a hard word to win as a prize.

The courage to see the world for what it was, to hear the words that ought to be listened to and fight against the words that ought not to be spoken. Then came the theories that the world gave, and afterwards understanding how to put them through the correct filter. For there were some theories that were correct; some philosophies that would rule our world. And yet there were some philosophies, some maxims that were false, foolish, and should be disregarded or were tyrannical because they did not allow all to be viewed as equal. Some philosophies exulted some and then ridiculed or oppressed others. As for the revelations, there were many, but they all had to be learned by us, humanity falling down over and over, stumbling, making a fool of itself, and taking a long time to stand. Yet when we do stand, it was all those times that we did make fools of ourselves and fumble that make the stand all the more precious.

And that is when one learns the ultimate courage.

"Fitzwilliam," I whispered.

"Yes?"

"When our children grow up, they might sometimes say the wrong thing, embarrass themselves and become the butt of jokes because they exposed themselves to something ridiculous. They might aspire to greatness and then find out that they were terrible at what they attempted to do, they will be despised because they chose to believe different than someone else, or they are bad at something that will cause others to point and laugh. And whenever they do, we have to forgive them and tell them one thing."

"What?"

"We must tell them that we are proud of them, that they are still worthy of being believed in as long as they have something good to fight for. And that they are not a mess, but simply they were brave for trying."

"I suppose we must. Yet what inspired you to think all this?"

"I thought it because no one ever said it to me. And I wished that someone had."

Darcy sat down on the bed, and I sat down beside him.

"My mother tried to teach me how to play the pianoforte," Darcy whispered. "I stopped learning however because I was terrible at it."

"I did not learn how to paint because I was awful at drawing."

"I also do not dance often."

"As you know, I barely can sing. And Jane, Kitty and Lydia stopped trying after they learned they had no skill at it whatsoever."

"Mary may be accomplished in some ways, yet your sister was terrible when she sang at the Aginfield ball."

"Yes, but she still tries, and every day that she tries, she has the right to be given another chance to try."

"Yes, yes she does."

"So, it is decided between us," I finalized. "We shall always convince others to aspire to greatness, yet we will not ever fear failure. It is all too wonderful, the journey of the human condition: all our tears spent on our defects and embarrassing moments, only to learn that we should have been forgiven for them long ago. The irony! It seems to be a tale told by an idiot."

"Yes, but it does not signify nothing, rather it signifies everything."

Darcy and I leaned forward, and we kissed.

## 8

# CAPTAIN WENTWORTH

The prince's invitation to St. James Court was widened to increase our number very quickly, and in a few days' time, we all traveled to receive our special honor amongst royalty and the highest of the aristocracy.

Wearing our finest, I sat in our carriage opposite Darcy, Georgiana, and Jane, while the Gardiners along with Isabella and Harriet were behind us, followed by Mr. Bingley, Miriam, Kitty, and the Colonel.

Jane expelled a sigh. "How often we are expected to dash about. I do so wonder what were to happen if we one day were to stand still. I bet the world would die of fright if that were to occur."

"I rather it be us than our aunt," I said. "Now that she is expected to be presented to the king, she is quite nervous."

"As she has the right to be," Darcy said, "for when it is your first time, it is daunting. Positively daunting."

"I hope the day will not end with us wishing to leave as soon as we arrive. Yet we shall see."

We arrived and were greeted by the members of court, and then we were presented before the Prince Regent, who as always, had many around him.

"The elusive Darcys!" he said, remaining seated while we all bowed to him. "Welcome to my humble abode."

"Humble?" Darcy said.

"Mr. Darcy, do you still not know a joke?"

"I understand it well, Your Majesty, however your surroundings are so prestigious that I am wondering if you are allowed to use the joke."

Everyone around us whispered at their exchange, and even I wondered at it! I knew Darcy to be curt with the prince, yet now this was public. No wonder Jefferson wished to remain in the room with us, lurking in the shadows. I would not be surprised if he had worried that he would have to defend Darcy from a royal guard who the prince ordered to maim Darcy.

"Ah, it is nice to see you still have your edge when it comes to wit, though you still are worse at it than I am!" the prince bellowed, to which everyone laughed. "And Mrs. Darcy."

"Good day, Your Highness," I said, curtsying, and also knowing that the prince seemed to enjoy us breaching convention and speaking to him upon re-introduction. "It is pleasing to be in your company once more."

"Your sweetness makes up for your husband's sordidness," he said, and then he turned to my sisters Kitty and Jane. "And these are the other Bennet ladies. I hear, Miss Kitty, that you are now wed to Colonel Fitzwilliam here."

"I am, Your Highness."

"A great pity that is."

"I beg your—" Colonel Fitzwilliam began, yet he closed his mouth and changed tactics. "A great pity for others, Your Highness, yet the most fortunate for me."

"Ah! And Miss Jane Bennet, the loveliest of creatures along with Mrs. Bingley here, and greetings Mr. Bingley."

"Greetings Your Highness."

"And," the prince said, turning to our Aunt and Uncle Gardiner, Harriet and Isabella. "I heard from the announcer when you entered, that you are Mr. and Mrs. Richard Gardiner, along with your beautiful daughters, Miss Gardiner and Miss Isabella."

"Yes, your highness."

"Relatives of the family?"

"Yes, they are," Mr. Darcy said. "They are Mrs. Darcy's Aunt and Uncle and are therefore our cousins."

"Very well, Mr. and Mrs. Gardiner, you and your lovely daughters are most welcome at Court."

"Thank you, Your Highness," Uncle Gardiner said. "It is truly a great honor to be in your presence."

"Wait till you become acquainted with me before you speak so," he said with a wicked grin. To which all the court erupted in very forced laughter. I felt quite remorseful at the lack of sincerity to everyone's girdle because the prince's jest truly was comical, and I laughed in earnest.

"Oh, yes," Darcy said under his breath to himself. "Yes, wait till you do become acquainted with him."

⊗⚜⊗

"However," the prince continued, "before you move to the edge of our company, I would very much like you to become acquainted with a captain who has done you a great service."

An announcer came forward and approached us.

"Honored guests, we shall introduce Captain Frederick Wentworth."

A tall and stern looking man approached, yet his severity soon relented when he smiled, and his face softened.

"Mr. Darcy, Mrs. Darcy, and company," Captain Frederick Wentworth said, bowing.

"Greetings, sir," Mr. Bingley said for the rest of us.

Captain Wentworth was an interesting man to appraise. His weight was quite proportionate to his height, for he was built solidly, yet not with too much mass on him. His hair was dark, his eyes were even darker, and his skin was more of the olive complexion. His face was a little long, but his height made it appear as if it was proportionate.

"Yes," the prince said. "I thought it fitting that you all meet each other, for it was through both your ends that a great injustice ended, was it not?"

"Oh!" I exclaimed. "Then this is the Captain Wentworth who assisted you in gathering evidence so that our friend could win the Trekenna Trial in America."

"I confess to pleading guilty on that score," Captain Wentworth said with a bow. "And you are the family who made a hero out of me. Therefore, I owe you thanks."

"Thanks is not required, sir," Mr. Darcy replied stoically, "for you have made us momentary heroes in turn."

❧

The banquet began and we were all called into dinner to begin the feast. Once we all sat in our proper and designated seats, the reason for our invitation soon came to light.

"Mr. Darcy and company," the prince began, "please regale us all with the particularities of the Trekenna trial and how a great injustice has now been brought to an end."

"Oh," Mr. Darcy began, "of course, your highness. Between Colonel Fitzwilliam, Mr. Bingley, and myself, I am sure we can recall every moment of it."

"You attended the whole trial then?"

"Yes," Mr. Bingley replied. "Every day of it."

The three men thus began their tale of how the trial progressed, and the attendees who sat at the table all listened with either interest, or they did their best to pretend to do so. When it came to the part of the tale when they appealed to the prince, Darcy told everyone how Georgiana and I urged him to write to the prince, and the prince interrupted.

"Oh, so it was Mrs. and Miss Darcy who asked you to write to me for aid?"

"Yes, Your Highness, it was no instinct of mine, and therefore my wife and sister must take the credit."

The prince nodded. "Then I thank you both. For here is where my part begins."

The prince began his narration of his achievements done on his end, and that was when it occurred to me that our whole invite to the Court was for the prince to show himself as the hero.

As his story came to a close, he ended it with telling us of finding Captain Wentworth.

"And now it is your turn, Captain," he said, "to give us your part in this remarkable tale."

"Ah, sir it is of little matter," Captain Wentworth said humbly.

"Indeed sir, your modesty is magnanimous right now. As a matter of fact, your pride seems strangely nonexistent. Tell us your story."

"Yes," Jane said, "please tell us."

All around the table asked him to continue, however it was Jane that Captain Wentworth stared at with admiration, and he had to remember himself and look down.

'Oh dear,' I thought to myself, 'Now that would be most unpleasant if he took a fancy to her.'

"Oh, very well," he said, "I shall begin."

⚜

Captain Wentworth's tale proved to be a brilliant and action-oriented one.

"I captained a ship named The Julia," Captain Wentworth said, "and it was one of the best posts to have, for it was one ship in the fleet of the West Africa Squadron, which as most know was assembled for the purpose of capturing and arresting slave vessels, especially our own Trade ships, and fine those who captained them. During our travels, we made berth at an island to restock our supplies, when I learned of a ship called the Trekenna who made it into their port, carrying enslaved cargo. The island was one that prohibited the slave trade and therefore the Trekenna had already broken the law under one territorial guideline. After making inquiries, we learned of their route, for they spoke of where they would stop next on their way back to New York, and so we quickly gathered our supplies, raised anchor and we went after them. Eventually we found them."

"You did?" A woman who sat further down the table gasped. "Did you capture those braggards?"

"Unfortunately, though we chased them, their ship proved the faster, and luck was not with us, at the moment. Yet do not fear, for providence may not have found me then. Yet it found me eventually, for one day I was here in London when I was called on by a dear friend of mine, Admiral Croft, who knew of my rendezvous with the Trekenna and had received word from our Royal Highness here, the Prince Regent. He told me that he wanted all the particularities on our chase and asked me if he could quote me on it all. I gave him my word, offered him my journal where I wrote all my daily entries of my time on the Julia, and he sent it to America."

"Where our friend, and my sister's fiancé, a Mr. Jason Whitfield," Mr. Darcy said, "used it to win the case along with the journal of a Spanish clerk, he won."

"Then the slaves are free?" Captain Wentworth asked. "For that, justice has prevailed and much has been won for it."

"Yet what happened to your journal after it all ended?" Isabella asked.

"Oh," Captain Wentworth said with a smile, "Mr. Darcy was good enough to mail it back to the prince and it was delivered back to me. Therefore, my inner thoughts and the chronicle of my adventures are now back in my care and locked away."

❦

At the conclusion of his tale, everyone exclaimed their praises, and it was quickly decided that Captain Wentworth was the most gallant man at the banquet. Mr. Darcy was a perfect addition as also being a gentleman's gentleman when it came to being a hero. Georgiana and I were quite dismissed by the multitude of having done anything, and that was to be expected. Whatever heroism we possessed was not of the sort that they considered acceptable, for we were still women after all.

However, as we ate, I had the good fortune to have been seated next to Captain Wentworth, and he was quite different in his views to my and Georgiana's actions.

"You were very humane to have encouraged your husband," he said, "as was your sister-in-law."

"Thank you, sir. Yet our actions were small compared to yours."

"In the eyes of the Great Redeemer, sometimes the small deeds that are good are as large as the greater deeds."

I nodded. "I hope you are correct, sir, for even in our most miniscule of virtuous deeds, I wish to believe they are being noticed by someone. Yet you are to be commended highly for what you did. A lesser Captain would have not pursued the Trekenna."

He laughed at himself. "I am a fussy sort, I presume, yet if that fussiness leads to fortitude, then I am lucky. And yet, you Mrs. Darcy, your accent does not sound like you are from London."

"No indeed, I am from Steventon in Hampshire."

"Steventon?" he said, his eyes widening in recognition.

"Yes, have you ever happened to have been there?"

"Oh, no," he said most hurriedly, "I have not had that pleasure. I have simply made the acquaintance of a family who was from there."

"What is the family's name?"

"Lucas."

"Oh, Sir William Lucas and his family?" I gasped, amazed that we had a mutual acquaintance.

"Yes, that would be them, I believe."

"I am a good friend to two of their children, Miss Maria and Mrs. Charlotte Collins."

"Mrs.—Mrs. Charlotte Collins?" he stuttered, flinching as he spoke.

"Yes," I said, reading his expression carefully. "She was the eldest of the daughters, and you might have remembered her as Charlotte Lucas."

"Yes," he said gravely, "there was a slight acquaintance on that score. Yes, I knew her a little."

"She was one of my closest companions in growing up," I said, and a part of me wished to know more behind the history of his acquaintance of the Lucas family, and with Charlotte to begin with. However, I knew it would be very intrusive and therefore I had decided to change the discussion. "I also live close to a family by the name of Austen."

"Oh, the clergyman?" Captain Wentworth beamed.

"Yes, you are acquainted with that family?"

"Yes, I am. A mere little, but still well enough. He has a charming family."

"I am on good terms with their brother, Henry, however I was very close with two of their daughters."

"Let me guess!" he said with energy. "Miss Cassandra and Miss Jane Austen."

"You do know them well, clearly."

"They might not remember me, but they are clear in my eyes. A devoted pair of sisters and I liked them both exceedingly."

"I cannot believe that you know them and the Lucases, and yet my family and I never have encountered you. How did you slip into Hampshire and become above or below my mother's notice?"

"Believe me, I did no such thing, for very little escapes a mother's notice. No, I met the Lucas and Austen sisters when both families had gone to visit Brighton."

"Oh, I remember it now. Roughly ten years ago, the Lucases went on holiday to Brighton to go sea bathing. Jane and Cassandra were invited to go with them as their daughters' companions, as were my sister Jane and I. However, our mother would not let us go because there was a gentleman who entered the neighborhood and she wanted us to remain in Hampshire to make his acquaintance."

"Oh, so you were all forced to remain home due to the art of matchmaking."

"Yes." I sighed, rolling my eyes. "And it all came to nothing. Therefore, we missed out on the wonderful joy that was sea-bathing. I daresay that a little sea-bathing would be a great pleasure."

"Have you never gone sea-bathing?"

"No, I have not. And I wish to."

"Yes, a little sea-bathing can set one up forever," he confirmed.

"To be a sea Captain, have any of you or your sailors ever jumped off the ship and into the vast ocean?"

"Oh yes."

"Really? Into so large a body of water where you do not know or sea the dangers?"

"When do dangers ever stop us humans from trying something?" He asked.

"Very true. Yet I do not believe I could ever gather up that much nerve."

"Oh, Mrs. Darcy, believe me, if you were on a ship for over a year, you would gather the courage."

"When the Lucases returned from Brighton with the Austens, they spoke much of the beauty of the place," I said, "yet Charlotte did not seem to have enjoyed it so."

"Oh," he said, avoiding my gaze and staring at his plate. "That is a great pity. However, Brighton, like all things, is not for everyone."

"No, I suppose it is not."

He bit his bottom lip and then he smiled forcefully.

"And yet another acquaintance of mine shall possibly grace the beauties of Hampshire."

"How so?"

"There is an estate there that my sister and her husband wish to purchase. My sister is named Mrs. Susan Croft and her husband is my superior in the navy, Admiral Croft."

"Oh, then the estate is Aginfield?"

"You know it?"

"Yes, right now it is under the name of Mr. Bingley over there. It is through him which Admiral Croft will make the purchase. I have often stayed at Aginfield Park myself."

"Have you?" he asked, interested.

"Yes, it is a comfortable home with much to recommend it."

"I shall extend your compliments of the place to the Admiral."

"You should. He will love the home and the estate around it."

"Thank you. And yet it is quite remarkable, that there is another connection between your history and my own."

"Yes, it is altogether a puzzlement."

"I suppose that it is."

No longer wishing to intrude on more of his history, I took another spoonful of my soup and turned to the person to my left as they asked me how I was enjoying London.

❧

As we returned to Grosvenor Square, I divulged Captain Wentworth's acquaintance with the Austens and the Lucases to Mr. Darcy, Jane, Kitty,

Colonel Fitzwilliam, and Georgiana when we were in the privacy of our dining room.

"Indeed, is the world that small?" Jane said. "For him to know two sets of our neighbors."

"Yes, it often is such," Georgiana said, "for I have learned all too often how miniscule the world can be under the weight of coincidence."

"It is more than that however," I said.

"What do you mean?" Kitty asked.

"I mean that there was something Captain Wentworth was not wishing to speak of. And I believe it had something to do with either the Lucases or the Austens."

"Well, that may be possible," Darcy said. "He very well might not have enjoyed the company or one in the party and he wishes to be polite."

"Yes," I said, not convinced, "that may be so. Yes, my dear, I shall not think on it anymore, for you are quite right most likely."

"I cannot say that I am, yet what I can say is that the banquet proved to be harmless and while the prince invited us, he must have done so to make our actions and his more recognized. Either way, I believe now we can finally be free to return. We are finally able to return to Pemberley."

I gave out a great sigh of satisfaction.

"Oh my, yes we will."

"Yes," Georgiana echoed, "and while I shall miss Jason, I believe that we earned it."

❧

Before I retired to bed, I went into the nursery where Lucy was sitting with Caiden and William. Both of my babies were asleep, and I stood there for a time, watching them as they were in the throes of slumber. My two beautiful boys—how complete and wonderful they looked.

However, even though seeing them in their cribs, it was not enough of a distraction to keep me from recalling Captain Wentworth, and what he was not telling me. More importantly, what was he afraid of? For fear is what I had seen in his eyes.

## ✻ 9 ✻

# ALARMING NEWS

O ur journey back to Pemberley was uninterrupted and uneventful. When we rode down the lane that led through the wide estate, every inch the carriages made was an immense relief for we were closer. Therefore, when we turned round the bend and Pemberley came into view, I broke out into a smile.

"We are back home, Fitzwilliam," I cried, "and our children are returned as well."

"Yes, all is to rights again."

Mrs. Reynolds was there to meet us as we all descended.

"You are all come!" she cried, "and we all are glad to see you."

"Thank you, Mrs. Reynolds," Georgiana said. "And I have wonderful news. Very soon, I shall bring you a fiancé."

"Will you? Then...you are engaged, Miss Darcy?"

"I am," she cried, embracing Mrs. Reynolds, who was taken by surprise.

"Oh," Mrs. Reynolds laughed, embracing her. "Be careful dear, I am an old brittle woman, so you might break something."

I took that time to go to the servant's carriage and help Lucy take down Caiden and William in their cribs.

"Oh, and there are the two boys!" Mrs. Reynolds cried. "The heirs of

Pemberley, Miss Darcy engaged, and you all returned, it is too much. And you all must be tired from your journey," she said as we followed her inside. "I have prepared refreshments, had your beds laid down, and have already prepared hot water to be drawn. You all still enjoy evening baths, I presume?"

"Yes, we still do fancy them," Colonel Fitzwilliam said. "And we recognize your efforts, Mrs. Reynolds."

"Oh, thank you, Colonel."

We all entered and sat down, ate some refreshments and Fitzwilliam asked Mrs. Reynolds how all had been in our absence.

"And a long absence it was," Mrs. Reynolds replied. "Though I know that you were off doing the best of deeds, I confess that we missed the house being so busy!"

"Well," Jane said, "we shall bring you much work to do now, and have the families been informed of our return?"

"Yes Miss Bennet, and they all have been made very aware that you are willing to begin lessons in two days' time."

"Thank you, Mrs. Reynolds, that is splendid."

"And to answer your question in full, Master Darcy, Pemberley has been running quite smoothly. There have been some disputes amongst the tenants, but it was resolved with ease, and you need not worry on that score."

"Thank you, Mrs. Reynolds."

After a moment she remained there.

"Forgive me," she said at last, "yet I must ask if you do not mind. Though I do not wish to remain a burden to you all and act out of place, however, I have never been to America, and I was wondering...what was it like? For you have been there twice now. Tell me, is it a grand adventure?"

"Oh!" We all cried at the same time, and then we all began to speak in unison, our words falling over each other like waves along a shoreline. We all stopped speaking and then one by one, we began to tell her about our adventures, which she enjoyed hearing of—even though it took us a half an hour to finish telling her everything, she listened with attention.

That night we bathed, dressed into our evening attire, went down to eat, all was comfortable, then we sat down in the drawing room, looking into the fire.

"In two days' time, Charles," Darcy said to Mr. Bingley, "you and I may take a look at Allenwell, which you need not worry about the distance. If we ride on horseback, we actually may reach it in an hour's time."

"Brilliant," Mr. Bingley said, and then he turned to Miriam. "If I like the house, I shall bring you to inspect it later to see if it is to your liking. I do not want you to be present when we go through all those particularities of the estate's trivial technicalities. House hunting should be more entertaining, and I want it to be for you."

"Thank you my dear," she said, "and I confess to not caring to listen to the proprietor's details about the walls, paneling and foundations."

"Then it is settled," Mr. Bingley said to Darcy. "In two days' time, we shall go."

☙❧

In two days, Jane had started her lessons with the children of Pemberley, Georgiana already missed Jason, and Kitty decided to distract her by convincing her to an afternoon ride on their horses. Miriam however assisted me in the nursery.

"I recall when my brothers were this small," she said while she cradled Caiden in her arms. "I was only five years old, yet I still held them."

"It shows," I said, crawling around with William. "You look natural in that position."

"Elizabeth..."

"Yes?"

"I think I am pregnant."

"What?" I gasped, turning my attention from William.

"I believe I am pregnant."

"How far along do you think you are?"

"It has been two months now."

"Then you are pregnant."

"I am afraid of telling Charles."

"Why so? Mr. Bingley would naturally be extremely happy?"

"Yes, but I do not wish to tell him and then I miscarry. I do not wish to give him false hope."

"You shall not," I said. "If you are pregnant, whether you lose the child or not, he has the right to know. Also, he loves you Miriam, and he would want to know all that surrounds you in this. He will want to be a part of the process, and even if you do miscarry, Charles is not made of weak inclinations. He understands that miscarriage is a natural thing through which the woman is not to be blamed."

"Then, I should tell him, then?"

"Yes, you should. Being with child is a great thing, and he should be allowed to be with you in every step of the way. All that I would recommend is that you wait for there to be an announcement to be made."

"Oh, how long should I wait?"

"A couple of weeks, however. Wait till the house hunting is ended."

"Very well. For two weeks, I shall allow this happy news to remain within me. Though it does feel as if it shall make me bubble over with excitement."

"I congratulate you, Miriam. I hope for your sake and happiness, that you have triplets!"

Mr. Bingley and Mr. Darcy returned from visiting Allenwell and Mr. Bingley had nothing but good to say of it.

"You shall love it Miriam," he said with enthusiasm. "It is a perfect size, the soil around the house is healthy and the house is very well situated."

"Then I shall not be happy until I have seen it," Miriam said. "Oh, to find a house so close to Pemberley, it would be nice."

Over our dinner, Mr. Bingley and Mr. Darcy regaled us with much information on Allenwell and it sounded like a suitable home. Although when their information ceased, Colonel Fitzwilliam had some unfortunate news.

"I have received word from my superiors," he began, "for a letter arrived today. I shall soon be called away to my duties and have to report to my old post."

"What?" Kitty cried. "You are being called back to the continent?"

"Yes, my dear. I very well may be called away to lead a regiment again on the Peninsula. War with the French seems to be never ending."

Kitty's eyes welled with tears. "I do not want you to go."

"I know my dear, but I must."

My heart went out to Kitty, for she clearly was filled with anxiety, and that was a painful state that I did not know what she truly felt. One can empathize and sympathize all that one wishes. However, one can only assume how one feels, rather than actually know. If Darcy and Richard's roles were reversed, then how would it have affected me? Would I be able to allow him to place himself in harm's way? In truth, I do not believe I would have let him.

"Then," Kitty argued, "I am coming with you. I shall follow your regiment."

"Kitty, I should like you to remain here where it is safe."

"I know, yet I shall not listen. Not this time, Richard."

"No, of course you shall not," Richard said gently, knowing Kitty's mind and mood. "There is no convincing you of otherwise, shall I?"

"Of course not."

"Then my love, at least you shall be beside me."

◈✦◈

"Are we close, my love?" I asked Darcy while our carriages were rolling down the road. The next day came and so came our planned day of seeing Allenwell.

"Yes, my dear," Darcy said, "we are very close."

Georgiana and Kitty remained at Pemberley, for both women chose to assist Jane in her teachings. Therefore, Colonel Fitzwilliam, Mr. Darcy and I joined Mr. and Mrs. Bingley for the outing.

In due time, we came upon Allenwell, and it was a fine house indeed!

It was not to the same level of Pemberley, however what was as great as Pemberley?

Upon our arrival, the proprietor named Mr. Worthington met us and after introductions were made, he began to show us the interior of the house.

I shall be frank. If I possessed the skill to describe perfect houses in detail and if architecture was the objective of this narrative, then I would go into much detail of Allenwell. Yet I lack the talent to discuss wall design and furnishings with any sort of flare. Therefore, all that I shall say is that Allenwell was the sort of home to serve Mr. Bingley's needs most perfectly. It had beauty and grace but was also well built and sturdy. After we all inspected the house and the grounds, we all nodded our approval and Mr. Bingley turned lastly to Miriam.

"Well, my dear, is this a home that you would love to live in?"

Miriam looked around once more and then she beamed.

"Mr. Bingley, I do believe that we have found our perfect home."

"Splendid!" Mr. Worthington cried. "Might we meet again very soon to have all the proper papers drawn up to transfer ownership to you?"

"Yes, you may, sir," Mr. Bingley said, almost giddy. "You may as soon as is possible."

Mr. Bingley had often described himself as being a man who when he did something, he opted to do it quickly. And his purchase of Allenwell would be done in the same style. As all was finalized, I could also see a deep tranquility within Darcy, and I knew the source behind the light in his soul. Mr. Bingley was my husband's bosom friend, and the strength that stemmed from their bond was also what strengthened them both. Therefore, to be in the same area of each other gave them much confidence on many levels—and as such, I was made all the happier for it.

The next day, I remained in the nursery once more and after an hour of crawling around with both my sons, I was met with a very unexpected surprise. Lucy, who had been with me the entire time, also witnessed the great event.

"It seemed to be a miracle!" I gasped.

"Yes, missus, it does seem quite wonderful."

"Please! Go and find Mr. Darcy, then have him come here."

"Right away, missus."

Moving with the speed of light and filled with energy, Lucy left me immediately and rushed to Mr. Darcy's study.

With my heart feeling as if it was swelled with pride and joy, I could not believe what I had just witnessed. Could it really have been? And if it had been so, then could the happy moment be replicated so easily?

I wondered if my feelings were what my mother had experienced when it came to my sisters and me when we were so little. I was not left to my own thoughts for long however when I heard the familiar footsteps of Mr. Darcy and Lucy. They entered and Lucy was indeed trailing behind him, for with his grand height, and her slight one, for every step he took, she would have had to take two of them.

"Elizabeth," he said, "what is it?"

"Fitzwilliam, it is wonderful! Caiden has taken his first step."

When hearing this, Darcy's eyes widened in surprise.

"He did?" Darcy declared.

"Yes! Oh, I am beside myself. He took a few steps and then he fell down again. I cannot guarantee that he shall do so again, yet if he does, I was hoping that you would be present to witness it."

"Yes, of course. Oh, my dear Caiden."

Darcy sat down and prepared himself.

"Now promise me that you will not be disappointed if he does not do so."

"I shall not. I promise."

"Very well."

I stood on my knees and took Caiden's hand in my own. Then I let go and he fell on his bottom, whaling out in laughter, showing that he felt no pain.

"Very well," I said, "Caiden, time for another try. Can you do it, for Papa?"

Caiden clapped his hands together and his energy was so brilliant that I could not contain how much I loved him, for he filled my heart with glee. I slowly removed my hands from his...and he remained standing!

"Oh, my boy!" Darcy cried. "My great boy!"

"Yes, he does seem great, does he not? However, do not come to him just yet." I then moved away from him, and I raised out my arms.

"Caiden, come to me. Caiden?"

Caiden laughed merrily and then he fumbled, falling to the ground. Yet he only rose to his knees then used his hands to lift himself up.

"He stood up himself this time!" Darcy gasped.

"Yes, he is a fast learner. Now Caiden, try my darling, I only ask for you to take one step. Caiden?"

Caiden looked down at the ground, and then he looked into my eyes. He raised out his hands to me—and he took one step.

As I rushed to him, I felt the tears flow down my face. I took Caiden in my arms and spun him around, for indeed at that moment, such a small moment felt like an eclipse of my senses. That was what it had meant to be parents, it seemed! Any small achievement that your children underwent seemed to be a large triumph, an accomplishment of the will and testament to their strength. One step for Caiden was a larger one than I had ever taken.

When I released him, Darcy stood up and he also approached me, wrapping his arms around me and our son.

"I am...Elizabeth, I cannot describe what I feel."

"You do not have to say anything at all, my love," I whispered. "All you have to do is be here. All you have to do is stay."

Lucy quietly left us alone while Darcy held me. Our son was in between us, perhaps wondering at why his parents were staring down on him thus.

The next day was Sunday. With it being one of the days that Jane had free from schooling, we all went to church, attending the service. Forgive me, I did my best to listen to the sermon, yet I could not tear my thoughts from William and Caiden, for I wished to remain with them—and the sermon that our clergyman delivered that day was so dry that I could not help but become easily distracted.

We all had returned home afterwards and sat down to our mid-day meal when Lucy entered.

"If you please ma'am, yet I have a letter for you."

"A letter on Sunday?" I asked. "That is most extraordinary?"

"The post just come, and it was sent express."

"Oh, that explains it, yet what is of so much importance that it should come to me with speed? Oh, it is from Charlotte at Hunsford. Would you all mind if I read the letter at the table?"

"It is suitable," Darcy said. "You may, my dear."

"Thank you."

I opened the letter and began to read. As I did so, I was startled more and more as I read on, so taken aback by shock that I did not know precisely what to feel.

"Lizzy?" Georgiana said, eying me closely. "You look quite flushed. Is the news of the bad sort?"

"It is...it is...the most alarming news."

"What is it? What has happened?"

"It is an acquaintance of ours. Charlotte has just written to tell me that Mr. Collins is dead."

"What?" Jane gasped.

"Yes. Mr. Collins is dead."

# POOR CHARLOTTE!

"That cannot be!" Jane cried.

"Yes," I whispered, "I believe that it is. Charlotte says it right here."

"Give it to me," Kitty said, walking over and snatching the letter from me, which I allowed her to do so with great enthusiasm. It was all so alarming, for while one understands that tragedy can befall someone one is acquainted with, it cannot hold disbelief at bay.

Kitty stood over the table and began to read it.

*Dear Elizabeth and et.*

*I have received word from Lady Catherine that you are returned to Pemberley, and I trust that your adventures were fruitful. However, I write to you now on a most grave matter. My husband Mr. Collins has unfortunately passed away.*

*The manner of his demise was quite sudden, and I rejoice that it was swift at least. He was unfortunately tending to his beehives along the edge of our estate. When removing the honey from one of the hives, he dropped it and it fell on the ground in a small puddle. We are not fully certain of what happened next, yet it can only be assumed that he slipped and fell, being knocked unconscious while he fell headfirst into the puddle of honey, and he suffocated to death.*

*This loss shall be felt all around, and I at least have one comfort in that he is now in a better place. I can only assume that by the time this letter shall reach you, the funeral service shall already be underway, therefore all I ask is that you offer a prayer to the Holy Redeemer for my husband's poor and pious soul.*

*Onto other matters, after the funeral, as you will have known, I must leave the Hunsford Parsonage due to the new Parson taking up residence there, for he shall be my late husband's replacement. Mary has also informed me that you and the other residents of Pemberley and Aginfield shall return to Hampshire in a little over a fortnight. This shall bring me much joy at this frightening time, your company shall be a blessing for me, for I shall have to return to Lucas Lodge once more, a daughter now widowed and returned to my solitary state.*

*I know that you shall pray for the soul of Mr. Collins and that is all the memory that I ask you to have of him. I cannot wait to see you, my dear friend...and that knowledge shall be enough to hold me fast and firm to my purpose.*

*Your friend and one time neighbor,*
    *Charlotte Collins*

Kitty lowered the letter and looked upon the rest of us.

"He drowned in bee honey?" Colonel Fitzwilliam exclaimed.

"Yes," Kitty replied, equally perturbed. "He actually did."

"I mean—it is very sad and of shocking degree," Colonel Fitzwilliam stuttered, realizing that he must have sounded insensitive, "yet...he really drowned in bee honey?"

"And not just any bee honey," Mr. Bingley added, "yet from his own beehives?"

"Yes, yes he did," I confirmed. "Well, at least it was, as Charlotte said, painless, for he was unconscious during it."

We all sat there, unwilling to speak, for I knew we all were thinking the same thing; death was always tragic, yet it was already hard to not see the reality when the person you had to lament was not well liked amongst the company. And the reality was...that the death was all too outlandish and comical!

Mr. Collins, our cousin and reverend to Lady Catherine de Bourgh, was always described as a ridiculous man at best, yet would he even be tied to it during his death? He lived under the judgment of being an idiot in many ways and yet to die in such an idiotic way, it made one unable to feel the tragedy at first, for all one could see was the comedy. Was the man not at least allowed to have a grave demise that invoked pity, where his name and identity would be redeemed by honor and piety?

"Poor Charlotte!" Jane said. "Imagine the state that she is in."

"Yes," I said. "She must feel a great pain now, and we are not close to her."

"Yet she knows why you cannot be," Georgiana said. "We all shall see her soon and therefore all that is left for us to do is offer Mr. Collins our condolences until then."

"I agree," Mr. Darcy said, and then he stood up and began to offer up a prayer.

"We pray for the life of Mr. Collins. Whatever his flaws, he was a fellow amongst our acquaintance who was pious and did possess kindness, therefore we offer up our condolences to him, and his wife Mrs. Collins. May his soul be released into the heavens and may he find peace and tranquility there."

"Amen," I said.

※

Before supper, I was in the nursery once more and this time Lucy was absent because Darcy joined me. I held William in my arms, he held Caiden's hands so that Caiden could use him for support in taking a few steps.

"Now that we are in secret," Darcy said, "I feel that I am allowed to say what I should not say, yet it is what I feel."

"You cannot speak in remorse for Mr. Collins because he made himself unlikable," I spoke for him. "And because his death was so ridiculous that it is hard to feel any sympathy for."

"Precisely. I understand his major flaw, which was that of a man who wished to please so much that he never knew how to please anyone, for he tried too hard. And his initial intention to marry one of you all to keep Longbourn in the family and not allow you to be forsaken was very noble. However, I cannot help but remember his treatment of Kitty after the rejection, his refusal to see Mary's feelings and how he hurt her indirectly, his telling your father to reject Lydia forever and call that being wholesome, and his constant meddling in our affairs by reporting much to my aunt Catherine and has led to me always thinking he shall be the bane of our circles. And now his death, it is a rum business."

"Yes, it is, an egregiously rum business."

"I want to feel remorse for him, I do, however it shall take me time."

"I understand. For pity for him cannot be conjured so within my heart so soon as well."

"Yet what do you feel in regard to Charlotte now?" he asked me quizzically.

"I feel remorse for her, I do, however..."

"A part of you still cannot deny that you view her marriage to Mr. Collins as a form of betraying you?" he finished my comment.

"How...how did you know that?"

"Because in some ways, it was. I know that Charlotte Lucas was viewing the match solely as a means to protect herself as well as support her family, and for that neither you nor I can reprimand her. She was a spinster who was given a means to rectify her situation, and what was she that society did not make her? She is heavily encouraged, to the point of being obligated, to marry as a means of securing her future. And yet, it still was an egregious error on her end, and she learned to see it very quickly. To marry for monetary gain is necessary even in the world we live in now, yet to do so when the man who proposed to you is the inheritor of the estate your dear friend lives on, it does seem quite callous."

"I always told myself that she did it with the intention of telling Mr. Collins to remain at Hunsford Parsonage, after my father's death," I said. "Yet now I am not certain. And I do not know what to feel. Either way, I must feel remorse for her, yet I am wondering if what she is undergoing now..."

"Is something she ought to undergo."

"Precisely. Even Charlotte recognized her mistake eventually. Do I sound cruel, Fitzwilliam, and vindictive?"

"Do not fear, my dear. Something tells me that this is a trial Charlotte Collins might need to undergo."

"I wonder what she is feeling now. Oh, poor Charlotte!"

# LOOKING TO THE UNKNOWN

The funeral procession was proceeding as one could be expected, Mary Bennet thought. She sat in the pew beside Anne and Lady Catherine de Bourgh. Yet every now and again, she turned her gaze toward Charlotte, who sat in the pew nearest to the altar, with Maria beside her. Behind Charlotte sat the rest of their family, all with the exception of Mr. Samuel Lucas, who Mary still did not know why was absent.

The substitute reverend, a man named Mr. Higgins who usually performed services in the neighboring parish, was giving a sermon at the pulpit about death and the peace one is expected to experience when life begins to re-open at the close. However, Mary took no heed to it. Usually, she paid attention to sermons spoken at Sunday services with great dedication, yet now she could not apply her mind to reflect on the words that were spoken.

There, in front of the altar, was Mr. Collins, who was resting in his coffin and his lifeless form inspired a range of emotions within her.

For months, she had been living at Rosings Park, employed as Anne de Bourgh's personal companion, and in all that time, she had learned much that opened her eyes. Anne not only had proven to be easy to be a companion to, yet Mary Bennet had discovered much...and the most valuable lesson she had come to learn was that she had escaped a most sad fate in not being the wife of Mr. Collins.

For so long she had been envious of Kitty for being the one to have been chosen by Mr. Collins for a wife, and then she had felt even more slighted when Mr. Collins had chosen to turn his affections toward Charlotte Lucas when she, Mary, had been standing right there to be the perfect substitute.

Initially when Mary had received the honor of being Anne's companion however, she was at first hesitant because she knew she would often be in Mr. Collins's presence. Yet her sense of duty and for a desire to be of some occupation called out to her—she therefore looked at this opportunity as a chance to change how others perceived her.

Only then would she begin to overcome her pain, for she found herself unable to see anything but the truth, and the truth was quite singular in that situation. Mr. Collins, though wishing to always be thoughtful and kind, often proved to be obsequious, redundant and an embarrassment to his wife, Charlotte. He often offended those without even knowing he was being offensive, his adoration of Lady Catherine de Bourgh was nothing far away from being obsessive, he lacked conviction for he was willing to always change his opinions to suit those he regarded as superior—and he often could be a hypocrite.

*I was such a fool to have ever liked him! Mary, you were a fool! And how had you not seen it before?*

Too many a time, she had seen Charlotte look down in embarrassment at something Mr. Collins had either said or done, and his shame marked her own.

Mary felt something touch her arm and she looked down to see Anne poking her, attempting to get her attention.

"What is it, Miss de Bourgh?" Mary whispered.

"What do you think she is feeling now?" Anne asked, looking at Charlotte in the other pew. "How deep do you think her pain is?"

"I think...that she is confused."

"How so?"

"For I believe that she is sad to not have the security of being wed, however she might also secretly be looking forward to being able to go home once more."

"Only one thing is certain," Anne said.

"What?"

"She feels remorse over the fact that she does not have it in her to cry."

Sitting in her pew, Charlotte Collins gave up trying to produce a tear. She indeed had felt sorry for Mr. Collins and all that he began to see in the end, however a part of her was angry with him. Though one could regard her feelings as being very un-Christian, she did not care.

She was angry that he had died on her!

Though never having been romantic, she did not require affection to wed, it was true, but it was not out of lack of desire for love, but of a distant memory of what love felt like. Charlotte Lucas, now Mrs. Collins, had never been a romantic because love was too hard—she had been under the spell of it once, and it nearly broke her. Thus, she shied away from needing passion from her life partner because she had accepted the fact, long ago, that she never would be strong enough for the real thing.

However, the least she would have liked was to have a like-minded individual to join her days with. A tie where there was at least a slight affection and mutual respect, yet there was not even that. For so long, living with Mr. Collins had proved to be a great chore! Time began to lessen the burden, most decidedly, yet the one consolation that she had received from her trial was that at least her future was secure. She had been protected from the rocky shores of an unknown future where she would be the butt of jokes, the perennial spinster that none would ever choose.

However, all had come to naught. Mr. Collins passed away not two years after their marriage, and she was left with little to nothing. She was right back to where she had begun.

What was worse was that part of her wondered if this was all her own doing? And therefore, this was what she had deserved? She married a man who held the future of her friends in the palm of his hand and accepted him rather than be selfless and have encouraged him to shift his attentions from Kitty to Mary. She knew that Mary had liked him. Only someone stricken with blindness of judgment could not see it—like Mr. Collins. Therefore, perhaps she ought to have done so, making Longbourn stay fully in the hands of the Bennets, yet she was vain—no, she was ambitious. And her ambition had cost her much, including the close bond she had experienced with the Bennets. It was true Mrs. Bennet held her plainness in comparison to her daughters over Charlotte's head, yet that was not any of the daughters' faults. It was not over Elizabeth's especially, who was the one that Charlotte was now fully jealous of.

Yet there was that other part of her, the part that she would not think about, that she also felt that she was being punished for. Yet she banished that thought as quickly as she had considered it. That result was not her fault. That man was not her problem, for she had done her duty.

☙❧

However, she then thought on to Elizabeth and wondered at how she had received such news. Would she be thrilled, for Mr. Collins had passed on and Charlotte did not produce any children with him, so Longbourn was now free from going to that quarter, or would she think kindly on Charlotte and be merciful?

Upon marrying Mr. Collins, Charlotte did wonder if there was ever the chance that she could have convinced Mr. Collins to remain at Hunsford Parsonage till the end of his days, forever being the reverend there, while the Bennets remained at Longbourn. Yet soon into their marriage she had learned that Mr. Collins was secretly too spiteful for that impulse initially. Over time, he may have softened at the idea, however at first, he was still bitter that Kitty had refused him. Oh Kitty! Who would have ever believed, that of all characters in their tales, her actions would prove to affect so many, and be the one to have made one of the wiser choices?

Yet Charlotte knew in her heart that Elizabeth might never believe that her intentions had been good initially. For who would?

Therefore, it was only fitting that she be dealt this blow, she realized.

Poor Mr. Collins, she thought.

Poor herself.

How ironic it should be that she, she who had prided herself for so long on being practical, had been thwarted, for even the practical could not long outrun fate.

As such, looking to the unknown that was her fate, she took comfort in one thing: at least she would be returning home, to Hampshire. At least she still had Lucas Lodge, as the Bennets all must have been happy that she did not have Longbourn.

# WELL WORTH THE FIGHT

"Now we shall still have Longbourn," Jane said as we all prepared to leave. "My heart goes out to the poor Mr. Collins and Charlotte, however I also cannot help but think of our parents, and our mother must be feeling some relief at the moment. Though it is awful to suggest such a thing, yet I know where her mind shall linger."

"Yes, she will be very much at ease," I said. "Yet I hope she shall be sure not to speak of it so loosely and never check herself."

"Lizzy, I am not certain of it. Yet I hope so."

The month of our staying at Pemberley had come to an end quite quickly and it was time for us to away to Hampshire, yet there was no real anxiety or resentment on the matter, for we were leaving for Longbourn and Aginfield. We had received word from Jason Whitfield that he would journey there when time allowed him, and he would remain with us at Aginfield for the duration. Therefore, it felt as if we were simply going from one home to another.

Thus, in one carriage was Mr. Darcy, Jane, Georgiana and myself. Colonel Fitzwilliam, Kitty, Mr. Bingley and Mrs. Bingley were in the second carriage, Lucy and another servant was seeing to my babies in the third along with Jefferson, and our luggage was stored with some servants in the fourth.

"Will Mary return to Longbourn?" I asked Jane as we rode along.

"Unfortunately not," she replied. "When I received a letter from our father, he spoke that she has to remain at Rosings Park with Anne de Bourgh. She has proven to be quite a valuable asset to the estate."

"I am not surprised, for Mary always was a useful sort of person, and therefore I can guarantee that not only is she essential to Miss de Bourgh, she might also be another person who Lady Catherine would like to utilize as her Right Hand."

"It would give my aunt another person to oversee and order around," Darcy said, "which she would love, yet I know very well that Anne would not want Mary to leave. Due to Aunt Catherine very rarely allowing Anne to leave her supervision, Anne is very lonely."

"Indeed, she was only allowed freedom in America," Georgiana said. "Cousin Thomas knew how to talk to her ladyship, and he was successful at being a good father that he immediately knew how to protect Anne from her own mother."

"Yes, and we here have no idea how to continue to help Anne find liberty. Yet we can only hope so. It is very well that Mary stays with her, for Mary is the sort who does not look to wed clearly and therefore she is the best sort of thing to happen to Anne."

I sighed. "Such an interesting turn it has taken. If you were to tell me a year ago that one day Mary would be the preferred companion of Miss Anne de Bourgh, I would never have believed it."

"It goes to show you," Jane said, "that everyone does have a place where they belong."

She smiled gently and then looked out the window as the scenery rolled on by.

The journey to Hampshire went swiftly and we were returned to Steventon where we first came upon the Austen house.

"Wait stop!" I cried. "Please Fitzwilliam, stop the carriages."

"You're about to do something reckless, aren't you?" he asked lightly.

"Yes!"

"Stop the coach, Nicholson!" Darcy said. "And order the rest to stop as well!"

Nicholson stopped the carriages and Jane and I jumped out.

"Come Georgiana!" I cried, "for they shall be happy to see you as well."

"Brilliant!"

The three of us jumped out of the carriage and were soon followed by Kitty from the other carriage.

"Jane!" I cried, "Cassandra! Austens, we are returned!"

"We hear you, Elizabeth!" Cassandra said, coming from around the house from the back lawn. "You are all returned to us! Jane, come out of the house! The Darcys are here!"

Soon the front door opened, and Jane Austen emerged with the rest of her family.

"Elizabeth! Jane! Georgiana and Kitty!" she cried. "Sorry, I was—"

"Writing, we know!" Kitty said. Cassandra, Jane Austen, and the rest of the Austens rushed up to us and we all hugged one another.

Cassandra was delighted. "You are returned to us. Oh, Charlotte will love that."

"Is Charlotte already returned to Lucas Lodge?"

"Yes, both Charlotte and Maria."

"How is she?"

Cassandra turned to her sister, and Jane Austen turned to me.

"It cannot be so easily described. When you are settled at Aginfield, tell us, so that we can all go to see her together."

"Very well," Mr. Darcy said, replying for me. All the Austens turned and looked up at him in awe, for he still inspired it within them.

He bowed, then gave them a special smile. "Miss Austen, Miss Jane and all the rest of you Austen lot. How are you all?"

Jane and Cassandra Austen smiled shyly at him and then curtsied.

"We are well Mr. Darcy," Cassandra said. "We trust you have had a pleasant trip in America."

"Oh, we have many stories to tell on that score," he replied. "Perhaps even too many, even for you Miss Jane."

"There is no such thing as too many stories told to a writer, sir," Jane Austen replied, smiling. "And I am like a dry rag, ready to absorb all within me."

"You are dangerous then!"

"Yes, I am, for the pen is mightier than the sword! Oh and Mr. and Mrs. Bingley and Colonel Fitzwilliam!"

"Hello Miss Austen and Miss Jane," Mr. Bingley said. "It is pleasing to see you once more."

"Indeed, it is," Mrs. Bingley said in return. "And Miss Jane, how has your writing been progressing?"

"Slow and fast all at the same time. Fast in the sense that it is not possible, yet slow in the sense that I cannot write as quickly as the thoughts come to me."

"Is that normal with writers?"

"Oh, I have often heard so."

"Well, forgive me for sounding direct, yet is there a chance that you shall be favoring us with a reading of yours? I have read *Sense and Sensibility* as well, and quite reveled in the technique of it. Is there anything else you have written that you would be willing to give a presentation on?"

"Oh, I usually do not give readings at all," Jane Austen said, "yet, since it is you, Mrs. Bingley, I think I should be up for the task."

"Oh, thank you."

Our meeting with the Austens did not last long, for we had to get on the road again to Aginfield and then meet my parents once more.

Therefore, we extended our farewells and left for Aginfield. Once we arrived there, it was unique to be there again, for this time we knew that it would be the last time we resided in it, for soon it would belong to another.

"What day shall Admiral Croft arrive to inspect Aginfield?" Colonel Fitzwilliam asked Mr. Bingley.

"I expect him to arrive in two days' time," Mr. Bingley said, "and I believe he is more in favor of purchase than not."

"That is very well."

"It is, and therefore I shall hope to give away Aginfield with a clear conscience. For that is where the rub is. A house begins to become more than just a house to one, but rather, it becomes a character in our lives. I shall always remember when Mr. Bingley was here—just as I shall always remember when Mr. Bingley was me."

"Do you think yourself apt to change your identity any time soon, my dear?" Mrs. Bingley laughed.

"No, I hope not, yet one day our son might be born, and he shall be the next Mr. Bingley, and then his son shall be. And then further down the line, there will be many Mr. Bingleys. Eventually, I, this Mr. Bingley will be no more, yet I shall take comfort in knowing that I was him for a time."

"I cannot tell whether to enjoy your mystical confession, my love, or whether to cry."

"Just smile and forgive my sentiment right now," he said, kissing her cheek.

༺❀༻

"Oh, it is all too much!" our mother cried when we finally arrived back at Longbourn. "All of my children are returned to me!"

"Hello mother!" Jane and I cried.

"Oh, Mr. Bennet is coming, he is just really slow. Mr. Bennet!" she cried. "Come out here immediately and greet our family."

"I am coming my dear," Came our father's voice and slowly he emerged from out of the house. "Oh, look we have our throng of kin."

"And with two additions," I said, emerging from the carriage, holding Caiden, while Georgiana also emerged holding William. "Mother and Father, behold your first set of grandchildren, William and Caiden."

"Upon my word!" our mother cried. "You have done well Lizzy! You not only gave your husband one son, yet two. That was well done."

"Well, I do believe Mr. Darcy had something to do with this act as well, my dear," our father answered dryly.

"Oh, do not be so scandalous in your speech, Mr. Bennet!" Then she turned back to me. "But Lizzy, yes well done, for when a woman does not give a man a son, she has quite failed."

"Ah, then that means you failed me?" Mr. Bennet added, enjoying the fact that his wife dug herself into that insult.

"Oh, nonsense," she cried. "I never did any such thing."

I rolled my eyes and then our mother turned back to my sons.

"They are lovely," she said, "and yet they are twins?"

"Yes."

"But they look very different."

"Oh, so you can see that as well?"

"Yes, they look very much so, and it is so ironic. Mr. Darcy, Caiden is the one who looks like you."

"What?" Mr. Darcy said. "You can see that?"

"Yes, it is quite clear. Caiden is the one who will be the spitting image of you."

"And what of William?"

Our mother then turned to William and looked down on him.

"Oh, my word..."

"What is it mother?" I asked.

"Mr. Bennet...he looks like you."

"What?" our father said.

"Mark my words, I can see it, he will grow up to look like you."

"Mrs. Bennet, surely you cannot be so accurate—it could not..." Our father came up to William and looked down on him. It was most remarkable for I had never seen my father look so amazed, no hint of cynicism or sarcasm, just pure innocent amazement. "Does he really look like me?"

"Yes, he does," our mother said, also subdued. "It is quite remarkable, is it not?"

"I...yes. Yes, it is." Emotion filled my father's eyes and he stepped back, trying to conceal his wonder. "Well..." He turned to our mother, and she looked up at him in quiet alarm. "What is it?"

"Nothing it is only...with that look on your face," she said. "With that amazement and pride, it made you look as you were when you were twenty-five years old."

My father grew red in the face, and he muttered under his breath, which I understood. This purity of emotion was too much for his base nature and for so long, I do not believe his heart had been touched in such a way. Therefore, he must have felt naked to the world now. At the moment, I had only wished that I had allowed us to bring my sons sooner, for if they could invoke this response from their grandparents, then their influence was a powerful one. I would never forget, not all my days, how William and Caiden had brought such a sight before us.

⚜

"Well then," Our father said after he gathered his resolve, "it is freezing outside, and I do not want our grandsons to have their first time at Long-bourn in getting a cold. Let us enter."

We all did so with alacrity for once we thought of it, we did realize that it was quite freezing.

Once we did, our mother greeted everyone individually and whatever intimidation she once felt for Mr. Darcy, she had now quite lost. She wished to hold William while Caiden took a few steps for everyone as I held one of his hands.

"Oh, Lizzy," she cried, "he has your spirit."

"Thank you, mama," I said, "but my loving husband has let me know that he shall not be satisfied until I have also given him a daughter."

"Oh, daughters usually are of no consequence to their fathers," she replied. "You are very different, Mr. Darcy."

"I hope so, Mrs. Bennet," Darcy replied.

"Oh Mrs. Bennet, that is not even true!" our father replied. "A daughter can be quite valuable to a father. It is only through entails that a son gathers more importance, and only then."

"Well, your tone has quite changed, Mr. Bennet."

"I...oh dear, I have no witty reply at the moment. It is quite strange."

We all laughed in response and then after we all spoke of our time in

America and in meeting the Prince Regent a second time, eventually the conversation steered to the loss of Mr. Collins.

"I shall miss him," our father said. "For his correspondence always rendered such an amusement to me, that I shall have no choice but to lament his passing."

"You are still an observer of human folly?" I asked.

"Yes, I am."

"I have soon learned that in such circumstances, a little goes a long way, Father."

"Yet never regarding Mr. Collins. His words of misguided wisdom would always be a constant source of diversion."

"Well," our mother said in a huff, "while I shall always mourn the dead, I cannot help but find the matter justified."

"Mother!" Jane cried. "That is unkind."

"And I am sorry for it my dear, but I refuse to not be heard on this subject. After his indelicate reaction to Kitty's refusal, to his marrying Charlotte Lucas instead of transferring his affections to Mary, and his constant hints at wishing to take over Longbourn. Pray, I cannot feel too much sadness over that odious man! I do feel sorry for him, for it was very hard how young he passed away as, and it is a great tragedy. Yet now I at least do not have to witness Charlotte Collins taking my place here and having to witness you all be destitute and cast against the terrible ways of the world."

None of us attempted to reprimand her further, because though she was vulgar in her words, what did she say that did not come from a rational fear and a desire to protect us? She was correct, in all essentials—if our father had passed away before we all were wed, our fates would have been awful, resulting in poverty and being homeless. Charlotte Collins still had a home in Lucas Lodge when Mr. Collins died, yet if our father had passed and we were single, our mother would have had nothing but a feeling of failure in that she could not protect us from the horrors of losing everything.

"And yet," Georgiana said suddenly, "now I am confused. If Longbourn was entailed to the male line and Mr. Collins was the inheritor, who shall inherit it now that he has passed?"

All of us looked to our father who actually looked entirely at a loss!

"I...I had not known about it, yet I am not certain. My brother is deceased, his son has followed after him and perhaps there may be a distant cousin of mine, yet I do not know."

"You do not know?" Colonel Fitzwilliam asked, squinting his eyes.

"Yes, perhaps the courts could find one, yet it will be a surprise if they do. All of my cousins, to my knowledge were all women, therefore I can only assume that one of their sons would inherit it."

"And yet, there might be another solution."

"What do you mean, Richard?" Kitty asked.

"It is just a thought," he said, standing up and beginning to pace, "and Mr. and Mrs. Bennet, please do not assume that I am doing this to be selfish, yet I am only thinking of Kitty's comfort."

"What do you mean?" our mother said, but I set my mind to work swiftly, and I did believe that I began to see what Colonel Fitzwilliam was hinting at.

"I mean, Mr. and Mrs. Bennet," he began, "that if the court and entail are so content to only allow an inheritance to pass through the male line, then perhaps we can use such bigotry and injustice in our favor. What I am saying is that courts would naturally accept any plan of *any* man inheriting over a woman. To the point where they might even allow it to be passed down to a son-in-law of yours, Mr. Bennet."

"Colonel?" Our father said leaning forward. "Are you implying what I presume that you are, sir?"

"Yes. I have seen it before, sir, and you have an attorney in your family, we shall have another with Mr. Whitfield marrying Georgiana as well. Between their powers, I am certain that we could get them to argue your situation where the entail enlarges to incorporate your sons-in-laws as your heirs. Or at the very least, the court will let you adopt one of us as your son in name and therefore be allowed rights to it. Sir, with your permission, I humbly request that you consider me. Please, for the sake of your daughter Kitty and yourselves, let us at least fight to have me inherit Longbourn. This way, if I do, when either of you unfortunately pass away, the other can remain for I shall run the estate, and when Longbourn is left to Kitty and I only, she shall always have a home, and so will our children."

"Oh, dear Colonel," our mother said. "Do you really think it is possible?"

"I know it is. The courts, wills and contracts will not allow any of you rights to keep your home, Mrs. Bennet, then let us use such a practice against them and return it back to you all."

"Oh Richard," Kitty cried, standing up. "Longbourn would actually become ours? I would not lose our home?"

"No, you will not, Kitty. The Bennets will not lose Longbourn, not if I have to say anything on the matter."

"Oh Richard!" she cried, embracing him and they kissed in front of us all, and we tastefully averted our eyes, pretending like the impropriety was not happening as long as we did not see it.

"Well, Mr. and Mrs. Bennet?" Colonel Fitzwilliam said, turning to my parents. "What say you? Do you think it is worth the fight?"

My father at first did not smile, then his eyes sparkled, and he grinned.

"Colonel Fitzwilliam, I think it is well worth the fight."

## ❧ 13 ❧

# TIME HEALS ALL WOUNDS

**M**uch was thought of and put into motion very swiftly. Our father proposed to Colonel Fitzwilliam that they visit the Philips residence the next day and then they planned how best to phrase their argument.

Meanwhile during the day, Jane and Cassandra Austen came to visit so that we all might walk to Lucas Lodge and see Charlotte and Maria. Jane, Kitty, Miriam, and Georgiana joined us while William and Caiden would remain at Aginfield with Lucy.

Thus, I was at liberty to see my old friend. Although how we would approach one another would be a strange thing. I honestly did not fully know what to make of Charlotte sometimes, yet she was in a time of inner turmoil, and as a result, she still did deserve my sympathy.

Our company arrived at Lucas Lodge and Lady Lucas greeted us kindly.

"I express my apologies for Sir William not being present," she said, "he is in town at this time."

"We understand," I said. "And we are most sorry for—"

"Jane, Elizabeth, Miss Darcy, Mrs. Bingley and Kitty!" Maria hurried into the room. "It is wonderful to see you again."

"Maria!" Kitty cried. "It is nice to see you as well. How did you find Rosings?"

"It was, well..."

"Elizabeth!"

I turned to the sound of my name and in the doorway stood Charlotte.

⚜

She looked—well, she looked as Charlotte always looked; calm and collected. I wondered at what she would have thought upon seeing me, yet she seemed to actually be a little reserved, not from coldness but from nervousness.

She and I had seen each other after her marriage to Mr. Collins, however I could only assume what she was feeling now. All her plans and schemes had come for naught and now she would have to suffer with knowing that she had lost in the end. Unless I was completely in error of what she was feeling.

"My dear Charlotte," I said gently, "I am so sorry for your loss." Deciding that it would be better to forget how her past actions vexed me, I decided to release it all, and thus I went up to her and embraced her. I felt Charlotte sigh against me, and she wrapped her arms around me. "I do not know what you are feeling now."

"I feel many things, and I am having a hard time describing any of them."

As we all remained at Lucas Lodge, I was able to speak with Charlotte in confidence while we sat away from the rest of the company.

"Now that we only have each other to confide in," I began, "tell me what you are feeling."

"As I said," she began, "it is so confusing that it is quite difficult to know how to describe. I feel some proper reactions to my new state, as well as some guilty ones."

"Guilty ones?" I asked, curious.

"Perhaps I should start with the 'good'. I feel quite sorry for my husband. He was too young and what was more, he was finally beginning to see his faults."

"Was he?"

"Yes, he was. I am not blind, Elizabeth, and you know that I was aware of my husband's character upon entering the married state."

"Really?" I laughed. "For I believe it was you who once told me that you thought it wise and sound that it was best to show more affection than one felt, and not less...and that it was better to know as little about your partner in advance. You told me that years ago."

"I did," Charlotte said, looking forlorn. "Yet that was after I had learned something, and I was telling you from experience."

"What are you talking about?"

"Oh, nothing of importance," she replied dismissively. "Do not worry on it."

From her shifty stance to her averting her eyes, I knew that she was hiding something, and for a moment I wondered how deep the unknown within her was, and how much did she do of which I was not aware. However, everyone has a right to their secrets, and then was not the time to ask her to put me in her confidence.

"But," Charlotte continued, "it was very cruel the joke that life played on Mr. Collins. He did not die a fool, and I cannot explain what moment the alteration began. Yet Lizzy, he began to improve."

"In mind?"

"In many things. He seemed to gather an understanding that he was obsequious and also that he was too yielding to Lady Catherine. It still took him awhile to begin to gather any sense of resolve, but he did his best to improve his sense, and he also gathered a bit of humility. He grew to see that he was not perfect, that he did not pay as much attention to how he affected others. And so near the end, he tried to change. It was so strange, and when I say that life played a cruel joke on him, it is because it was quite heartbreaking that he died just as he began to improve—and just as I was beginning to gather affection for him."

"You began to finally fall in love with him?"

"Oh, I cannot call it love truly, but it was respect."

"Well then take heart."

"And then there is that which makes me feel quite guilty."

"You can tell me anything you like," I said. "And you know that I shall not repeat it."

"Thank you," she said, "you are a good friend, Elizabeth, even though I might not deserve it."

"Do not speak so, Charlotte."

"But I must. Elizabeth, I do not think you will believe me now, but I never wished for Longbourn to be taken from your family. I thought when we wed, I could convince Mr. Collins to always remain at Hunsford and that being a reverend for all his days would be best, yet I know that you might not believe me. Yet believe this, all that I did was just to secure myself from being a burden to my parents. I was an old maid to some, and therefore I was frightened, Lizzy. I know that now."

"Charlotte, that is a very common fear."

"Yet what I shall tell you now is not so common."

"What?"

"Elizabeth," she said, her voice growing heavy, "I was sad of his passing, believe me, yet a part of me was happy to be free again."

I looked down, for I knew what sadness she must have felt to be telling me this cold observation. She was not proud of what she felt, clearly, yet she also needed to speak of it.

"I was happy that I had the chance to be Charlotte Lucas and return to Lucas Lodge. My fate is undecided and hopeless, it is true, but it is no longer my fault, and my family cannot look on me so. I did marry, and the man passed away, therefore I am not to blame for being home once more. It is not my fault that I am a burden."

"Charlotte, you must not look on yourself so."

"Thank you and you are correct. I should not do so, and now that I am single once more, I shall find myself wishing to broaden my own reflections. I have come to learn something of myself."

"And what is that?"

"That I am not always correct. I prided myself on my sense and judgment, yet sometimes using one's head can still lead to betraying one's heart."

"Charlotte," I said, taking her hand, "I understand that you must consider economy but if you ever were to consider marrying again, then please try and do so not because of desperation, but because there is mutual respect for one another, and some natural affection."

"I sincerely doubt that marriage shall find Charlotte Lucas twice," she answered on a sad note.

"I am not sure of that. One can never know. Time heals all wounds however, and soon you shall be on the mend."

"On the mend? Yes, Lizzy, I believe that if there is one thing that I can control, I can control that."

# 14

# A CERTAIN LOOK

That night we had a dinner party at Aginfield where Cassandra and Jane Austen attended, along with Sir William Lucas, Lady Lucas, Charlotte, and Maria. Of course, our parents were present and before the dinner began, Miss Jane had informed Miriam that she had brought pages of a book that she had just thought up an idea for. We all sat down and prepared for what we hoped would be an amusing pleasure as she raised the pages and began to read.

*Emma Woodhouse, handsome clever, and rich, with a comfortable home and happy disposition, seemed to unite some of the best blessings of existence; and had lived nearly twenty-one years in the world with very little to distress or vex her.*

*She was the youngest of the two daughters of the most affectionate, indulgent father; and had, in consequence of her sister's marriage, been mistress of his house from a very early period. Her mother had died too long ago for her to have more than an indistinct remembrance of her caresses, and her place had been supplied by an excellent woman as governess, who had fallen little short of a mother in affection.*

*Sixteen years had Miss Taylor been in Mr. Woodhouse's family, less as a governess than a friend, very fond of both daughters, but particularly of*

*Emma. Between them it was more the intimacy of sisters. Even before*
*Miss Taylor had ceased to hold the nominal office of governess, the mild-*
*ness of her temper had hardly allowed her to impose any restraint; and*
*the shadow of authority being now long passed away, they had been living*
*together as friend and friend very mutually attached, and Emma doing*
*just what she liked; highly esteeming Miss Taylor's judgment but directed*
*chiefly by her own.*

*The real evils indeed of Emma's situation were the power of having*
*rather too much of her own way, and a disposition to think a little too well*
*of herself: these were the disadvantages which threatened alloy to her*
*many enjoyments. The danger, however, was at present so unperceived,*
*that they did not by any means rank as misfortunes with her.'*

Jane continued to read on, and we became acquainted with her
creation, Emma Woodhouse. From what I gathered, Emma was not the sort
to suffice for any form of heroine, for she seemed to be quite the
misguided young heiress to Hartfield. When her governess, named Miss
Taylor, married a man named Mr. Weston, Emma had convinced herself
that she had made the match herself, and therefore she made the decision
to begin to help others around her find their happiness through matrimony.
In short, she had appointed herself both Cupid and Aphrodite regarding the
matters of love, and it was clear that it would not come to a good end. Her
father loved her, yet he had no backbone and then a character entered
named Mr. Knightley who did wish to check her, but she did not take heed.
While I thought him to speak good sense, he also struck me as the sort of
man who spoke what he would and always called himself just for doing it
while often men such as him pride themselves on their good sense so often
that they ruled over others too much, and their extremity could lead to
rudeness. There was a large difference between honesty and rudeness and
only time would tell which one Mr. Knightley possessed.

However, Jane Austen had only written the first chapter, for she was
finishing another project at the same time as she had written this. Therefore, her reading concluded with her last paragraph.

*"With a great deal of pleasure, sir, at any time," said Mr. Knightley, laughing; "And I agree with you entirely, that it will be a much better thing. Invite him to dinner, Emma, and help him to the best of the fish and chicken but leave him to choose his own wife. Depend upon it, a man of six or seven and twenty can take care of himself."*

Jane Austen then lowered the pages and nodded, bashful.

"The end...for now!"

We all cheered and clapped.

"Most accomplished and witty," Colonel Fitzwilliam said.

"Yes, very good," Lady Lucas said. "Yet I wonder, are we meant to like this Emma Woodhouse?"

"Most certainly not!" Jane Austen laughed. "As a matter of fact, I am beginning to think that she shall be a character who few besides me would ever actually like."

"Then why write her?" Mr. Darcy asked.

"Because sometimes, I have found, it is the imperfect people who need stories written about them, for imperfect people read them—and need to learn from them. I have written heroines who were quite the perfect sort of creatures before, to be the perfect models to our lifestyle, and yet should it follow that that is the only way to teach someone how to improve their own natures? Emma is proud, wealthy, and so used to believing herself right on all scores that she will not see that she can be thoroughly wrong, and often is. How many 'Emmas' have you met? Think of it, haven't we all met those in our circles who are proud, are given much authority and wield it in harmful ways?"

"I can speak as a first-hand authority and have seen that often," Miriam said.

"As do many of us," Mr. Bennet said.

"Precisely, and therefore, I have decided, that if I do write this book, I shall keep Emma as she is in hopes that the Emmas' in the world who read this book can see themselves in the character and therefore learn how to improve, as she does eventually."

"As such," Georgiana said, "it can therefore be said that Emma Woodhouse is a heroine of the people, for she is the people at its most base."

"Precisely, Miss Darcy, and her failures are a grander version of our failures. Therefore, if I write her to reform, then her reformation will always be the readers' reformation."

"Well," I said, "I encourage it, Jane, for I think I shall like this novel, when you ever complete it."

"Thank you."

"However, there is one other work that I always wondered if you would think to finish."

"What is that?"

*"The Watsons."*

"Thank you!" Maria cried. "You see, Jane? Elizabeth agrees with me that if you had only finished it, it would have been a great tale."

"Oh, you honestly both like that one!" Jane Austen appeared shocked.

"Yes," Cassandra said, "and they are correct to, for Emma Watson was also a very good heroine who it seems we shall never know the fate of."

"Oh, very well," Jane said, rolling her shoulders, "I solemnly swear that if I finish all my other projects, may I live long enough, I shall finish *The Watsons.*"

"That would be delightful," Maria cried.

"And I should test your desires," Jane Austen said, "for I have been invited to an engagement party in Lyme and they have asked for a reading. While I planned to read an excerpt of *Sense and Sensibility*, perhaps I should read *The Watsons* and see how the audience responds to it."

"Well—but you said an engagement party in Lyme?" I asked.

"Yes, it shall be the engagement party of the son of Lady Russell, Mr. Edward Russell."

"What a coincidence!" Mr. Bingley cried. "For we have been invited to the engagement party."

"Really?"

"Yes, we could all be a company."

"Oh, that would be delightful!" I remarked. "I can scarce believe the luck of it."

"Oh, you shall love Lyme," Sir William Lucas said.

"Yes," Charlotte said, "for I have heard it often said that it is quite lovely."

"Oh," Jane Austen exclaimed, "you have never been?"

"No, I have not."

"Well, then if you like, this will be a perfect diversion for you. My invitation has allowed me the chance to have two companions. Naturally, my brother Henry is always dashing here and there with his wife, the Countess."

"What?" Charlotte gasped. "Yet what about Cassandra?"

"I cannot attend unfortunately," Cassandra said, "for someone has to remain here to look after everyone."

"Oh, but Cassandra, I would never wish to take your place for something that would be so enjoyable."

"Cassandra," her sister said, "tell them the truth."

"Oh, very well," Cassandra murmured, "I do not like the sea."

We all could not help but laugh at her admission.

"Do not like the sea?" Miriam asked. "Truly?"

"Yes, I do not know why, but I really do not like the sea. I did when I was young, yet I no longer do, and I will not have my current dislike of it affect Jane's happiness there. And therefore, Charlotte and Maria, what do you say?"

"Oh," Maria answered, "I am invited as well?"

"Yes," Jane said, "you are."

Maria jumped up and squealed in delight, turning to Lady Lucas and Sir William.

"Mother, Father, I am to go to Lyme!"

Both parents expressed their effusions of joy for their children while also thanking Jane Austen for her kind offer.

৩✦৩

"Yet Mr. Bingley," Sir William Lucas said jovially, "I have heard a report that is flying throughout the neighborhood that you are interviewing a new candidate for who shall live here in Aginfield."

"You are correct, Sir William. Tomorrow I am going to meet an Admiral Croft along with his wife."

At this confession, I saw Charlotte's head turn most abruptly and look to Mr. Bingley.

"Admiral Croft?" she said. "Pray, is his wife's name Mrs. Susan Croft?"

"Yes, it is."

"Were those the people you had met before in Brighton?" Sir William asked Charlotte.

"Oh," Charlotte said, her voice growing weak, "yes, I did make their acquaintance."

I considered my memory of my time at Court at the Prince's banquet, and my mind resorted back to Captain Wentworth, and the same look of unease that he had on his face then was the look that Charlotte's expression masked. Though I should have chosen to not voice my questions and curiosities at the present time, I still decided that it did not hurt to discover more of the secret—if there was a secret at all.

"Yes," I added, "and at Court, we have had the good fortune to meet Mrs. Croft's brother, a Captain Frederick Wentworth."

Charlotte's eyes darted towards me, and within them was a look of shock, alarm, and disturbance—yet what was more curious was Jane Austen's expression. She also looked upon me with disquiet and her attention shifted from me to Charlotte, then back to me.

Charlotte was hiding something from me.

And Jane Austen knew what that hidden thing was.

❦

"I believe you have made his acquaintance as well," I continued, "for he mentioned meeting you."

Charlotte turned and looked at Lady Lucas who looked down at her hands, her expression furtive...and now my instincts could not be in error. The mention of Captain Wentworth caused an inner stir between them all that was not of the good sort. And yet it did follow that if there was a story here, every story had a protagonist/ a hero, and an antagonist, who sometimes is also regarded as a villain. There was a history here that remained in the shadows and to my utter surprise, the look of guilt that covered

Charlotte's face, of disquiet in Lady Lucas's, and of familiarity in Jane Austen's, it had me believe that Charlotte might not have been the protagonist in this situation. She very well may have been the antagonist.

And yet, why should I have been surprised? For when it came down to fundamental facts of one's nature, Charlotte had proven to not always make the right decisions yet believed herself to do so.

"How did you find Captain Wentworth?" Charlotte asked smoothly.

"I liked him very much, and he has proven to be quite the hero," I added, "for it was he who's account of tracking the Trekenna Ship led to us being able to fight for the freedom of slaves, Charlotte, therefore if you ever preferred his company, then he is one friend who you ought not to be ashamed of, for he has done some honorable deeds."

Charlotte smiled. However, I could tell that she was losing her resolve by the way she looked upon me, and then Mr. Bingley added his knowledge of the captain.

"Yes, and I also had the good fortune to speak with him. He is a most well-informed and well-learned man, and he had found great profit in being at sea. My sources at Court have told me that he has made 20,000 pounds during the war, for he originally fought against the French a couple years back in the beginning of the Peninsular War."

Charlotte turned to look upon her mother who was alert at hearing this detail brought to light.

"Truly?" Sir William Lucas asked.

"Yes, for he originally Captained the naval Ship the Edward, and he found victory often during his naval battles against Napoleon's forces. Yet when he had received special attention among the royals, he requested to then be a Captain in their West Africa Squadron, in hopes of heading the anti-slavery operations there. However, now he has found his fortune as well as his honor."

"And this Captain Wentworth," Sir William Lucas said, "his brother-in-law is an Admiral?"

"Yes, Admiral Croft," Kitty answered.

"Well, then a navy man should live in Aginfield. That shall be most interesting. I once knew a Baronet who owned a large estate but lived so beyond his means that he went into debt and had to retrench. Instead of fully doing so, he learned that it would be best to retire to Bath where he could live less expensively, and he rented out his estate. When his attorney told him that the best option would be to consider naval captains as a tenant, the man objected thoroughly to renting out his home to a Navy man!"

"Why so?" Mr. Darcy asked.

"He strongly objected to the Navy on two points, which he found to be offensive. His two strong grounds of objection were thus: first, as being the means of bringing persons of obscure birth into undue distinction and raising men to honors which their fathers and grandfathers never dreamt of; and secondly, as it cuts up a man's youth and vigor most horribly. A sailor grows old sooner than any other man, he claimed. And a man is in greater danger in the navy of being insulted by the rise of one whose father, his father might have disdained to speak to, and of becoming prematurely an object of disgust himself, than in any other line."

"Nay that is very severe indeed," Cassandra said. "And he ought to have a little mercy on the poor men. We are not all born to be handsome. The sea is no beautifier, certainly and sailors do grow old betimes, I have often observed it. They soon lose their youth, but then, is it not the same with many other professions, perhaps most others?"

"Indeed," Maria added. "Soldiers in active service are not at all better off, and even in the quieter professions, there is a toil and a labor of the mind, if not of the body, which seldom leaves a man's looks to the natural effect of time. The lawyer plods, quite care-worn, the physician is up at all hours and traveling in all weather."

"And we must be thankful," my sister Jane added. "The Navy, I think, who have done so much for us, have at least an equal claim with any other set of men, for all the comforts and all the privileges which any home can give. Sailors work hard enough for their comforts, we must all allow."

"Very true," Charlotte said at last. "And from what I did recall of Captain Wentworth, he did labor very hard to achieve all that he has been given."

"Yes, he has," Georgiana replied. "And from what I recall of the man, he appeared to look well and hearty."

"Well, how was he as you had remembered him, Charlotte?" Maria asked her sister.

"I cannot tell you in full," Charlotte said vaguely. "For we were so often in the company of others that being so much in a crowd made it impossible to gather an accurate depiction of his character."

"Was he handsome?"

"He was regarded as handsome."

"Was he agreeable?"

"He was by no means disagreeable."

"Was he a man of information?"

"All of his statements seemed correct."

"Oh, you are impossible, Charlotte!" Maria cried, "and it vexes me."

"Maria," Lady Lucas chided, "it is not Charlotte's fault. Besides, it is Admiral Croft who is coming to Hampshire, and not this Captain Wentworth, therefore you need not gather a curiosity about him, for you shall never make his acquaintance."

"Oh, very well, yet at least we shall have a new arrival in Hampshire and that is enough to satisfy me."

"Very good, Maria. Very good."

We all continued to speak on the arrival of Admiral and Mrs. Croft yet all the while I glimpsed Charlotte's face, which possessed a certain look that made me curious.

As such, I had decided to come to a decision: I would find out what was the truth that hid beneath the surface of politeness.

## 15

# THE CROFTS

The day came and Admiral Croft and his wife arrived precisely around the time they had informed us, which was 1 o'clock in the afternoon.

They arrived in a chaise and four and we all were prepared to greet them. When they descended, they both appeared to be of the jovial and attractive sort. When I use the word 'attractive' I imply that they felt comfortable to be around and possessed an air of being very open people.

Mrs. Croft, though neither tall nor fat, had a squareness, uprightness, and vigor of form, which gave importance to her person. She had bright dark eyes, good teeth, and altogether an agreeable face, though her reddened and weather-beaten complexion seemed to indicate that she had been at sea often.

Admiral Croft appeared to be older; he was of a good stature and height, not being overbearingly tall. His hair clearly was once a rich blonde, yet now there were streaks of gray running through it, and he was in uniform.

"Admiral Croft and Mrs. Croft," Mr. Bingley said, followed by Mrs. Bingley. "You are most welcome."

"And very well met," Admiral Croft said. "My good Mr. Bingley, since

I have been relieved from duty at present, I was in need of a humble abode to remain in, therefore your post was a godsend."

"You are indeed, and this must be Mrs. Croft."

"Good day Mr. Bingley," she said, curtsying. "I am pleased to make your acquaintance."

"And this is my wife, Mrs. Miriam Bingley."

Miriam came forward and then made all the proper introductions to the visiting couple. Mr. Bingley turned the Crofts attention to the rest of us and we were all introduced.

We entered Aginfield, sat down and began to become acquainted with this seafaring couple.

"The war between France has been mostly on land," Admiral Croft said, "therefore there was no need for me to be employed at present and I have been able to stumble upon peace. My wife here then decided that it would be wonderful to retire into the country for a while, for we have come to that age where we enjoy tranquility."

"And a change in society as well," Mrs. Croft answered with a smile. "Yet I found that we already have a mutual acquaintance with you all."

"Are you referring to your brother, Captain Wentworth?" I asked.

Her eyes were warm. "Yes. You remember him, I see."

"He is not one that is easy to forget," Miriam said, "Your brother is a most admirable man, Mrs. Croft.

"Well, with your permission I will tell him so. And very soon, after our purchase of Aginfield, he shall come and visit."

"Oh, will he?" I asked, curious. "That will be a most welcome addition to the confined circles that Hampshire revolves in. It will make our mother pleased, and you all shall find yourselves the center of attention and many looks when you come."

"We do not fear being gaped at like we are novelties," Admiral Croft said, "for it happens every time that we go into another port. The perks and drawbacks of being a seaman is that you are always the new face that people see."

It became decided amongst us that both Admiral Croft and his wife were a pleasant sort of people with much conversation and information, and after we all partook in refreshments, we all joined the Bingleys as they showed the Crofts around Aginfield. Each room and the furnishings proved to be to the tastes of the naval couple and by the end of the evening, the Crofts planned to stay in the Drunken Prince Inn so that they could take another look at the estate on the morrow, just for good measure.

They dined with us at Aginfield at supper time, yet they left afterwards to make it to the inn before the time had grown to be too late.

After they had left, we all sat down by the fireplace and talked of what our impression of them was.

"I believe that they shall be excellent tenants," Miriam said. "And they were a very good sort of people."

"They also clearly had a mutual respect for one another," Colonel Fitzwilliam said, "which was very pleasing. The Admiral and his wife respected each other in a very good manner."

"Yet will they say yes to taking up Aginfield, I wonder," Mr. Bingley said. "For if they come the next day and do not like it upon a second inspection, then I shall have to find new tenants."

"They looked optimistic on purchase, Charles," Mr. Darcy said, "so rest assured."

"Was I pleasant enough?"

"Yes, you were."

"Did I say anything that was rude?"

"No, you did not."

"Was I too overbearing?"

"Not at all."

"Did I also look presentable?"

"Yes, you did."

"You know that appearance is everything."

Mr. Darcy chuckled. "Charles, you looked fine."

"Yes, my dear," Miriam said, "do not fret. You were splendid."

"Very well, I shall stop worrying and believe it."

"You ought to," I answered with a smile, "for right now you sound like my mother."

"No, I do not."

"Yes, Mr. Bingley...you very much do."

Eventually we all retired. I thought on the Crofts, and if I should inform Charlotte of Mrs. Croft's brother coming if they do reside there. Yet to do so, I had to acknowledge what there clearly had been between the two of them, and that had to be addressed first.

## 16

# A HISTORY BEHIND THE
# HEARTBREAK

The next day, my first tactic in uncovering the truth was not to address Charlotte first, but rather, I went to the Austen house and decided to first accost Jane Austen and Cassandra on the matter.

When I arrived at their home, I found Jane Austen and her sisters washing clothes in one of the backrooms of the house. While Cassandra and some of the rest in the household were taking the wet clothes to the clothesline behind the house, Jane was still stirring some petticoats in a large pot when I sat with her.

"It must be a great luxury," Jane said, "not having to wash your own clothes."

"I admit I am fortunate in that way," I said, "yet unfortunate in others."

"And how could Mrs. Darcy be unfortunate?" she asked lightly.

"Because you seem to be in the confidence of Charlotte in regard to Captain Wentworth and I am not."

Jane Austen looked at me with alarm and then she turned away.

"Elizabeth, I do not know what you speak of—"

"Jane, you are lying. I saw how you and Charlotte looked at each other at the mention of his name."

"I..." Jane stopped cleaning and she remained still. "It is not my story to tell really."

"I know, but tell me a little, and I shall confront Charlotte on it."

"I am not sure that she wishes to ever speak of it."

"And I did not wish for her to marry Mr. Collins and therefore become the eventual mistress of Longbourn over my mother. Yet she did. Charlotte Lucas has turned out to not always be what she appears to be. And if I am to believe she is a pale reflection of the woman that I once knew, help me to comprehend it all, please."

"You must begin to understand," Jane said, "that her engagement to Mr. Collins, though it was a terrible move on her part, was out of desperation."

"I know, but..."

"It was her fixing a mistake."

"A mistake? What do you mean?"

"It was Charlotte making up for the one time she had been proposed to before."

"Before?"

"Yes. A man had proposed to her once. And she refused him."

I felt as if I could have been knocked down with a feather.

"Charlotte?" I gasped. "She refused a proposal?"

"Yes."

"Practical and unromantic Charlotte?"

"Yes, practical and unromantic Charlotte."

"Why would she do such a thing?" I was truly stunned.

"That is something she has to explain."

"Then.. Jane, was the man Charlotte rejected Captain Wentworth?"

At first, Jane did not reply, and then she chuckled.

"Amazing, is it not? How one mistake of hers led to her making another. But I had sworn not to speak of it."

"It is too late for that now. Jane, was the man Captain Wentworth?"

☙❦❧

"Yes," Charlotte replied, for after I had spoken to Jane Austen, I then decided to proceed straightaway to Lucas Lodge, where I had found Charlotte at home sitting alone in the sitting room, sewing. Upon seeing her, I asked her to tell me the truth of her acquaintance to Captain Wentworth, informing her of what I had seen transpire between Jane Austen, Lady Lucas, and her. And thus, she began to tell me the sad story of her history with the captain.

"Yes," she repeated, "I did refuse him."

"I..." I stuttered, "I do not understand."

"When I was in Brighton on holiday with our family and Jane Austen accompanying us, we had made the acquaintance of Captain Wentworth and his friends, who were named Captain Harvill and Captain Benwick. We were often thrown together in each other's company, and...I fell in love with him."

"You did?" I could barely believe my ears. Charlotte, who had always insisted on marriage to not be a matter of romance, was now telling me that she had in fact suffered the slings and arrows of love's aim.

"Yes, I did," she whispered, wistful. "You have seen him, Elizabeth. He is handsome and fascinating. Charming, of great conversation, and filled with much heart. Even I, who am not usually a romantic, could not help but have a change of manner and mindset when I beheld him. And for him to like me...me? You have seen me, Elizabeth, I am no beauty."

"You are not ugly, Charlotte."

"But nor am I handsome. I am simply tolerable—but *not handsome enough to tempt anyone*. I know what I am, and I always have. Therefore, to have this remarkable man take an interest in me was overwhelming—and I fell in love terribly."

"Yet I do not understand...if your designs were always to marry for the sake of having a future, then why did you resist him?"

"Because I was persuaded to refuse him."

"By whom?"

"By my mother, Lady Lucas."

"Lady Lucas?" I gasped. "Why would she influence you to do so?"

"Because of his situation at the time. When you see Captain Wentworth now, you see a man who is successful, yet he was not so then. He had genius, brilliance, and charisma to be sure, as well as nerve, yet he had no fortune, no future in sight at the moment and still had to make his way in the world. Therefore, my mother could not but view him as a fortune hunter. We have never had much money in our family, but our title has rendered people to believe much in us. And therefore, my mother worried that he was attempting to take advantage of me. And if not so, she also convinced me of the fact that him being poor, I was throwing my life away if I chose him. I would have no happiness for I would be low and to marry a man with nothing to recommend him, I would ruin myself and my name."

I sat there in amazement at this confession.

"How long ago was this?"

"It was around nine years ago."

"So then, you gave up on love, and fell prey to over-persuasion."

"Yes, my mother had persuaded me. Therefore, when I engaged myself to Mr. Collins, it was quite an ironic thing. I had rejected the man I did love yet accepted the man who I did not. I had no one else to blame but myself, you see. I might have been persuaded, yet the decision still should have been mine in the end, and therefore I deserved Mr. Collins. I deserved my mistake and no better, for I know I hurt Captain Wentworth, and he deserved better. Therefore, my suffering was my due and a proper punishment. And last night at the dinner party, when my mother and I heard that not only has he found his fortune, yet he has also earned renown, there was great shame, and we were both made aware just how in error we had been."

"How do you feel toward your mother now?"

"I am at that moment where I am having a hard time looking upon her. Her refusal to accept my choice in Captain Wentworth led to me never being given an offer for years and then reduced to finding my best option in Mr. Collins. She senses that I am angry, yet she avoids me as much as I avoid her."

"Why do you not talk to her of it?"

"What good will it do?"

"It will give you closure."

"But it will not change anything."

"No, it cannot. Yet sometimes you shall have to learn to speak up, Charlotte. For God sakes, look where your actions from not speaking up has led to? You were persuaded to refuse him and turned away from the right man by your own mother. I want to feel sorry for you, but I cannot because you are allowing yourself to wallow in self-pity that is mingled with martyrdom. Speak up now, or you never will. It is that side of you that retreats that allied you to Mr. Collins. You knew that it was wrong, I knew it—we all knew it."

"You knew what would happen if I did not."

"So, you fear the world's reaction and you use that as an excuse for your actions. I tell you now, it does not. I am sorry for you, I am, but as you say, you never allowed yourself to do what your heart told you to. And I agree that sometimes one should listen to one's headfirst, yet this was not one of those moments."

Charlotte suddenly began to burst out crying.

"Charlotte," I said, my heart softening, "I did not mean to..."

I then stood up and walked to the window, looking out at it while she wept. In the few times that I saw Charlotte cry, she never liked to be held, but always wished to be left alone.

"Am I able to turn around now?" I asked.

"Not yet," she said still weeping.

I stood there, looking out at the window and saw Maria coming in from the yard.

"Maria is entering the house, Charlotte."

"Right," she said, wiping her eyes, and then I turned to her as she did her best to look presentable.

"I did not mean to hurt you."

"I know," she whispered. "All that I did, I did to myself."

"Then I am sorry for it. And now I know the history behind the heart-break, and I hope that you will recover from this, Charlotte. I hope that you find happiness."

"Thank you."

I walked up to her and embraced her.

"Very soon we shall leave for Lyme," I whispered. "Look at this as a chance to start over. Forgive yourself, and let your past remain in your past. Look forward and you shall be able to make yourself anew."

# 17

# NO MORE RAIN

**D**ays later, I was still surprised with all that I had learned of Charlotte, and it frightened me in some ways. She and I had been friends for years and never did she confide in me about that. Reflecting on the situation, I comprehended why, for such a painful memory was perhaps something she did not wish to think about.

I still felt that I needed to speak on the matter, but I did not wish to inquire to Charlotte more on it for I knew it caused her pain.

Therefore, I visited the Austen's once more and sat with Jane Austen as she was preparing some clean pages for her writing.

"You must not blame her for not telling you," Jane said. "For she did not want anyone to know about it. The only reason that I knew was because I was present to have seen the letter that he had written to her with his proposal, therefore she had no choice but to keep me in her confidence."

"I know," I admitted. "Yet I cannot help but be somewhat beside myself."

"I can see what you might be feeling, therefore I am not going to say it was wrong. And you must not blame yourself for being firm with Charlotte. I daresay that she needed to hear it from someone."

"Thank you, for I was feeling guilty."

"Telling someone the truth can lead to one feeling so. Yet it can be necessary."

"Imagine if she had married Captain Wentworth, it could have all turned out differently I suppose, but it didn't."

"No, it didn't. And I am sure that deep within her, she has wondered what it would have been like to have accepted him."

"I am afraid to ask, do you think that she still loves him?"

"I am sure she does."

"Really? How can you be so sure?"

"Because she was recently wed to Mr. Collins. As such, being his wife would give her no choice but to truly regret refusing Captain Wentworth even more, and now she must miss the chance she once had."

"Yes, yes she must. Jane?"

"Yes?"

"I have no choice but to forgive her, don't I?"

"It is hard, yet you have no choice, for now that you know her history, you now see that Charlotte Lucas was not giving way to convention because she was cold. Rather she did so because her heart was broken...and she was the one who broke it herself, and herself alone."

⚜

Eventually I returned to Aginfield where there was a wonderful announcement waiting for me. Mr. Bingley informed us all that Admiral Croft had enjoyed the look of Aginfield and he was willing to purchase it.

"This leads to me feeling most willing now to purchase Allenwell and I shall therefore be a landowner of Kent," he said with a big grin.

"That is wonderful, Mr. Bingley," I said.

"Oh, and here is a surprise. As it so happens, Admiral Croft and Mrs. Croft were also invited to Lady Russell's party at Lyme."

"Truly?" I asked, surprised. "How so?"

"It is quite wonderful," Miriam said, "yet they have made her acquaintance in London and one of Lady Russell's relatives served under the Admiral in the navy and Lady Russell was grateful to the Admiral for looking after her nephew."

"How extraordinary," Georgiana said. "Yet around this time of year, I believe it is only natural for extraordinary things to occur."

As we sat there, there was the sound of a carriage approaching down the lane and we all went to greet it. As soon as it came to a halt, the door was opened by the coachman and Jason Whitfield emerged, jumping down and approaching his fiancée.

"My beautiful Georgiana," he cried.

"Jason!" she exclaimed and then jumped into his arms.

Yes, Georgiana might have been correct; that was the time of the year where extraordinary things happened.

⚘

Jason had arrived after visiting his eldest brother, Victor, at the family estate.

"He shall let us remain there until I find a suitable home for us in London," Jason said to Georgiana as we entered the house. "I wish for us to have a home immediately upon marriage. Yet finding the correct place to live is not something that one should do lightly, I feel, and I wish for you to also have a say in the place we live. Therefore, when the time is most convenient, I would like for us to inspect homes together."

"Thank you for considering my feelings, Jason. I should like that."

He expelled a sigh of relief. "Brilliant. And while I know you are used to living in the country, I am sorry that we must permanently reside in London. It is just that as a lawyer, that is the best place for me to find work and be bountiful regarding a good income."

"Do not worry, I do enjoy town—well parts of it at the very least."

Between Jason's arrival, the Crofts purchase, and the invitation to Lyme to loom over our heads, there seemed like nothing, but good fortune, was finding us at present. I almost believed that life could not get any better, however I was happy to have been proven incorrect.

For one day, while we all went to Longbourn for a dinner party, and I had taken William and Caiden along—and they both were walking a little —I was in for another declaration of good news.

As we all convened in the sitting room, the men with glasses of port and the women with tea, my father stood up.

"I have an announcement to make, and I fear that I cannot wait until dinner to make it."

We all turned to him as he stood with his glass in his hand.

"A little over a fortnight ago, I had my wonderful sons-in-law over to visit and one of them made the delightful suggestion of me seeking legal action in order to have the entail changed to incorporate not only a male heir by blood, but by family relations."

"That would be me!" Colonel Fitzwilliam declared, to which we all chuckled.

"Yes, that would be you. Well, very soon after this suggestion, we took it to my cousin Mr. Philips in Meryton, who as you all know is an attorney. Then Mr. Whitfield arrived here a couple of days ago to also offer his expertise, and now today, I have learned the product that has spawned from their labors. The court and the legalities have all been ironed flat and...the entail has been widened to include heirs from marital relations."

"Mr. Bennet!" our mother cried. "Are you saying what I hope you are?"

"Yes, my wonderful wife, for despite our differences, I now see that you are wonderful. The contracts have been drawn, and I can now include Colonel Fitzwilliam into the entail, he shall inherit Longbourn, and Kitty shall be your successor."

"Then," Kitty whispered desperately, "Longbourn will stay in the family!"

"Yes, one day you shall be its mistress, and Mrs. Bennet, when the sad case of my departure from this earthly realm does come, you shall always have a home, and that home will be Longbourn."

"Oh, Mr. Bennet!" My mother forgot herself and embraced our father, who embraced her in turn. To see them so at ease with one another and loving, it made me content in seeing that it only took a lifetime for them to find each other again—and remember how much they once were in love.

"Well then," she sighed, "I admit that I am most glad."

"Yes, the storm clouds have gone from our prospects, and no more rain shall oppress us on that score. Now there is only the calm without the storm. Be glad, my dear, be glad."

## ❧ 18 ❧

## LYME

Throughout the days at Aginfield, we treasured our time there because we knew it would be our last. Darcy and I often took Caiden and William to Longbourn where our mother, who managed to always overcome her nerves to be happy in seeing them, and our father could not help, despite himself, secretly favor William, the one who resembled him.

As for Mary, it was most strange, for in all that time that we were there, she wrote to us from Rosings Park often, which was not always her way in the past. She had never been the best correspondent, however now that she had two nephews, she wanted to know often of them. While we at first were vexed with her initially for not journeying back to Longbourn to see them, we learned very quickly in her first letter that this was no fault of hers:

*Dear Elizabeth and Mr. Darcy,*

*How has your journey been from America, to Pemberley, then from Pemberley to Longbourn? Indeed, you do often seem to be a family on the move. I have received many positive reports of my nephews. Are there names William and Caiden? For I do not wish my report to be wrong on that score, and I heard they are strong and healthy baby boys. I congratu-*

*late you on your good luck, and it is nice to have new additions to our family which I shall be happy to meet.*

*As for me not doing so at present, then I must apologize in advance, for I shall be frank with you. As the companion of Anne de Bourgh, my time is not my own, and while it may appear as if I am using my employers as an excuse to being cold in paying my respects, I speak the truth. Lady Catherine would not find it suitable for me to leave at the present and has not granted me a choice of departure for Longbourn. You have met her Ladyship, and she is not one to be gain-said. Also, if I were to leave, I would be leaving Anne alone for at least three weeks and I have grown to feel an affection for her and regret her being constantly lonely, therefore I do not wish to allow her to feel abandoned even briefly at this time. Nor do I wish Lady Catherine to be upset with me.*

*I know you must think ill of me for my lack of resolution, but I just do not wish to offend anyone. And, if I may be allowed to be honest at this time, Lizzy, and Mr. Darcy, I feel useful now. I feel as if I am of some importance in the world, and that sense of being utilized and having a place amongst my peers has become essential to me.*

*Yet I do wish to meet my nephews, and as soon as I have worked under Lady Catherine's employ long enough to have gained more ground of assertion at Rosings, I shall further do my best to persuade her to allow me to visit Pemberley, if you will still allow me to visit.*

*I believe now that I have gathered a larger acquaintance with the ways of the world, I have earned a perspective, a point of view—I have just begun to live. And I believe that when I do return to Hampshire or visit you all in Kent, you shall find me greatly improved.*

*I do wish for Caiden and William to know that I am their Aunt Mary, and that I shall love them.*

*Yours etc.*
*Mary*

*p.s. - How are Kitty and the Colonel? Tell them I wish them well. And tell Jane to write to me.*

When Darcy and I had read the letter, even he was gently touched by Mary's desires to meet our sons.

"She is changing," he said. "We have not seen her; however, this letter indicates a clear alteration in her nature."

"Yes," I added, "she has clearly, as she so put it, developed a better knowledge of the ways of the world, yet I see that it has sprung from an inner need of desire, as she has told us. Mary was always a serious lady who wanted something to define herself with, and I think that lack of a goal or occupation led to her not fully knowing where she was going half the time, or what she ought to be doing. She did much to keep herself busy, yet she never was fully of use to anyone and being the source to anyone's happiness—and like all of us, she did deserve to be so."

"And Anne is dear to her mother, but she needed someone who wanted to be of use to her."

"Therefore, it could be said that Mary and Anne might have been perfect companions for one another."

"Indeed. I never would have suspected that bond to form between them both, yet it makes sense. Whatever imperfections your sister has, her intentions are always very well, and now that her experiences in life have been widened, she has had many chances to improve herself."

"And we cannot be angry with Mary, for she is correct. If Lady Catherine does not desire her to leave Anne or Rosings at present, then she will have no choice but to remain."

"Yes, but I worry for Mary," Darcy confessed.

"Why so?"

"Because while I could be mistaken, my aunt might have finally found one Bennet girl who she could control. I worry that she would abuse that power and always wish to rule Mary."

I glanced at him. "You think she would do that?"

"I think it is possible she might do that, even if she had no idea that she was doing so."

"Well, though this is a long-term plan, maybe after we attend this engagement party at Lyme, we write to Lady Catherine, informing her that we wish to visit Rosings Park to pay our respects and have her meet our children. While we do so, we can make sure to check on Mary and see how she is being treated."

"Though that will pressure us to not return to Pemberley even sooner, for my aunt will want us to remain there as long as she possibly can convince us to. Yet it will be beneficial to attend if she says yes of course."

"Curiosity will get the best of her," I said with a grim smile. "For she now has two more nephews, and where marriage can cause scorn, children are the perfect olive branch. Also, I can be passive for long enough; she will want to make many suggestions of how I should raise William and Caiden, and she also will insult me on the way I have been a mother, I assure you. Since I have won so much, I believe I can sacrifice my pride for a while and let her believe I am listening to all her advice. Maybe that shall make her love me after all."

"Whether she does or not," he said, kissing my forehead, "it matters not, my love. You are the perfect mother."

"Thank you, my dear."

Fitzwilliam left me alone so that I could write back to Mary, which I began to do so even before I knew what I was going to say.

*Dear Mary,*

*Thank you for telling us of your condition, and we are very happy that you wish to gather a bond with your nephews. We are in hopes that after we return from our trip to Lyme in two months' time, Lady Catherine shall look forward to a visit from us, to which we shall write to appeal to her.*

*If you would be so kind as to speak to her on our behalf, informing her of our wishes—and if you could also delicately hint that I am wishing to visit not only to gather a further acquaintance with her ladyship, yet also because now that I have my two sons, I would love to hear her experiences as a parent to learn what advice she could offer, for I am new to the role of being a 'mother'. If you would do so, Mary, then that would be wonderful for us, and we would appreciate your efforts.*

*As for you being a suitable companion to Miss de Bourgh, I am very glad that you have found something to your delight. I am happy you are of use to her; and to Lady Catherine as well, for you always were a very learned woman with much to offer. Mary, you always deserved to be recognized for your studies and efforts and I am happy they are now being noticed. Therefore, as long as Anne is treating you well and you both are of importance to each other, if Rosings is vital to you, then it is all well.*

*As for Caiden and William, they have now both begun to walk a little. They can take four steps each before they fall down. Caiden tries to speak, and it is most amusing and touching to the heart. And William looks like our father! Yes, our mother says so, she says that he will grow to look as our father did when he was young. I cannot remember our father as being any age but what he is now. Therefore, if she is correct, when my sons grow, we shall see what our father looked like when she and he married.*

*I shall tell Kitty and the Colonel that you asked about them, and they are quite well and very blissful, and to tell Jane to write to you about the lessons she gives at Pemberley.*

*Inevitably we shall see you soon.*

*Your sister,*
*Elizabeth*

I looked at how I wrote my name and saw that it looked like chicken scratch and might be illegible, yet I knew that it would do, so I folded the letter and placed it in the envelope just as my sister, Jane, entered.

"Lizzy!" she exclaimed.

"Jane, what is it? Is something wrong?"

"Oh, no it is most wonderful. Mrs. Bingley is pregnant!"

"Oh, so she has confirmed it?"

"Oh, you knew already?"

"She told me of her suspicions, yet she was worried of saying anything in case she was in error—or in case she miscarried and therefore did not wish to raise false hopes."

"Oh, I see. Well, come into the sitting room, for Mr. Bingley has informed all of us of the matter and we are all having a glass of punch."

"Very well, before you join us, read this," I said, handing her Mary's letter. "She wishes for you to write to her as well."

I walked past her and down to the sitting room where all were assembled and were congratulating Mr. Bingley and Miriam. I approached them and added my well wishes to the fortunate couple. Mr. Bingley was overjoyed, and Miriam actually seemed to be glowing—and indeed I wondered if I had looked so when I was with child, for if such news made one look so marvelous and divine, then I did see why pregnancy was hailed as truly an incredible state a woman could be in.

News very quickly spread over Hampshire that Mrs. Bingley was pregnant, and many came to pay their respects, including the Austens and the Lucases.

All throughout the Lucases visit, I saw Lady Lucas look at Charlotte very furtively. There seemed to be a mixture of guilt mingled in with resentment, and I wondered what was behind it.

"You are not in error," Charlotte said when I confronted her on the matter. "She and I have a strained relationship now, for I am still quite dejected. I told her that, despite the objection I would have received upon marrying him, I should have still enjoyed and liked to have been wed to Captain Wentworth. She replied that it was not sound and that at the time, I was perfectly logical for rejecting him. I did not have the heart to argue on the matter, so that is not why she looks on me so."

"Then what is the reason?"

"She is angry with me for not having any children while Mr. Collins and I were wed."

"Why should she be? If you had a child in that time, then that would have made widowhood even more cumbersome for you. Both economically and romantically. Raising a child would take more from your pocketbook and eligible gentlemen are less likely to consider a widow who has children from a previous marriage, for they usually only want their own."

"Yes, and that was the way that I had viewed it—except for the luck of marrying once more, for I find it unlikely that any shall chose me. Yet that is not how she views it. If I had a child and it was a girl then yes, that would have been unfortunate. However, if it was a boy, then..."

"Then he might have been able to have inherited Longbourn, no matter how young he was," I finished for her.

"Yes."

"By god, that is preposterous, and terrible."

"I know, Lizzy. I know and I do not share her ambition on the matter."

I turned and looked at Lady Lucas and wondered at what point she went from being simply a caring mother to one who schemed so.

"Charlotte? What happened to your mother?"

"Disappointment...that was what happened to my mother. And an immense fear of failure. I have failed in the eyes of some, and she is angry that she cannot find a way to solve it."

I shook my head and turned away.

❦

The days rolled on and eventually the time came for when we all had to leave for Lyme. Since all preparations had been made in due time and Jefferson had seen to it that we would depart precisely at the hour that we planned, it was mid-spring and we set out on our next adventure. Mr. Darcy, Colonel Fitzwilliam, Kitty, Jane, Mr. Bingley, Miriam, Georgiana, Jason Whitfield, Jane Austen, Charlotte, Maria, my two sons and I were headed to Lyme.

## ❦ 19 ❧

# THE TONGUES OF THE TON

A
s we journeyed to Lyme, we stopped at inns along the road, and each time we did so, I noticed that Charlotte began to look more and more like her old self. She smiled and laughed often, was quick to offer a joke, and if one compared her to the person who I had met when I saw her upon first returning to Lucas Lodge, versus the woman who was now, the alteration was extreme to say the least.

Charlotte Collins had needed to get away.

Or at least be reminded of the fact that she had initially been Charlotte Lucas, and Charlotte Lucas, even in her most sensible and logical state, still had once had much life to her.

Eventually we arrived at Lyme, and it was a lovely place that was equally quaint, large, and was nothing short of a breath of fresh air.

"Look!" Jane and Kitty cried, "it's the sea!"

The sight delighted me. "Yes, yes, it is."

It was quite lovely and all the words in the world could not describe it, but I liked it very much upon first impressions, and hoped that favorable impression would continue upon closer inspection and after gathering a better acquaintance with the town of Lyme.

We arrived at The Queen's Right Hand Inn, which was very lovely in my eyes while also being quaint and very comfortable.

We told the innkeeper that we had arrived for we were a part of the Lady Russell party and he informed us that Lady Russell had changed her plans.

"Changed plans?" Mr. Darcy stated threateningly, to the point where he slightly frightened the host. "What do you mean?"

"Oh, forgive me, I did not mean the party was changed, I just mean to imply that location of her visitors changed. She has rented out the Cumberland Plateau House on the outskirts of Lyme, for it to be a more luxurious stay for your party. Mind you, she has also volunteered to still pay for the room and board of any who wish to remain here at the inn, in case there proves to not be enough space at Cumberland. Yet upon my last being informed, there still is space at the Plateau."

"Oh, well," my husband said, looking much less daunting, "in that case, I admit to preferring to stay here at the inn and I shall consult my party."

He consulted us and we confirmed that we preferred to remain at the inn. For in case we needed to leave the party, which would be a three week long engagement, we could do so easier if we were to depart from the inn rather than at Cumberland.

As we were shown to our room, I asked Darcy about the history of Cumberland.

"It's a large estate that was built by a Frenchman named Julian Claude de Lafayette, who was one of the French Doughier who won land here after the Norman Invasion," he explained. "Since the French won the Battle of Hastings, many of them made their fortunes and also took land, building large homes as well. Lafayette did so, and had Cumberland built, just as my ancestors did. Of course, improvements have been made over the years and it has been thoroughly modernized."

"Oh," I gasped, "that is right! I was told before."

"Yes, the name Darcy, taken from the name D'Arcy, was actually a royal name that goes back to the Renaissance."

I gave him a wry smile. "I should not be surprised."

⁂

We all settled into our lodgings, each couple placed in a room while those who were single took more to a room—except for Jason, who was the only single male who had his own room. Yet Charlotte and Maria stayed in one room, while Jane Austen, Jane and Georgiana took another room.

After we were all settled, we knew that we had no choice but to travel to Cumberland to pay our respects and meet the happy couple.

Our ride took no more than half an hour before we arrived on the outskirts of Lyme and along the lane of the great estate.

When we arrived, footmen tended to our carriage and as we stepped down before the steps, the doors opened. A small throng of people descended, all of which I did not recognize, however the older woman at the head I presumed was Lady Russell.

"Greetings Mr. Darcy!" the older woman said. "You are arrived, and you are most welcome. And I am surprised that you have taken time from your busy schedule to honor my son."

"It seemed like a party that I could not deny the pleasure of," Darcy said smoothly. "And might I introduce you to the rest of my party?"

Darcy offered her all our names and I was correct; she was Lady Russell. She was of medium height, had handsome features though her face was very much not symmetrical on both sides, her teeth were clean and white, her skin was wrinkled in some places, yet she still appeared quite sleek-looking, and she was also medium in weight, not too thin, yet not large either.

"Well," she said, "I welcome you all to Cumberland, and this is my son, Mr. Edward Russell and his fiancée Miss Ariella Elton."

"It is nice to meet you Mr. Russell and Miss Elton," we all said individually, and we were profuse in our congratulations on their good fortune. They replied with the customary civilities and then we all entered Cumberland. The rest of the people in the crowd were other family members and friends.

As we sat down to tea, pleasantries were passed in between us and then Lady Russell inquired of where our luggage was.

"Oh," Colonel Fitzwilliam said, "we instead opted from remaining at Cumberland to remain at The Queen's Right Hand."

"You chose to remain at the inn?" She gasped. "Upon my honor, you are a most unique lot."

"Or just humble in needs of accommodation," Jason Whitfield replied. "We can enjoy the comforts at the inn and rather have your spare rooms be occupied by those who would prefer the honor."

"And you?" she said, looking at Jason narrowly. "You are a most fascinating addition, for I know little of your history."

"Oh, I do not wish to waste moments talking of myself. Not when there is an engaged couple who wish to celebrate their finding each other."

"Oh, we shall spend the next couple of weeks talking of nothing but each other," Miss Elton said. "Pray, let us hear all of how you have been."

"Very well," Jason said, "I have had the wonderful honor of becoming engaged to Miss Darcy."

"You both are engaged?"

"Yes," Georgiana echoed. "We did so when our family had visited America."

"You visited America at this time of year?" Mr. Edward Russell asked quizzically.

"Yes, we did," Mr. Bingley added.

"Oh," Lady Russell said, "yes, I do recall hearing something about that in the papers."

"You still read newspapers, then?" Darcy asked her.

"Oh, yes indeed. You know that I love remaining informed. Now you were all involved in some business...a trial of some kind."

"Yes," Jason said, "I was the attorney at that trial."

Jason proceeded to tell her the history of the trial, from our intervention to the Prince Regent's assistance.

"Good gracious," a woman named Fanny Crawford said. She was one of Lady Russell's nieces and was Mr. Edward Russell's cousin. Lovely in appearance, she had very beautiful red hair and wonderful skin. Sitting there, she presented a very striking picture and had a very delicate voice that was smooth to the ear. "That is quite a story. And to think that it resulted in a happy ending."

"Yes, it did so indeed," Kitty said.

"Yet I confess to being very happy you are all come," Miss Crawford added, "for I should like to gather a further acquaintance with you all, for I have heard quite the highest praise of you."

"Oh," Jane said, "we should be delighted, however you are sure to be disappointed, for sometimes people can embellish the truth."

"Oh, no not at all, I have heard good reports of your deeds from another source, and one not at all inclined to exaggeration."

"Yet am I not deceived," Mr. Russell said, "that our party here also contains Miss Jane Austen, the writer of *Sense and Sensibility.*"

"We do indeed!" Miss Elton exclaimed.

"Thank you so much for the invitation," Jane Austen replied. "And Lady Russell, nothing would give me more pleasure than to be present at your party. And Mr. Russell and Miss Elton, I hope that the reading I give shall bring you much pleasure for your engagement party."

"Miss Austen, it will indeed."

※

After we had finished our tea and cakes, we were shown around the grounds of Cumberland which were large, expansive, and very well groomed. Lady Russell took our compliments with delight, despite the truth that this was rented out to her, it was not her home necessarily, yet we all decided to overlook that at present.

While we walked onward and we developed more ease with our hosts, I inquired at why they chose to have a three-week engagement party to celebrate their happy moment, for usually that was not the case.

"It was out of a desire to finally celebrate being together once more," Miss Elton said. "Mr. Russell and I were separated for so long, with him being away in India, that we promised one another that we would celebrate by having a number of guests join us in Lyme for a holiday. I always found Lyme to be the perfect place to enjoy oneself. It is by the sea, comely while also being homely, and there are more amusements than one would know of initially."

"We have been here only for a day, and we are already struck by its charms," Miriam said. "And for most of us, we have never been to Lyme before."

"Oh, once you are here for a week, you shall wish to come back one more time every other year," Miss Crawford said. "It takes a toll on one's soul."

"And I may not have been clear on all the details of our excursions," Lady Russell said, "therefore I pray you brought a lovely ball gown, for we shall be giving a ball here in Cumberland. We shall also invite some of the prominent families in Lyme to our dance as well."

"Oh, Mother!" Edward cried. "Even if they did not bring one, they have enough to purchase a hundred."

"It need not be so," Georgiana said, "for worry not, we came sufficiently prepared for a ball, just in case one were to present itself, which it has the tendency to do, we have come to learn, when there are more than ten families of the ton in the vicinity of each other."

"Very well thought out."

"And yet," Miss Elton added, "you, Miss Darcy, are now engaged as well and therefore this should not just be a celebration regarding Mr. Russell and me, but you and Mr. Whitfield should also be given your due."

"Oh, do not trouble yourselves—," Georgiana began.

"No, we do not wish to remove attention from you and your—," Jason added.

"Oh now, I insist," Miss Elton said. "For only one thing could strengthen the enjoyment of our company and that would be if our guests did not just celebrate one engagement, but also two."

"That would be most delightful," Lady Russell said. "And it shall be to my liking as well. Therefore, Miss Darcy and Mr. Whitfield, I will brook no refusal, and when all the other guests arrive, we shall now celebrate the engagement of my son and of your sister, Mr. Darcy."

Jason and Georgiana smiled at her, and then turned to Darcy, uneasy. His scowl was so customary, and all were immune to it that they took his quiet and stoic appearance as normal, yet I knew that he was slightly annoyed. For the party to also be extended in celebration to include Georgiana's engagement would bring attention to us in ways he may not have wanted. After all, now there was no way that we could leave earlier if he wished to.

"That is most unfortunate," Darcy said to me.

Hours had passed and Darcy and I were in our bed at The Queen's Right Hand Inn, and we were looking up at the ceiling.

"Yes, I can see your mind—and you might be correct."

"We shall be the center of attention always, along with the Russells. People will wish to know everything about Georgiana's engagement."

"Do not worry, Georgiana or Jason shall never let slip the improper side of their courtship."

"Yes, but being in such a situation, leads to us remaining under scrutiny. When the ton leaves Cumberland, they will know stories about us, and where stories are, very quickly are they followed by gossip, rumor and defamation of character."

"I would say that you are being an alarmist, my dear, yet I cannot deny that you do have a point. Tell me truly, Darcy, are we in a den of serpents?"

"My dear, I wish to say so, yet when it comes to social fatality, serpents are tame compared to the tongues of the ton."

# 20

# WALKING BOTH AWAY &
# TOWARDS A PROBLEM

The next day, more guests arrived, and they consisted of some members of the Proudfoot family, the Weston family, the Goddards, and the Smiths.

While we had left William and Caiden at the inn the first day with Lucy, the next day, we brought them to Cumberland. It was the perfect inclusion to our party, for William and Caiden became the center of attention.

"Oh, they are just darling!" Miss Crawford said.

"And they are twins?" Lady Russell asked.

"Yes, but they look different," I said.

"That is the best then, for that shall make it easier upon them."

"Yet, I have often found with twins," Miss Elton said, "that sometimes they spend much time wishing to know which one came out first, and therefore which one was the minute older?"

"They would argue of such a thing?" Darcy asked.

"Oh, very much it is possible they might do so," Charlotte Lucas said. "I have heard that as well."

"And it makes sense, for it will be most confusing for them when it comes time to inherit," Mr. Smith said. "Therefore, tell us Mr. and Mrs. Darcy, which one is the oldest?"

"Oh dear, I do not think I should say," I said, hiding the fact that I honestly had no idea who was the older one! In the midst of the chaos of giving birth, I never took notice. And Darcy, in the midst of seeing his wife give out in pain, he did not have time to care which one came out first. And yet, now that I thought about it, it was best if I did not know really.

"And," I added, "I do not think we shall ever tell them."

"You would do such a thing to your sons?" Mrs. Proudfoot gasped. "How so?"

"With great ease. If they do not know who the eldest is, and therefore do not know the heir, then they shall have to earn it. He who deserves Pemberley gets Pemberley."

The rest in the company turned to Darcy.

"That is the best option to our dilemma," he said, agreeing with everything I said as if it was long deliberated upon.

"Well then," Charlotte Lucas said, "I find that to be a marvelous idea."

"I disagree," Mr. Weston said. "For if they do not know, then it shall incite chaos in its wake, and they will spend too much time competing."

"Or it will teach them initiative," Charlotte said. "By earning something, they show whose nature is best to inherit."

"And besides," Jane Austen added, "who is to say that it is less civilized than the oldest inheriting?"

"Mr. Weston," Kitty said, "I see what you are feeling. With the heir being the inheritor, it makes everything less complicated."

"Precisely."

"Yet perhaps, that is the way it should be: complicated. Inheriting a grand estate such as Pemberley is not something that should be dealt with from birth before a parent has learned which son's nature is the best equipped to run an estate. What if in this case, the older brother wishes to be idle and not have an empire on his hands? Then the younger one could be the successor. You are correct that it might bring competition between them—however I have learned, in my wanderings, that competition is within human nature and is not something that can be extinguished. It is a wave that one must float over eventually, but always encounter."

"Pray," Mr. Weston said, "you give your opinions very decidedly for so young a group of persons." He then looked on the gentlemen in our party. "Do you teach your ladies to speak so?"

"We taught them nothing," Mr. Bingley replied, "and therefore we can take no credit. All we can declare is that they have taught themselves."

"Quite right," Jason added.

Mr. Weston and the rest looked on us all in wonder, and then Miss Crawford leaned forward and looked at our sons carefully.

"So," she began, changing the subject, "Which one is the one to look like his father?"

※

"Mr. Weston's comment did not dampen our appearance in everyone else's eyes," Charlotte said as we left Cumberland that day. "Do not fear. I spoke with many of the others in confidence and they always found Mr. Weston to be a stuffy sort of man. Though I daresay William and Caiden were everyone's favorites."

"Yes, I believe that my sons are very good at being emblems of peace," I said, and then I eyed her closely. "You seem happier, Charlotte."

She gave me a warm smile. "Yes, I suppose I am,"

"Then Lyme is already doing you much good?"

"It is not only Lyme. It is the distance. I am away from Hunsford and Lucas Lodge, and for a time, I can act as if my problems and woes are behind me. I know that I shall have to return, yet still, I am granted these moments of diversions, distractions, and I feel as if I can find myself again. And I can see that you are forgiving me."

I looked at her, uneasy, and I knew that she was reading my mind.

"Yes. I know that you never did anything to hurt me, yet I just felt anger for a while."

"You were not wrong to. Elizabeth...you were my dear friend once. I hope in time, I may have earned that again."

She touched my shoulder and then looked out of the carriage window as we drove back to the inn.

※

The next day, the rest of the guests were arriving, and some were in the sitting room, awaiting us for when we arrived and others were still in their rooms, making sure the servants unloaded their things correctly.

Upon arrival, we made the acquaintance of another set of guests, the Prices, the Thompsons, Lady Heywood, and—"

"Admiral Croft and Mrs. Croft!" Jane cried.

We all turned and entering the sitting room was Admiral Croft and on his arm was Mrs. Croft.

"Miss Jane Bennet!" Mrs. Croft cried. "At last, we meet again."

"Yes, we do, and the rest of my family is in the company as well," she said, turning and looking for us, yet she did not need to look far before we all walked toward the Crofts.

"Admiral and Mrs. Croft," Colonel Fitzwilliam, Kitty and I said. "It is wonderful to see you. How have you all been?"

"Lovely, we have," Mrs. Croft answered, "we have been staying with my older brother at his townhouse in London until Aginfield becomes open to us."

"Well," Mrs. Bingley said, "as you are aware, we have now completely vacated the estate and you can take possession of it once you leave Lyme."

"We look forward to it," Admiral Croft responded. "And we do quite enjoy the people of Hampshire. Yet we have a treat for you all."

"A treat?" Maria Lucas said, coming forward. "And what would that be?"

"Oh, Miss Maria, this does affect you as well, and your sister and Miss Austen. We have brought another acquaintance of yours that we thought would be a wonderful addition to our party."

"Yes, it is—"

"Ah, timely met!"

We all turned to who had said that.

"Timely met indeed," Mrs. Croft said. "This is my younger brother, as you all know, Captain Wentworth."

It was most extraordinary...for walking toward us was Captain Frederick Wentworth!

"Mrs. Darcy," Captain Wentworth said warmly, approaching me, "and Mrs. Fitzwilliam, Miss Bennet, and Mrs. Bingley."

He bowed when seeing us and we all curtsied in return.

"How fortunate," he continued. "When my sister told me that your company was to be a part of the engagement party, I was very much surprised and took great delight in it. Yet where are Miss Darcy and the rest of the lot? For I am so used to seeing you all together, that I do not know how to see the set of you without the other half."

"Oh," Kitty said, "they are about, yet let us introduce you to our friend who is also a part of our group. This here is Miss Maria Lucas."

Captain Wentworth turned to Maria and bowed to her.

"Miss Lucas, it is a pleasure to meet you."

"Thank you," Maria said, smiling, "yet the title of Miss Lucas belongs to my older sister, Charlotte. I am simply Miss Maria."

"Charlotte?" Captain Wentworth said, his smile and voice faltering.

"Yes, Charlotte Lucas is the eldest in her family," I said for Maria, eying him delicately and with immense pity. Captain Wentworth was in for a shock indeed—yet so was Charlotte. And nothing would be there to soothe their agony. "She is also in our company as well, and I am sure that she shall be delighted to see you again. For I recall that you are acquainted with her."

"Oh...yes," he said, alarm filling his eyes and then he quickly attempted to dismiss it with a false look of amazement. "I am shocked is all, for I did not anticipate to meet another lady who I have known before."

"Yes, and..." My eyes shifted as I was distracted and looked at something over his shoulder. He followed my gaze—poor soul! For it had been Charlotte he had been looking on as she was approaching us. As he turned to her, her eyes fell upon him and she recognized his person. Her footsteps ceased immediately, she stopped where she stood and then beheld him with alarm, fascination, and pure dread.

In that moment, I did feel great sadness for her. For at least Captain Wentworth had a moment to realize that she was here, but she was given no warning and this first look was her introduction into seeing him again. This moment would cause them such pain that might linger all throughout their days here at Lyme.

When the silence between them had the danger of being noticed, I spoke up once more.

"Oh, dear Charlotte! You are so surprised at seeing him again that you are speechless. Look, Captain Wentworth has done us the wonderful honor of joining this engagement party. Is it not a delight?"

"Oh!" she said, closing her eyes and breathing heavily. When she opened them again, her face was quite red. "Yes, forgive me, I am simply surprised by your appearance is all. Good day, Captain Wentworth. It is a...pleasure to see you again."

"Miss Lucas," he said, bowing his head slightly. "It is nice to see you as well."

"Oh," Maria said, "forgive me, that is my error. My sister no longer bears the name of Lucas. She is now Mrs. Charlotte Collins."

"Collins!" Captain Wentworth said, unable to hide a certain sharpness in his tone. "Oh, I do recall now, and I offer my congratulations, Mrs. Collins."

"Thank you," Charlotte said. "Yet your well wishes, though accepted most readily, are no longer necessary. For I am recently widowed."

"Widowed?" Miss Crawford said coming forward. "Oh, dear me, I had never learned."

"Oh, I did not wish to dampen this happy occasion with my own grave history."

"Yet I am sorry for you. You must feel greatly in distress and hope-lessness."

"Yes, you must," Captain Wentworth said. "For it is indeed a painful moment in your life, and yet, you are correct to be determined not to over-shadow this happy moment for the Russells with gray clouds. It is very selfless and is the path that you should follow." Then his eyes narrowed on Charlotte and there was a hint of malice and demand in them. "And speak of it little."

"Yes, I...I agree," she whispered, very much in dread of him. I did not know what to do because while Captain Wentworth's attitude was filled with malice, I could not deny understanding his resentfulness. He was a man who was rejected by a woman who—I shall be frank—had given him encouragement and then did not accept him when he deserved better.

His coldness and his desire for her to not speak of Mr. Collins was an impulse that I could not help but understand the inspiration of. And therefore, I did not know what to do—whether to leave it be, or to defend Charlotte.

"I can understand so," Miss Crawford said. "Yet I must ask...and then I shall forever hold my peace. Was his passing peaceful? How did it come about?"

I started to say that it was too difficult for Charlotte to speak of, yet Charlotte had already begun speaking, for which I did not know why. I could only see that she was so flustered that she was distracted and was so keen to be speaking to anyone else but Captain Wentworth, that she was willing to answer any question without thinking first.

"Oh, he was working with his beehives one day when he fell down and knocked his head against the tables and then suffocated."

"He passed away while looking after his bees?" Captain Wentworth repeated suddenly. "Oh, well, that is most—unfortunate."

"Yes, how alarming," Miss Crawford said, then she squeezed Charlotte's shoulder and walked away. I felt so terrible for her, for her husband to die in such a pathetic way while the man she rejected had survived naval battles would naturally satisfy any internal need for retribution that Captain Wentworth might have wanted. And as for Miss Crawford...she appeared as being a nice woman, yet I did not fully trust her. She gave me the impression as being the sort of woman who was very proficient in looking mannerly and considerate of others but would as soon turn around and tell everything about a person to another, being false and deceitful. Therefore, I did not feel very certain that when she walked away from us, she would not tell everyone how Mr. Collins died. If she would do so, then Charlotte's bad fortune would be at the base of their jokes for the rest of our time at Cumberland.

❦

"Yet we have another addition to our company," Maria said, "who I believe has made your acquaintance, Captain. Miss Jane Austen is here. I shall go to fetch her, and she shall be overjoyed to see you."

Maria turned and left to look for Jane Austen while I turned back to the Crofts and the Captain.

"Come, let me take you to Mr. Darcy, for he shall love to see you once more."

"Very well, but wait," Captain Wentworth said. "There are two more guests to Cumberland who are great friends and colleagues of mine for whom I am waiting. I would like for you to make their acquaintance, for they would love to meet you, Mrs. Darcy, Miss Darcy, and Mrs. Fitzwilliam. They have a fondness for *strong* women."

I avoided looking at Charlotte, for I knew full well that Captain Wentworth was trying to slight her as well as avoid her. Charlotte did not know what to do but stand there, on the other side of Kitty, looking down at the ground.

"Oh, I can guess who these friends are!" Mrs. Croft said.

"Yes, you can, sister, and they will be most happy to see you as well."

"Captain Wentworth!"

We all turned, and Jane Austen approached, being led by Maria. As she did so, she averted her eyes to Charlotte who exchanged a quick glance with her and then turned back to the captain.

"Miss Austen," Captain Wentworth's smile was sincere. "We meet again."

"I can scarce believe it sir," Jane said, approaching him with forced ease. "When Miss Maria had told me that you were present, I thought she was putting a joke on me."

"Indeed, she was very serious. I offer my congratulations as well, for now you are a published author."

"Thank you, sir."

"Is there any chance that you shall favor us with a reading while we untalented lot remain here at Cumberland?"

"I promise that I will not disappoint on that score—whether the listeners enjoy the reading or not is another matter."

Very soon we were joined by Mr. Darcy. The rest of the men in our company and Jason were introduced to the Crofts, who took to him most readily.

Lastly to join our conversation was Captain Wentworth's comrades, Captain Benwick and Captain Harvill.

Their arrival was a breath of fresh air, for they were not acquainted with Charlotte or knew of the history she possessed with their charming friend. Therefore, they met her with ease and Charlotte easily began to take to Captain Benwick, who was most sympathetic to her recently widowed state.

⚭

Eventually we all joined the rest of the guests and began to shift our attention to where it was owed: the engaged couple. At this point, there were forty people there in total—at least that was what I had counted, and we all gathered in the dining room where we all sat down in the immensely long hall for a mid-day meal. Before the food was presented, Mr. Russell stood up with his glass raised.

"Our wonderful guests," he began. "No, I must be frank. You are all so large in number that I feel as if I am beginning to suffer from stage fright."

We all chuckled politely and then quieted down when we saw that he was to continue.

"On behalf of my officious mother and my lovely fiancée, I thank you all for coming to my welcome home party as well as my engagement party. You are witnessing the coming together of two people who are matched in both mind and soul, and to see you all here, witnessing our ties and our beginnings to an intangible bond, I am therefore speechless. Well, not really, yet it feels so to me now."

Mr. Edward Russell turned to his left and took Miss Elton's hand in his own.

"Miss Elton...my dear Ariella, when I left for India, never did a day go by that I did not think of you. Always you were in my thoughts, and I wished for you to be by my side. Yet now I am returned, and it is now no longer a dream. Now it shall be a great reality. Miss Elton, when you first accepted my proposal, I felt as if I had strayed into a fantasy, and when I returned, a part of me worried that the fantasy would come to an end. Yet the fantasy was not fiction. Yes, it was always real. Thank you for marrying me, my beloved friend. And you shall make me the happiest of men."

Miss Elton stood up, moved by her fiancé's words and he kissed her hand as all the men at the table stood and clapped while we ladies also applauded but remained seated.

As we did so, I stole a glance at Captain Wentworth, and I saw him once more looking at Charlotte. She looked at him briefly before she looked down as well.

჻჻჻

After the meal was ended, I eventually found that Charlotte had gone onto the terrace by herself, making it appear as if she was just looking at the view of Lyme. Knowing that she was viewing it as her great escape, I decided to go out and join her.

Acting nonchalant, I walked out, and she turned when she heard my footsteps, but her shoulders slackened, and her expression relaxed when she beheld that it was only me.

"Remain calm," I said, and then I stood next to her as we looked at the view.

"It is a wonderful sight," she said.

"Yes, Lyme is quite beautiful."

"Yes, it is."

"Charlotte, I had no idea that Captain Wentworth would attend."

"I know you did not."

"I am so sorry."

"You have nothing to apologize for. I was foolish for thinking I could spend my entire life never seeing him again."

"How are you feeling right now?"

"It felt—Elizabeth it felt awful. I feel utterly shaken and exposed to the world for my sin of foolishness. I am a fool!"

"We all are sometimes."

"And he despises me now."

"No, he does not."

"Yes, he does. You know it, for you have seen it."

"I saw a man who is angry and bitter—and perhaps wants retribution. Yet it is not hatred. Though I admit to not knowing fully, for his mind is his and it is hidden from us. And I am sorry for your pain."

"I thank you, Elizabeth, and you are too good. Yet, if I am to be objective this time, I should confess to myself that it is my fault and therefore who more should suffer than I do now? Yes, I ought to be blamed, and I ought to feel it. Therefore, feel it, I must. I feel so blind now! For I came here, thinking I could escape my painful memories, even for a little while, and fate taught me a valuable lesson: one cannot escape one's past forever and to think one can is pride...it's blind hubris."

"I see how it must hurt, to think you have outrun something and only to find that you have only run faster towards it."

"Yes, I truly have been walking away and towards a problem all at once. And that problem was Captain Wentworth."

## 21

# SUCH IS THE WAY OF
# RESENTMENT

As we returned back to the inn, my sister Kitty moved beside me, and she whispered in my ear.

"Elizabeth, you are most observant, therefore I must ask you something."

"What is it, Kitty?"

"Are you aware of any prior history between Charlotte and Captain Wentworth? For the way that they looked on each other signified a more in-depth acquaintance than just the slight one they claimed to have. Mark my words, Elizabeth, there is more between them than they are letting on. And I believe that the captain insulted Charlotte slightly."

I was quite torn for I wanted to confide in Kitty, yet Charlotte had never given me permission to do so, therefore my hands were tied and I could not divulge anything.

"I have not any idea," I lied. "Yet I observed the tension between them as well and I am most curious about it."

"Is there...is there any possibility that you might ask her? You are her closest friend and I believe that she would take you most readily into her confidence. I do not mean to pry, it is just, if there is something amiss, then we ought to know of it."

"I agree," I said. "Worry not, I shall ask her very shortly." Kitty was put at ease. She walked onward and I was left alone, yet I was near Charlotte and Maria. Charlotte walked on without contributing much to the conversation, yet Maria, who was excited from meeting so many new people and being seen by many in turn, was talking away of their success, but not to her sister's delight, for she then had turned her conversation toward Captain Wentworth as her chief subject.

"The captain is a kind man and was most attentive to me, yet he is not very gallant toward you, Charlotte. For as we talked together, I asked him what he thought of you, and he said that you were so altered that he should not have known you again."

Charlotte bit one of her lips, nodded and continued walking.

Maria had been oblivious at the moment, and though she usually possessed the feelings to make her respect her sister's emotions in a common way, she was perfectly unsuspecting of inflicting any particular wound, it appeared. All I could do was wish that Maria had held her tongue, yet Charlotte was clearly most affected by this report, and it would affect her self-confidence most acutely.

⊙⚜⊙

The next day, we all met at Cumberland for a mid-day meal once more and we planned for an afternoon walk after it to enjoy the views and nature of Lyme.

While we had done so, there was much talk and discussion, yet our Navy men were the chief attraction, for their lives had been so full of action and adventure that they had many stories.

"Being a sailor or captain of a ship leads to eating some strange meals," Captain Harvill said as he sat opposite Captain Wentworth. "Frederick and Benwick, do you remember what we ate when we pulled into port in Spain?"

"Oh, yes, squid!" Benwick and Captain Wentworth said together.

"Squid, really?" Miss Crawford exclaimed. "And how did it taste?"

"Absolutely delightful," Captain Benwick said, "as long, mark my words Miss Crawford, as long as it is cooked properly."

"And how does one cook it?"

"Harvill," Benwick said, "you tell her, for you are the cook between us."

"Are you?" Jason asked Captain Harvill.

"I had no choice," Captain Harvill said, "for it was either learn to cook or learn to eat raw food. Believe me, that was a wonderful incentive to learn to cook."

Everyone laughed.

"Good heavens!" Miss Elton said. "Was squid the most unique food you had ever eaten from the sea?"

"Would you believe that it was not?" Captain Wentworth said. "One time, I tasted a fried starfish!"

"You did not!" Maria cried.

"Yes, I actually did. And to my surprise, it was delightful."

"Upon my word," Lady Russell said, "I would have never believed it."

"Well, there is something even more extreme," Admiral Croft said. "And this I believe was the most bewilderingly and surprisingly delicious."

"What?" Jane Austen asked.

"Oh, I know what it was!" Mrs. Croft said.

"Octopus!" Admiral and Mrs. Croft said together. "Yes, it did taste very good."

"You actually ate octopus?"

"Cooked and ate octopus," Admiral Croft said. "Yes, the sea makes a strange diet and food selection for anyone who tries to traverse it, Lady Russell. A strange diet indeed."

❦

Eventually the subject of the discussion shifted to the ships in the navy and there was a general ignorance of all naval matters throughout the party, making our naval guests very much questioned, especially by Maria and Miss Crawford.

"My first ship was the Asp," Captain Wentworth said. "Yet you shall never find her in the Navy List. She eventually became quite worn out and broken up. I was the last man who commanded her there. In truth, she was hardly fit for service when I did finish with her, and therefore she was reported fit for home service for a year or two. And so, I was sent off to the West Indies."

"Oh, the West Indies!" Miriam cried. "I have always wished to go there."

"Perhaps you shall one day, Mrs. Bingley. I can assure you that it is worth the adventure."

"Yet you mentioned that the Asp was not a very well-maintained ship even before you were given her?" Jane asked.

"Yes, she was worse for wear, undoubtedly. The admiralty entertains themselves now and then, with sending a few hundred men to sea, in a ship not fit to be employed. But they have a great many to provide for, and among the thousands that may just as well go to the bottom as not, it is impossible for them to distinguish the very set who may be least missed."

"Oh, Frederick, you exaggerate," Admiral Croft said. "What stuff you younger fellows talk! Never was there a better sloop than the Asp in her day. You were a fortunate man to get her. And you know perfectly well that there must have been twenty better men than yourself applying for her at the same time, yet you were the sort to gain her as your prize. Lucky fellow to get anything so soon, with no more higher connections than the one that you had. For usually to get a ship like the Asp, you have to have many friends in high places, and you did not, but used your charisma as your guiding light."

"I felt my luck, Admiral, I can assure you. I was as well satisfied with my appointment as you can desire. It was a great object with me, at that time, to be at sea...a very great object. I could not bear to be idle and I wanted to be doing something."

"To be sure you did, for what should a young fellow like you do ashore? And for half a year? If a man has not a wife, he soon wants to be afloat again."

"Yes, you are correct, Admiral." He smiled and then his eyes rested on Charlotte. "I desperately wished to be at sea, for I had no wife at the time. Therefore, at sea, I went. With great enthusiasm and alacrity."

Captain Wentworth proved to have not made his point well enough yesterday, for he wished to continue to display his feelings to Charlotte, perhaps in hopes of making her feel what he once had, and such is the way of resentment: it often leads to spite.

# 22

# MORE UNFOLDING OF HEROES

A fter our meal was finished, we all took a walk over the grounds of Cumberland and we spoke more on Mr. Edward Russell and Miss Elton, asking them of how they first met, when they began to fall in love, and they unfolded their story.

They had met at a ball and the rest of the women in the party practically swooned, for to them, that was the perfect meeting to a fiancé, especially to Miss Crawford, whose sensibilities could not help but to be touched.

However, the walk did not last very long, for many in our company were not great walkers, and those of us who were, were left to return back to the house with the others.

As we re-entered Cumberland, we were all in for a surprise for the hour had come when it was time for Jane Austen to give her reading.

Therefore, she took some pages from her portfolio, a stand was brought for her so that she could place the papers on them, and she began to read.

*'The first winter assembly in the town of D. in Surrey was to be held on Tuesday, October 13<sup>th</sup> and it was generally expected to be a very good one. A long list of county families was confidently run over as sure of*

*attending, and sanguine hopes were entertained that the Osbornes them-*
*selves would be there. The Edwards' invitation to the Watsons followed, of*
*course. The Edwards were people of fortune, who lived in the town and*
*kept their coach. The Watsons inhabited a village about three miles*
*distant, were poor, and had no close carriage; and ever since there had*
*been balls in the place, the former were accustomed to invite the latter to*
*dress, dine, and sleep at their house on every monthly return throughout*
*the winter. On the present occasion, as only two of Mr. Watson's children*
*were at home, and one was always necessary as companion to himself, for*
*he was sickly and had lost his wife, one only could profit by the kindness*
*of their friends. Miss Emma Watson, who was very recently returned to*
*her family from the care of an aunt who had brought her up, was to make*
*her first public appearance in the neighborhood, and her eldest sister,*
*whose delight in a ball was not lessened by a ten years' enjoyment, had*
*some merit in cheerfully undertaking to drive her and all her finery in the*
*old chair to D. on the important morning.*

*As they splashed along the dirty lane, Miss Watson thus instructed and*
*cautioned her inexperienced sister—*

*'I daresay it will be a very good ball, and among so many officers you*
*will hardly want partners...*

Jane Austen continued her reading for another twenty minutes and it
was as enjoyable as when I had read it. When she finished with her last
line of 'Carefulness and discretion should not be confined to elderly
ladies, or to a second chance,' added his wife, 'They are quite as necessary to young ladies in their first', she lowered the papers and we all
cheered.

"Very accomplished," Captain Wentworth said, the most pronounced of
all our compliments. "Very accomplished."

"Thank you for your kind words," Jane Austen said. "I wrote it in 1803
actually."

"And have you finished it?" Miriam asked.

"No, I have not. For some reason, I had not the inspiration to."

"I cannot believe it," Lady Russell said. "For the character Emma
Watson is a very delightful sort of creature, and enjoyable."

"Indeed," Captain Wentworth said. "She is a character who understands compassion, openness of temper, good manners...and loyalty."

"Yes, she is," Maria said as Charlotte remained silent. "You see Jane, I have often told you that you should have finished this one. I have told her, believe me! Therefore, I shall be bold Jane, let us all implore her to finish it."

There were pools of requests for Jane to finish 'The Watsons', to which she chuckled and rolled her eyes.

"Oh, very well!" She sighed. "I am undertaking the revisions of many of my finished novels now as well as still writing another project. Yet once I finish it all—and if I am lucky to live long enough, then I will return to the 'The Watsons' and I shall complete it."

"Oh, I do hope so!" Maria cried.

Jane Austen threw back her head and laughed. "I do believe that you shall get your wish, for Maria, I feel as if I am as healthy as a horse."

❧

"And yet, Miss Austen," Captain Benwick asked, "is there ever the chance that you shall write a story where a navy man is a hero?"

At this there was a lot of cooing.

"Oh, is this where I am told what I shall write now?" Jane Austen replied wittingly.

"Oh dear, did I sound like one of those?"

"Yes, sir, you did sound like one of those poor and infamous souls who always have to offer a suggestion to us poor writers. Sadly, for you, we cannot be demanded so, and sometimes cannot write something that our instincts do not believe in. Yet fortunately for you, I am very much open to writing a story where a navy man is a hero."

"Oh, you were simply teasing me."

"I could not help but do so, I confess. Yet since you are so presumptuous as to suggest things to me," Jane Austen said, not serious or critical to Captain Benwick at all, but was light and amused, "then I have the right to ask if I may use your name."

"My name?"

"Yes, Captain Benwick. If you want to suggest that I use your profession, then might I name a character after you?"

There was a general uproar among the guests, and they all began to cry out for their names to be used as well.

"Are you sincere?"

"Are you afraid?"

"Not so, actually. I suppose I do not fear the pen and something such at all. In fact, I feel quite the contrary and welcome my name lasting forever."

"Very well," she said.

"And if you are not against the name of Harvill," Captain Harvill added, "then I am most open to being written in as well."

"Vanity works well on us sailors, clearly." Admiral Croft laughed.

"And why should it not?" Captain Harvill asked. "We are soldiers on the sea, Admiral. Any day it can swallow us up, therefore the greatest thing would be is for a writer to remember us with no harm coming to us at all."

"Too true. Too true."

"Well then," Charlotte said, smiling, "if you are willing to allow Miss Austen to use your names, then it might also help for her to hear some stories about your times at sea."

"Oh," Admiral Croft said, clapping his hands together, "that is where I come in. While Captain Wentworth over there had a ship that was faulty in the Asp, I had a worse ship when I first became a Captain, and she was named The Diana. And I knew pretty well what she was, before that day. I suppose because I had no other discoveries to make, I grew to love her like she was my right arm practically. Ah! She was a dear Diana to me. She did all that I wanted. I knew that she would—I knew that we should either go to the bottom together, or that she would be the making of me; and I never had two days of foul weather all the time I was at sea in her."

"With me," Captain Harvill said, "I had a ship called The Dauntless. And I had the good fortune, in my passage home one autumn season, to fall in with the very French frigate—which if you do not know, is a French war vessel—which we engaged in battle with. I brought the Dauntless into Plymouth; and here was another instance of luck. We had not been six hours in the Sound, when a gale came on, which lasted four days and nights, and which would have done for poor old Dauntless, in half the time. You see, from our encounter with the French vessel, the Dauntless was so much in disrepair that I felt the ship was going to fall apart all around me. Therefore, I worried all the while that she would have done so, and I should only have been a gallant Captain Harvill, in a small paragraph at one corner of the newspapers; and being lost in only a sloop, nobody would have thought of me."

The whole room of guests shuddered.

❦

"Well," Captain Benwick said, beginning his narration, "for me, I was given a ship called The Dominus, and she was a beauty, and those were pleasant days when I had the Dominus. How fast I made money in her!"

"Oh of course, that is what it is all about!" Captain Wentworth laughed.

"Yes, it is. A friend of mine, and I, had such a lovely cruise together off the Western islands—the Hebrides to be precise—Poor Richardson! You know how he wanted money, remember that, Frederick?"

"I do." Captain Wentworth explained to us, "Another captain that we know, Richardson, he also desired wealth, and had a heart of gold."

"Yes, he wanted it more than I did," Harvill said. "It was not from being infatuated with the ecstasy of gold, you must understand. It is only that he has a wife, and he is a very excellent sort of fellow. I shall never forget his happiness after he married her. He desired wealth just for her sake, and therefore I wished for him to find luck the next summer, thinking he might find his fortune then. Luck was found the next summer, yet it was not for Richardson's sake. But rather, it was Captain Wentworth here who found his pot of wealth that year."

"Aye," Captain Wentworth said, somber. "I found it in the Mediterranean. And I suppose I found it because I was never even looking for it or thinking I would ever be the soul to ever be given a good ending. And yet I was, I was."

The captains proceeded to tell more stories of their adventures on the sea, to which we were all thoroughly enjoying.

163

"Well then, Miss Austen," Admiral Croft said at the end of it, "I hope that you have enjoyed our set of memories. Were they sufficient?"

"You have given me much and more," Jane Austen said, "for before us all was more unfolding of heroes and at every part in a story where a heroic deed is required, I may call upon your memories and may they fill the page I write them on."

## 23

# WHAT IS TO BE DONE?

"Yes," Jane Austen said as I visited in her room at the inn, "I have noticed it all."

Upon our leaving Cumberland, she wished to retire to her room and write some more, yet I needed to speak with her before she did so. To make matters clear, I acknowledged all that I had seen pass between Captain Wentworth and Charlotte, and she had noticed it all as well.

"He is not only angry, from what I could see," Jane continued, "yet he is also perhaps looking for revenge—seeking what he regards as justice, or a reckoning at the very least."

"It is a very ungentlemanly thing to do," I commented. "And quite impolitic, for it may lead to him appearing very ungallant toward her in our company. However, I cannot pretend to act like I do not know what he is feeling now."

"Precisely," Jane replied. "And his actions are all stemmed from wounded pride of being jilted—and from being betrayed. For that is what it feels like when someone you love turns their back upon you because of one's position in life."

"Is that what you felt when Tom Lefroy did not offer to marry you?" I asked gently.

Jane chuckled sadly and then put her quill down on her desk.

"Well Elizabeth, I want to say that I handled it well. And I wish to also say that if I were to see him again, I would be forgiving, at ease, and mannerly, but I cannot. I was very angry, very disappointed in him. And it did feel like a betrayal. For it was, in some ways, and reacting to such an act with passivity and serenity is not something I am sure that I could do. Therefore, I shall leave such perfection of manners to my heroines, for they have the right to be better than myself."

"So, you understand Captain Wentworth, then?"

"Yes, I do. Perhaps more easily than I understand our dear Charlotte. That does not mean that I do not believe she should be damned for her actions, not in the slightest. And we must be there for her, for she is quite aware of her own mistake. But as for them both, what can we do, but look on them and hope that peace grows where there is now division and separation?"

"I do not believe that Captain Wentworth would ever be directly evil to her."

"No, he would not. He would simply just make comments that appeared off-hand-like, where no one would know he was insulting her; only she would know it."

"I thought, with her coming, this holiday would be a retreat for her, and not a prison."

"There is still a chance that she may find some diversions here to her liking."

"It does not need to be hard to endure, if Charlotte were to do the right thing."

"And what is that?"

"She needs to confront it. She needs to speak to him."

"I do not think she has the strength, Lizzy. She is a very sensible and kind woman, but to do so would mean that she would have to break decorum. It is not in the nature of many to be willing to speak up so and would rather avoid."

"Precisely, and if she were to avoid it, the problem might grow."

"It has grown enough, for we are entering their story at the end of it all."

"It does not have to be an ending for them. If she confronts the matter, then it could be a whole new beginning. Or if the captain were to know of it..."

"Lizzy, what are you thinking?"

"I'm thinking that if the captain knew that the problem, the very reason that he was rejected was because her mother objected to the match, would soften him. He would see the logic of the matter."

Jane Austen looked at me knowingly, for she saw where my mind and thoughts were directed.

"Yes, perhaps you are right. So tell me, what is your suggestion of who should make him aware of the true source of this fact?"

"Who do you think he trusts more? You, me, or my sisters?"

"While our words would hold some weight with him, it might not be as strong as if he would learn of it through another more intimidating avenue."

"Intimidating?"

"We are Charlotte's friends, Lizzy. Captain Wentworth might be aware that anything we say of her would be in her interest—we would try to absolve her in his eyes because we would be in her confidence. Therefore, what say you to Mr. Darcy?"

"Have my husband speak to him?" I laughed. "Jane, that is preposterous."

"Is it?"

"I do not know if Darcy would enjoy having to do such a thing, not to mention it means that my husband would have to do some acting, which he would despise! For he only knows how to tell the truth."

"This is a truth."

"Yes, that he would be scripted to say, therefore he would feel as if the whole conversation were a lie."

"Well then, what say you to Colonel Fitzwilliam?"

"I..."

I leaned back when I thought of Richard as a candidate. Though his acquaintance with Charlotte was little at best, he was a very gallant man, as well as a humane one. Therefore, he would be more compliant at doing a service to ease Charlotte's suffering somewhat.

"Ah, the Colonel might suffice."

"Yet do you think he would be willing?"

"Even if he does not listen to me, then I shall ask Kitty to influence him. She can convince him to do practically anything."

"Very well. Let me know how this all ends when it is done, but make sure not to tell Charlotte you are doing it."

"Why not?"

"Because believe me, this is something she will not want to have help on, even though she needs it. This is something that she will rather suffer in silence and then hope for a miracle to present itself on its own."

I smiled and stood up, preparing to leave.

"Oh, and Lizzy?"

"Yes?" I replied, turning back to her.

"What say you to the title *Mansfield Park*?"

"Well, I cannot give a ready opinion, for I do not know the contents of the book."

"It is one of my older compositions that I am working to re-edit. It follows a girl who was brought to the estate Mansfield Park as a child, and it is a charity case. Then she grows to be the right hand of the mistress of the house, only to fall in love with her cousin while she lives there and spends her time wondering if it shall all come to rights in the end.

"Then why not name the book after the lead character?"

"Oh, Fanny Price?"

"Yes...if that is her name."

"Because of redundancy for one. I shall name *Emma* after the lead character, and also because, though the story follows Fanny Price, it is not only about her. It is about her coming to the estate of Mansfield and how her relationships with those characters define her as well as how she defines them. The connection is manifold."

"Then it is suitable. Is it your favorite of your works?"

"It is very much Cassandra's favorite, yet I do not think I can speak for all on that matter."

"Then Mansfield Park is well enough."

I turned and left, thinking to myself that though it was a suitable title to a book, it would never fascinate some as the title *Sense and Sensibility* had. And, therefore, while it could very well be a great book, I knew that if Jane were to be remembered for a certain great work, it would be another book in her canon.

⬥

I walked to Lucy's room and found her looking after Caiden and William.

"How are my two beauties?" I asked her.

"Oh, they are splendid, yet they are hungry I believe."

I began to feed William and Lucy fed Caiden.

"William is learning to try and speak now."

"He is?"

"Yes, of course they are not words that are discernible, yet that is not the point I believe."

"No, it is not. As long as he is beginning to find his voice. He was so quiet before and it gave me peace yes, but actually, I am happy that he is speaking."

Then, as if he comprehended my desires, William began to make gurgling noises and cried out, not sadly but with exclamation.

When he finished the milk, I kissed him, put him on the floor and was amazed at how tall they were both getting.

"I hope they are not short because of me. And not because the world worships tall, or because I find shorter men to be inferior in any way, it is simply that if they are not, their father will always look like a giant to them. I want them to be able to stand as tall as their papa."

"Usually, sons are either a little less or taller than their fathers. They shall be of good height, but if I am allowed to predict the future now, they will not be as large as Mr. Darcy."

Caiden got to his feet and then took a few steps toward me, grabbing my petticoat and pressing his head against my knees. I did so love them terribly, and I feared spoiling them.

Eventually William and Caiden got sleepy, so I handed them over to Lucy and left. As I had done so, being out of the nursery room felt as if I was leaving a sanctuary, for the issues, little or great, were returning to me, and the matter of Charlotte also did so.

Therefore, for her, was our next step the correct one? In the matter of friends, what is to be done? And how does one know if it is the right thing?

## ❧ 24 ❧

# TWO ACTORS

With speed, I had gone to Kitty and the Colonel's room, accompanied by Darcy. In the security of the room, I told the history between Charlotte and Captain Wentworth to them.

"Truly?" Kitty asked. "Charlotte received a proposal from the captain?"

"Yes."

"And she refused him?"

"Yes."

"Good heavens, that was foolish beyond all comprehension."

"You forget, Kitty, that then, Captain Wentworth did not have any wealth."

"Yes," Kitty sniped, looking at Colonel Fitzwilliam, "because wealth is something I care about deeply."

"Oh," I sighed, "Kitty, Charlotte is not you."

"Yes, and I do not understand what she was about, and I admit is a greater simpleton than I would have ever taken her for."

"What makes you say that?" Richard said, looking at her with a most amused expression.

"I mean that with a woman who was trained to consider the concept of matrimony as the highest degree a woman could receive, to then reject a man who not only she felt a deep connection to but also one that she would be fortunate enough to have received attentions from is beyond me. While it should not be set down that every woman should be apt or forced to accept any man who fancies to marry her, this is different. Lizzy, I am fond of Charlotte, but she always was regarded as plain. There is beauty in that plainness, for there is goodness in her, but Captain Wentworth has a wider look to him regarding pulchritude."

"Do you find him attractive, my love?" Richard asked, warningly.

"Not in the slightest, for he is not you, you stubborn mule," she said, kissing his chin, "yet still in the eyes of the world, he is satisfactory."

"And he must feel the same thing," Darcy replied, "for he is a pleasing and agreeable fellow, and I like him immensely. Therefore, for Charlotte to reject him must make her foolish on that score."

"But she was persuaded to refuse him," I said.

"Could anyone have persuaded you to refuse me?" Darcy cocked an eyebrow at me, looking deep into my eyes. "Say that I was not wealthy, but meager and of a profession, would you not have fought for me?"

"Oh," I said knowingly, "I understand now."

"Precisely, you would have been too stubborn."

"Yes."

"And Charlotte was not. Charlotte, when it mattered, did not fight for him. And that is how the captain looks at it. She did not fight for him when he needed her to. The reason that we are wed is because you fought for me. Kitty and the Colonel here are married because she fought for him. See how her crime appears in his eyes now?"

"Yes, I do."

"Then I am not sure that our doing anything about it would change that. When the facts are laid bare, Charlotte may not have been the one to have refused him initially, yet she was. Be it her mother's influence that sparked it or not."

"And yet, Fitz," Richard said, "he will be resentful, yes, and I do not blame him. However, I see Elizabeth's reasoning. He still needs to know that she did care for him. For the sake of peace here at this party. If he knows that she was persuaded and pressured, it does not lessen that she made the wrong choice, but that her first instinct had been to accept him.

We do it for his peace of mind as much as for her own. And then there lessens the chance that they will have any scenes that may arise which shall be unpleasant to more than just themselves."

Darcy groaned and leaned forward.

"It is just... I am not good at lying."

We all laughed at this.

"Yes, my dear," I said, "we know."

"Yet Darcy," Kitty said, "this is not a lie. All is true, Charlotte did reject him because of her mother's rebuttal."

"Yes, but the conversation will be staged. I am terrible at line delivery."

"Now you make us appear as if we are two actors who have to memorize our parts," Richard said with a laugh.

"Yes."

"Why so?"

"Because we are."

"Fitz, no we are not. We are simply letting the good Captain know a truth. We are exposing veracity and putting an end to ignorance."

"And though I disagree with Charlotte's giving in to her mother so easily," Kitty said, "I can see that this is a mistake that Charlotte did not do out of malice, but weakness and the natural inclination to obey her mother. This was a mistake made out of love, not hate or indifference. Such mistakes should always be given the right to be rectified."

Darcy looked on all of us, and me last of all.

"This is a bizarre scheme, my love, even for your creative mind."

"It's because it did not come from mine. It came from Jane Austen's."

"Oh!" Darcy remarked. "It would come from her, wouldn't it? Only a writer would think of such a scheme."

"Or a wife, I must admit," I said. "Yet this time, it did not come from this wife." For then, I had pointed to myself.

"Well then, we shall engage the captain in polite conversation, and then..."

"We can easily tell him of Charlotte's poor state," Richard said, "and casually acknowledge her sad history."

"Precisely," I said, clapping my hands. "There you see, you are not two actors in this drama."

"Yes, we are," Darcy said, "and we shall do the job most poorly."

"Speak for yourself, Fitz," Richard said. "I find this highly amusing."

"You would!"

"I do!"

"Oh, quiet yourself."

"No, you quiet yourself."

"No, you quiet yourself."

"No, you quiet yourself."

Ah, I thought, the cousins resort to their childhood.

## ❧ 25 ❧

# SITTING ALONE

T he next day, all met at Cumberland and the ladies of the party were asked to individually go to the pianoforte and display their talents.

As Charlotte remained seated, Georgiana was asked if she would give the honors first, for her talents at the instrument were said to be unparalleled.

She smiled bashfully and then stood up, giving her fiancé, Mr. Whitfield, a fleeting look.

"I never knew that you played," he said, smiling at her.

"You shall see." She gave him a fetching smile.

Remaining in her seat, Charlotte watched them both and witnessed the mutual affection between each other, and it made her feel slightly forlorn. She, Charlotte, had allied herself with a man who she had little affection for, if any, and never did she find repayment. As she looked around the room of the guests, she saw Mr. Darcy sit with her friend, Elizabeth, and Colonel Fitzwilliam with Kitty as well, and they all were content in their union. There was no emotional disquiet or regrets, and that was most greatly opposite to her state.

A part of her wished that Mr. Collins still lived, and not just as her protector, but that he was a constant companion, even if a flawed one. And his recent improvement of character before his demise had opened her chances of having some domestic felicity with him. It was instantly preferable than being at Lyme where her past had come back to haunt her in such a way.

'Oh, Mr. Collins!' She gasped in her heart, 'I feel such ironic and conflicting sentiments. I am happy to be free while also equally burdened at losing you.'

Charlotte directed her attention to Jane, Maria and Jane Austen, who all sat near each other, alongside Lady Russell and Miss Crawford. She however, remained in the back of all the guests, where none noticed her, and she was left to the peace of her own company while Georgiana moved to the pianoforte and Mr. Whitfield followed her, to be the one to turn the pages.

As such, Charlotte, who kept her attention on the happy couple, was so occupied in the perfect pair they made in standing up together that she did not notice the person who sat in the empty seat next to her until they did so, and she turned to see who it was.

"Captain Wentworth?" She gasped.

"Yes," Captain Wentworth said. "Sitting here would give me a better view to the scene, now would it not?"

❦

Charlotte's emotions were in disarray as she beheld him sitting there, looking at her smoothly, yet also coldly.

"Oh, I see, yet this seat is not the best," she rushed out quietly.

"Is that your way of telling me that you do not wish me to sit near you?"

"I did not imply that, I can assure you. I just did not think this seat so advantageous to the performance."

"There are less heads in my way at this angle. However, I daresay that when it comes to musical performances, it is not the visual that is most important, but the sound the player makes and the quality of it."

Georgiana began to play. Her skills were not exaggerated, and she was as much the proficient as all rumors had claimed her to be.

"Masterful, is she not?" Captain Wentworth said.

"She does play infuriatingly well," Charlotte said.

"Indeed, I have never heard her equal."

"Nor have I. In Hampshire, we do our best to possess such a talent at playing, yet I have never been able to acquire such skill."

"Just as you say," Captain Wentworth whispered. "Because you would not take the pains to aspire to such excellence."

Charlotte swallowed in apprehension, for she felt the offense of his statement all too keenly.

"You'll make me quite ashamed of myself."

"If obtaining superiority of talent or virtue, Mrs. Collins, then perhaps you should be."

Charlotte fisted her hands and put them in her lap, greatly affected.

"I never pretended to possess any talent at the pianoforte, or ever desired to be known for my talent at it."

"Yes, from what I recalled, you never did."

"You are remembering my playing at the halls in Brighton, I see."

"Yes, I am remembering it. As I remember everything else."

"That was a very enjoyable holiday."

"Yes, it had begun that way. And judging by your attitude or indifference, it would have remained that way to the very end."

"Captain Wentworth..."

"Yes, they were better times, for I remember when you would call me Frederick."

Georgiana had finished playing. Everyone clapped politely, and then it was the turn of the next obliging young lady, which turned out to be Miss Elton with Mr. Russell as her page turner. When they began, he also proved to be of the musical sort, for they began to sing a duet while she played.

Under the cover of the singing, Charlotte began to speak once more to the captain.

"You wish to speak of times long past, Frederick?"

"It is not so long ago."

"Nine years and a few months, to be accurate."

He slanted her a glance. "You pay attention to the time? I am flattered."

"Yes, I did, Frederick. And is there something that you wish to speak of?"

"You are quick to confront what I imply."

"I confront it because I know that you wish me to."

"Still not original in your decisions then? And relying upon others to begin them?"

"Frederick, stop insulting me," Charlotte hissed. Frederick looked at her, smirking, for his intention, though not a charitable one, had been to provoke Charlotte into her spirits being arisen.

"Your feelings are hurt?" he asked. "I know the sentiment and sensation of one's feelings being hurt all too well."

Charlotte bit her lip and looked ahead.

"You are angry with me, aren't you?" she whispered gently.

"Yes..." he replied slowly. "Very much so."

"And you are seeking revenge."

"No, not revenge, Charlotte. I am seeking what could only feel like retribution. Justice. Yet you would view it as revenge."

"I do not blame you," Charlotte said suddenly.

"What?" Captain Wentworth said, alert and surprised.

"For wanting your reckoning upon me," she replied smoothly. "You proposed to me because you loved me. I refused you even when I should have done otherwise, rejecting you in a painful way. Then years have passed and the years which have destroyed my youth and bloom have only given you a more glowing, manly, open look, in no respect lessening your personal advantages. Not only does this give the advantage of appearance, it also has given you wealth when I rejected your suit due to your lacking in economy. And here I am, Charlotte Collins, widowed to a reverend who I only had married to save myself from ruin."

Charlotte turned to him, seeing how he was stricken with her frankness. It suited her well, for she knew that only by being honest with him completely would she put him off his guard and make him cease his cold remarks that were aimed at wounding her.

"Yes, that is what happened, Frederick. I was motivated by necessity, and from the fear of living my life under the fear of being labeled a spinster. For I was never again given the offer of a proposal, and I will not shy from that fact. Frederick, I was little and made poorly enough that I will never deny it. I was honored by your proposals and should have been more so in action rather just in compliment. I never gained the favorable admiration from another man, and perhaps that was fortune's way of punishing me for what I did to you. So do not look upon your past as one to feel wounded, but to enjoy your triumph and be satisfied by it."

Captain Wentworth did not move a muscle, frozen by her confessions.

"Find peace, Captain Wentworth," she said gently. "You have won, and I have been punished. Therefore, you need not seek your retribution; fate has done it for you."

"I..." he began, at a loss of what to reply, "well...I..."

The music ended and everyone clapped once more. Charlotte, seeing that Wentworth was now at a loss of what to say, as well as not wishing to be in her company, stood up and approached Elizabeth.

"Eliza," Charlotte began, "I am going to open the instrument, and you know what follows."

Elizabeth, taking her meaning, looked around the room and felt suddenly very self-conscious.

"You are a strange creature by way of a friend! Always wanting me to play and sing before anybody and everybody—if my vanity had taken a musical turn, you would have been invaluable, but as it is, I would really rather not sit down before those who must be in the habit of hearing the very best performers."

"And you know very well," Charlotte said, smiling through her inner turmoil, "that while playing the pianoforte does require some skill, it is more about how you feel when you play something than how you play."

Elizabeth merely shook her head. "Tell that to my mediocrity in talent."

"Then let us be mediocre together. Come my old friend, we often played together at parties back when we were in our teens and at Lucas Lodge. Let us see if we can bring our old times right here to Cumberland."

Elizabeth looked on Charlotte and saw the necessity of submitting, and the need for them to return to a simpler and happier time. So, she stood up and chuckled.

"Very well, if it must be so, it must." Elizabeth turned to Lady Russell and Miss Elton. "There is a fine old saying, which everybody here is of course familiar with: 'Keep your breath to cool your porridge'. And I shall keep mine to swell my song."

Therefore, together Charlotte and Elizabeth walked up to the piano and they both began to play a duet while Elizabeth began to sing.

⚬⚬

It is a truth, universally acknowledged, that what is not perfection can still be regarded as beautiful. Though often the world praises an ideal, sometimes the diamond that is flawed shines even more radiant than one that is cut with flawlessness.

Charlotte and Elizabeth's performance was pleasing, though by no means capital. Charlotte played while Elizabeth played and sang, yet as they did so a magic seemed to engulf them—a harmony of the music and the human movement toward ease and comfort; their abilities matched one another so much so that they proved to be enjoyable to watch and listen to. Therefore, despite their limited skills, the audience could not help but enjoy every moment of their duet.

Yet between them, there was a harmony as well, a synchronization of will and instincts. They were no longer two women performing at Cumberland, but the Charlotte and Lizzy who performed together often at Lucas Lodge when they were in their teens. All the history and rifts that had occurred before now had faded away as time had become undone and they were returned to their simpler state.

For one moment, Charlotte Collins had become Charlotte Lucas again and she could fall so easily into the welcome abyss that was reliving one's past in a moment where it gave her pleasure.

Together, they finished their song, and everyone clapped, smiling at them. Charlotte and Lizzy looked at each other and smiled, feeling the old camaraderie that had once bound them so and it was welcome.

Charlotte, despite herself, could not help but turn and look on Captain

Wentworth, who stared at her and Elizabeth, transfixed. Then, recalling himself, he clapped gently and then stood up and changed to another seat.

⚜

Later that evening, the Darcy Company returned to the inn, and Charlotte went to her room to change while Maria wished to spend more time in Miriam's room, telling her of something that Miss Crawford had spoken of.

When finally left alone in her room at the inn, Charlotte sat down in a chair and looked blankly into space.

She did not know if it was prudent for her to tell Captain Wentworth the truth of everything she had felt, yet she could not apologize for it. If she had said nothing, he never would have known what she was feeling, and that seemed of greater importance, at the moment. He might no longer seek his justice upon her, for he could see how she was punishing herself. Self-inflicted penance could always erase a person's desire to pursue their road of retribution.

Yet perhaps she had made matters all the worse, and they would remain more in each other's company, ill at ease. Tomorrow could bring anything.

Glancing at the wall in front of her window, she felt that it resembled her own path, blank and bare. Therefore, briefly, she released her anxieties and wept. Once the tears escaped her, she felt the catharsis of telling the truth, of exposing herself to the side of confrontation, and then displaying her feelings rather than keeping them within. There, sitting alone, Charlotte made peace with herself.

## ❧ 26 ❧

# IF THE WORLD IS A STAGE

"Your sister plays the pianoforte extremely well," Captain Wentworth said as he played billiards with Mr. Bingley, Mr. Darcy, and Colonel Fitzwilliam.

"Thank you, Captain," Mr. Darcy said. "I shall tell her of your compliment."

"While Miss Elton, Miss Crawford, and Lady Dalrymple played with great superiority as well," Colonel Fitzwilliam said offhandedly, "it was the duet between Mrs. Darcy and Mrs. Collins that was my favorite."

"Thank you, Richard," Mr. Darcy replied, doing his best to sound natural. "Too little she ever performs and therefore it is a rare pleasure."

"Yes," Captain Wentworth said. "Her air is unaffected and artless, making her playing lovely to be heard."

"Yes," Mr. Darcy said, "and Mrs. Collins, well, she bears her trials most effectively, to recover so well after her recent disappointment."

"Does she?" Captain Wentworth said, playing his next turn and appearing indifferent.

"Yes," Mr. Bingley said. "She still must be in agony over the death of Mr. Collins."

"It is not simply that, that I speak of," Mr. Darcy added, "yet it was also from her long past. Do you not know her history?"

"No, I do not."

Out of the corner of his eye, Darcy saw Captain Wentworth flinch.

"Well," Colonel Fitzwilliam said, taking hold of the narrative. "I see no apprehensions on talking about it, for I believe it is no great secret. Nine years ago, someone was courting Charlotte Lucas. She has never given the name, but she told Kitty that she was greatly in love with him."

At the mention of this, Captain Wentworth missed his shot, but Colonel Fitzwilliam, greatly amused at the reaction, continued.

"One day, the man wrote to her with a letter as a proposal and Charlotte wanted to accept him, and she appealed to her parents to tell them of her answer, but her mother was against it."

Unable to help himself, Captain Wentworth looked on the Colonel blatantly, and began to listen in earnest and most attentively.

"So, her mother commanded her to refuse this man and eventually, she persuaded Charlotte to do so. Out of daughterly devotion and a sense of duty and obedience, Charlotte did as she was told, and wrote a letter of refusal to the man."

"Oh dear," Mr. Bingley said. "That must have been very hard."

"Yes," Mr. Darcy said, "very hard indeed. And for both of them. Charlotte has had to spend years knowing she put that man through pain, and he had to spend years undergoing it."

"Yes, it was a sad lot for them both. And to think, that man probably only ever knew that she refused him without knowing the reason why. That is a cruel fate."

"Yes, it is. Most cruel."

"Well," Colonel Fitzwilliam said, "her being here must be a great comfort to her then. She may undergo diversions that can bring her pleasure."

He looked to Wentworth who started and tried to appear indifferent.

"Yes," Captain Wentworth agreed, "yes, it could."

"Oh," Colonel Fitzwilliam said, "I believe this is now my turn. Well," he said, picking up his billiards stick, "here I go."

"That was bloody painful!" Mr. Darcy said, walking down the hall with the Colonel. They had finished their game and were moving to the patio to join the rest of the company.

"How so?" The Colonel asked. "For I thought we did spectacularly."

"I felt like I was forced to be putting on a farcical comedy, and I did not like the feeling."

"And this is how you act after you do a good deed, cousin?" Richard laughed.

"No, this is how I act after I have meddled in others' affairs."

"You remember the line from Shakespeare; all the world is a stage."

"Well, if all the world is a stage, then I want a better role in it. Because for a moment, I felt like we had fallen into a badly done production of *Much Ado About Nothing.*"

Richard emitted a hearty laugh. "Oh, I was going for *As You Like It in* my performance style, but to each his own!"

Both men continued to walk down the hall, bickering as close companions often do.

## 27

# IT'S ALWAYS SUNNY IN A BALLROOM

After Charlotte and I had played our duet together, I had moved away from her, amazed at how the smallest action could trigger an old sensation. Whatever estrangement we had felt before now had ceased and for a fleeting moment, I had forgotten that Charlotte had ever been anything else but otherwise, and we had performed together so often at Lucas Lodge that we very well returned to that memory in the present.

All I knew was that Charlotte had walked away from our duet looking more confident and therefore I was happy to know that she had at least found a moment of peace. Or perhaps was it hope?

I could not honestly tell.

⚅

The day of the ball came, and it was proven to be a perfect day for it, for it had rained terribly the day before and we worried that Nature would not be on our side; however even she proved to love a good ball.

Therefore, that evening, dressed in our finest, with Lucy tending to Caiden and William, our party rode to Cumberland with Jefferson sitting on the seat of the first carriage, alongside Nicholson.

As we approached Cumberland, the lane was outlined by lanterns along it, and it looked quite lovely.

"Exquisite," Miriam said, looking out of the window. "They may mostly be the company of the people we have already met over and over, yet it is still exciting."

"They have invited some families who live here in Lyme to vary up our company," Mr. Bingley replied, "so there shall be some more chances at stimulating conversation and there shall not be a want for dance partners."

Our carriages arrived, we descended and entered Cumberland with other couples. As we did so, we were greeted by Lady Russell, Edward Russell, and Miss Elton in the line of couples, then we entered the ballroom and there were roughly eighty people in total.

We were very soon met by Captain Harvill, Benwick, Admiral Croft, Mrs. Croft and Captain Wentworth.

"Ladies," Captain Harvill said when he approached our company, "you all look remarkably well this evening."

"Thank you, Captain," Jane, my sister, replied.

"And I must apologize in advance to your fortunate husbands, but I very much hope that you all shall reserve a dance for me this evening. Indeed, I do not want to sit out one set and I would take immense delight in dancing with the most beautiful set of ladies in the room."

"Their husbands get first reservations, however," Mr. Darcy said.

"Of course, they do," Captain Benwick said. "However, I shall be bold and ask Mrs. Collins to reserve the second dance for me if she is not otherwise engaged. As I am to dance the first set with Miss Crawford already, and if I were not, I would so much have wished to dance with you first."

Out of the corner of my eye, I could see Captain Wentworth wince at this request, but he made no other movement or gesture. However, under such a moment, when one is doing one's best not to look as if one cares about something, it becomes quite clear that one actually does.

"Thank you, Captain," Charlotte replied, looking quite flattered. "And I am not engaged."

"Good."

Captain Harvill requested Jane's hand, while Captain Wentworth requested the hand of Maria. Jane Austen and Charlotte were the only ones who were without a partner for the first set, yet Jane Austen was determined not to feel slighted.

"It shall not be the first time that I have had to sit out the first dance," Jane Austen said with a smile, "And surely it shall not be the last."

Charlotte also looked perfectly indifferent and at least they were not alone but had each other for company.

However, as we all moved to the dance floor with our partners, a most insulting thing had occurred. As Captain Benwick went to Miss Crawford to escort her to the center of the floor, he had been intercepted by another gentleman who had also gone for her hand. It became quite clear that Miss Crawford had forgotten that she had accepted two men's offers for her hand on the first dance. The scene was not loud or too public, yet those around them did notice and could not help but look on the scene.

"Oh, dear," Miss Crawford whispered, "I am mortified. My dear captain, I had quite thought I had you down for dancing the second set with me, and I granted Mr. Nelson here the first."

Both Captain Benwick and Mr. Nelson looked on each other with coldness and a bit of competition, yet if they hesitated, then the scene would become all the worse. Seconds had passed as both men waited for the other one to revoke his offer and let Miss Crawford be their partner, yet it was not to be so. Mr. Nelson at first said nothing, and neither did the captain, until Benwick remembered his honor and bowed to Mr. Nelson.

"Sir," he said smoothly, "the night is long, and I believe that you shall enjoy your partner as I happily offer her to you."

"Thank you, sir," Mr. Nelson said. "I am much obliged."

"And we may dance the second dance if that would be your pleasure," Miss Crawford said offhandedly. "For I am quite free."

"Alas I shall not be," Captain Benwick replied, "for I am quite promised to another."

Miss Crawford looked at him quickly before she turned back to Mr. Nelson and they both walked to the dance floor. Before I could even begin to feel pity for the poor Captain, there was a quick movement as a ball gown flashed past Miss Crawford and Mr. Nelson; the person in the gown turned out to be Charlotte.

"Excuse me," she said coldly to Miss Crawford and Mr. Nelson as she passed them, and then she approached Captain Benwick, who smiled upon seeing her.

"Mrs. Collins," he said, "I also forgot to tell you how remarkably well you look this evening."

"Thank you, Captain, yet I am just as much in need of good conversation as a good dance partner, and I believe that you are quite skilled in that way."

Captain Benwick blushed, and he was no fool. He knew perfectly well that she had come to his aid, a most gallant act, and should not be replied to with any less than the absolute of gallantry in return. Therefore, he took her hand in his own and he smiled warmly.

"I welcome any conversation with such an elegant young lady as yourself, Mrs. Collins, yet I must be bold and declare that I am no less attentive in conversation while in the middle of an invigorating dance than when sitting idle. And therefore, I must ask, may I have your hand for these first *two* dances?"

"You may, Captain."

"Thank you, now let us see if I am as good as I declare that I am. He gave her his arm," and together they walked to the dance floor and joined our set. The interaction between them did not go unnoticed and along the dance, I could see Captain Wentworth turn his gaze and behold Charlotte with his friend.

૭⁂૭

As the evening progressed, Captain Benwick and Charlotte danced for almost an hour together in their two dances, talking all the while and then afterwards, they spoke often while they both sat out a few sets. Indeed, an acquaintance seemed to be growing between them, and whether that acquaintance grew from desperation or like-mindedness, it was not to be determined, for I did not hear any of their conversation. Yet it must have been pleasing for Charlotte to have undergone a change for the evening, and the captain clearly felt in her debt.

As for Miss Crawford, she looked on them often as she spoke with others, and while I wished to label her as a harpy, I could not do so. For through the evening, she had clearly wished to make amends for her actions yet did not know how to best go about it. She seemed to be heartily ashamed of herself, or good at appearing so.

As for Captain Wentworth, he danced the first set with Maria, then the next two sets with Jane Austen, who regaled him with stories of her writing, and then he danced with Kitty, and Maria again. Yet, when it came time for the last dance, I was standing with Miriam, asking her of how she was enjoying the evening when I beheld Charlotte go to the punch bowl, only to be taken unawares as the captain was on the other side of the punch about to partake in the same refreshment.

They both looked on one another with utter confusion and alarm.

"Captain," Charlotte said at last.

"Charlotte," Wentworth whispered. "Oh, Mrs. Collins, forgive my slip. And I, well, I..."

He gestured to the dance floor, then he said nothing else, and then muttered something.

"I..."

"Yes?"

It seemed as if he wanted to ask her for her hand to dance, yet he could not bring himself to do so. Then he bowed swiftly and walked away. I was not alone in witnessing the interaction, because Miriam then turned to me.

"What do you believe was the cause of that?" she asked. "Surely, he doesn't dislike Mrs. Collins, does he?"

"I do not know," I replied, lying again, "and I cannot get on at all behind the meaning to his behavior. From the little I know, there is no conflict between them."

Such a situation could not help but to be an amazement for Miriam and she continued to speculate on what could have occurred between them both, while I replied every now and again with useless suggestions that I knew were not true at all.

As for Charlotte, she took her glass of punch and moved to the far side of the room, keeping to her own counsel.

After Miriam left to find Mr. Bingley, I was left alone to find Charlotte, for Mr. Darcy was dancing with Miss Elton. I looked and saw that she was still seated in a corner by herself, and while she perhaps preferred her singular attitude, I still thought it wise to join her.

Approaching in a casual manner, I sat down beside her, and she smiled at me.

"How goes your evening, Elizabeth?" she asked.

"Very well, and my husband has now fully begun to learn that it is best to stand up with any woman in the room and not regard it as a punishment."

Charlotte chuckled and then folded her hands.

"Yet how goes your evening?"

"Better than I expected."

"You do not need to conceal from me, Charlotte. I happened to see Captain Wentworth and your meeting at the punch table."

"Oh, you saw that?"

"By happenstance."

"It went much better than I expected."

"Oh, did you expect worse?"

She glanced down and smiled. "Yes, very much so. He was flabbergasted, Lizzy. And that is very much preferable to coldness of sly remarks. You are neither blind nor unobservant; you saw how he tried to wound me with his words and references to what I had done to him. And, so, I did the unthinkable; I told the truth about all that I had been feeling."

"Did you?"

"Yes, I did, for I realized something."

"What?"

"That it needed to be talked of. There are so many things that need to be talked of that never are. We call that being mannerly and keeping all in order, yet sometimes order needs to go hang!"

I practically burst out laughing at her declaration.

"Yes, I said it and I meant it. For it was very much true in this circumstance. Captain Wentworth needed to know that I realized I was in error and that I said no to the right sort of man and said yes to the wrong sort. And that I am fully aware of life playing a trick on me. Or at least fate doing so, by my ending being this way, what has happened that I did not deserve? I am being ungracious just now, for Mr. Collins was the one whose life met with the real tragedy. Yet in Frederick's eyes, he will only see my abysmal prospects and not my late husband's final destination."

"No, he would not think of him. And only you."

"Yes. It is not his fault."

"He has insulted you in some ways, and you defend him."

"He is worth defending now, in truth, and I was worth offending. And who is to say? If I were in his position, I might have acted worse to the person who had wronged me."

"Yes, I know the feeling."

"No one is perfect. Not Frederick, nor I."

"This is the first time that I have ever heard you call him Frederick."

"Yes, I do so in my mind, and I have to remind myself to always call him Captain."

"Yet, the way he looked, Charlotte, he clearly wants to apologize."

"Perhaps he does. Even if he does not and simply grows kinder to me, then I would be immensely happy."

"Captain Benwick was also attentive to you as well."

We both shared a glance and then chuckled.

"He only was grateful for my saving him socially, that is all. And nothing more. It's always sunny in a ballroom, it appears, because we look at one person's smile as a great encouragement and is like a beam of light. Yet in the morning, everything usually changes, I have often found."

# 28

# WILD & FREE

That day, the entire company of Cumberland took a boat ride along the coast of Lyme.

The ship was called the Ulysses, and we all boarded it, as it was a large merchant vessel, it was able to hold forty people with ease.

As we sailed along the sea, enjoying Lyme from every angle, Admiral Croft looked shifty in his stance.

"And what is the matter sir?" Jane Austen asked him.

"It is the unfortunate habit of a man who commands a ship to feel wary when he is aboard one while not being at the wheel of it," he said. "I do not like being on a ship that others are controlling, for I fear that they shall run us aground."

"The Admiral is too afraid of submitting to the will of others," Mrs. Croft said. "It has always been so, I've observed, when I traveled on board with him and his crew."

"You have been traveling on his ship with sailors?" Miss Elton asked.

"Yes, a few times."

"Indeed, she loves traveling with me," the Admiral boasted.

"What a great traveler you must have been, ma'am," I observed.

"Pretty well, I wish to call myself so. In the fifteen years of my marriage, though many women have done more. I have crossed the

Atlantic four times, and have been once to the East Indies, and back again; and only once besides being in different places about home—Cork, and Lisbon, and Gibraltar. But I never went beyond the Straights—that is the Strait of Gibraltar to be clear—and never was in the West Indies. We do not call Bermuda or Bahama, you know, the West Indies."

"I have not a word to say in response to that," Jane Austen replied, "for I could not have accused myself of having ever called them anything in the whole course of my life."

Everyone laughed comfortably, yet Maria was still filled with intrigue by all that Mrs. Croft had seen.

"Yet what is it like to live on board a ship for so long?" she asked.

"Oh, I do assure you," pursued Mrs. Croft, "that nothing can exceed the accommodations of a man of war. I speak, you know, of the larger ships. And I can safely say the happiest part of my life has been spent on board a ship. While Admiral Croft and I were together, you know, there was nothing to be feared. Thank God! I have always been blessed with excellent health."

"Oh," Maria then continued, "so you never suffered any sickness of any kind?"

"There was often a little disordered feeling always the first twenty-four hours of going to sea, but I never knew what sickness was afterwards. The only time that I fancied myself unwell, or had any ideas of danger, was the winter that I passed by myself at Deal, when the Admiral was in the North Seas. I lived in perpetual fright at that time and had all manner of imaginary complaints from not knowing what to do with myself, or when I should hear from him next, but as long as we could be together, nothing ever ailed me, and I never met with the smallest inconvenience."

"Oh, Mrs. Croft," Admiral said, "I may be older now, but I still can blush, and you are making me do so."

Everyone in the crowd marveled at the warmth of their relationship.

"Oh, yes, we sailors can face cannons, gunfire and our adversary's frigate, but we cannot take a compliment from the woman we love!" He sighed, content, and then turned to Mrs. Croft. "Thank you my dear."

We sailed onward slightly and then there was a huge rock that was amid the water.

"Oh, look there!" Captain Harvill exclaimed to us all. "Do you see that rock?"

"Yes," many in the crowd replied.

"That there used to be a fun pastime for us sailors. When we would sail along these waters, we would have competitions where we would sail near it, then we would jump from the ship and see who could swim the fastest. Do you not recall us ever doing it, Benwick?"

"Yes," Benwick said, "we did it often. You were never present for it, Frederick."

"No, I was not," Captain Wentworth said, "for if I had been, I would have won!"

"Oh, I doubt it," Harvill answered with a sly smile, "for I always proved to be the fastest one."

"Except for that one time," Benwick challenged. "I defeated you once."

"Only once!"

"Bet if we were to do it again, you would suffer defeat, Harvill."

"You are very lucky that we are not in the presence of many sailors now, or I would test that challenge, in our clothing and all."

"Yes, if only we would be allowed to do so."

"Then what is stopping you two?" Charlotte challenged.

"Propriety, ma'am," Harvill said, surprised at her question. "We would scandalize our guests here if we were to suddenly jump into the water."

"It is most sad then, that we keep you from such a fun pastime." Charlotte leaned over the railing of the ship and looked down into the water. "And if we were not here, then you would have done so?"

"Yes, but..."

"Then," Charlotte said, "it all comes down to honor."

"Honor?"

"At you being men who still believe in chivalry and gallantry."

"I want to believe that I contain both virtues," Benwick said, not comprehending what Charlotte was speaking of, as were we all.

"Very well, that is beneficial to know."

"Splendid," Harvill said, turning back to the others. "Well then, we also would—"

"Ah!"

We all turned in hearing Charlotte shout and then gaped as we all saw her fall overboard!

※

We rushed to the edge of the railing as we saw her body crash into the water.

"Mrs. Collins!" Benwick cried.

"Charlotte!" Captain Wentworth cried.

Benwick and Harvill were the first to finish pulling off their jackets, shoes, and hats, just as Captain Wentworth was removing his. Quickly Harvill and Benwick jumped into the water and swam to Charlotte who was floating on the water surface just as Captain Wentworth was about to jump over as well.

"No, Captain Wentworth!" Charlotte cried out, holding up her hand. "You are very much gallant where you stand, sir, for this is a competition between these two men."

"Charlotte," I cried, the truth dawning on me, "what are you about?"

"I might be about getting myself into trouble," Charlotte said, and then she looked back at both men who swam up to her. "You both said that you were gallant, chivalrous, and heroic you have proven to be in your instinct to save me. Now you are in the water, your reason for you doing so is to save me, making me the only reckless one amongst us."

"Mrs. Collins?" Harvill said. "Are you telling us that you intentionally fell overboard?"

"Yes. Please do not be angry with me. Look up at the people on board, and don't let them stop you from committing a favorite pastime. You are Captains of ships and masters of the sea! Why don't you show us who is the faster one?"

"Mrs. Collins!" Mr. Edward Russell called out from near us. "You are being preposterous."

Down below Charlotte looked at Captain Benwick.

"Captain?" she pleaded. "Don't disappoint me."

Captain Benwick looked at her keenly and then nodded, understanding her mood more than I.

"Elizabeth," Darcy whispered next to me, "has Charlotte gone mad?"

"I cannot be certain, my dear," I replied.

Captain Benwick turned and looked up at us.

"Cumberland Company! I admit that now that we are in the water, I have a great desire to put my friend's challenge to the test, and I want to prove to Mrs. Collins above all that I am the fastest on this ship! Would any of you be willing to place some bets and be prepared to be entertained?"

"I will!" Jane Austen cried out. "Yet not the betting part, for I have bad luck. Yet I would like to see you two race."

Admiral Croft turned to one of the sailors.

"Lower a rope for Mrs. Collins so to bring her up however."

"Thank you, Admiral," Charlotte said from below, "but do not trouble yourself as of yet. I am in no danger and the water actually feels quite lovely."

"Oh, but..." Lady Russell began. When she realized that there was nothing else to be done, we all turned to Benwick and Harvill.

"Have you all placed your bets?" Harvill cried out.

On the ship, we all took out one shilling from our purses and decided who we would bet on. I chose Benwick while Darcy chose Harvill.

"Very well," Mr. Bingley replied looking down below. "On my mark, Captains! 3,2, and 1!"

Both Harvill and Benwick pushed off the edge of the ship and were swimming with great speed toward the large rock that was thirty feet away.

"They are fast!" Maria cried on the other side of Jane Austen. "Look at them go."

There were many such remarks along our company as the two men swam, and the exclamations were little compared to our amazement. It actually was quite wonderful to watch them grow closer and closer until...

"Benwick won!" I cried out. "Benwick won!"

For those who had bet on him now were clapping with great enthusiasm as I turned to my husband.

"You sir, owe me a shilling."

"I'll repay it when I have overcome my annoyance of losing this bet."

⚜

Benwick and Harvill climbed the rock, and they raised their arms in triumph as we cheered for them once more.

"That was brilliantly fun!" Benwick cried out, "for I said I would win, did I not? And thank you Mrs. Collins for putting yourself in the situation to be saved, or we never would be happy now."

I turned to look at Captain Wentworth, who looked down on her in wonder.

"What the devil could have possessed Charlotte to do that?" Jane Austen asked as she stood next to me.

I shook my head in wonder. "I can only suppose that we were watching a woman who has labored so long under the weight of propriety that she is now beginning to rebel."

"Well, I have labored long as well."

I looked up at Jane Austen and saw a mischievous look in her eyes.

"I know that look," I said.

"I know you do." Suddenly Jane Austen grabbed my hand and yanked me along. Out of instinct, I grabbed Kitty's hand and pulled her, then she grabbed Jane's and we ran through the crowd.

"What are we about to do?!" My sister Jane cried.

"We are jumping as well!" Jane Austen said.

"Jane!"

"Just follow us, Jane!"

"Lizzy!" Mr. Darcy cried from behind me. I turned to see him gaping at me. "What are you..."

"I love you," I said, for it was all that came to mind. "And forgive me!"

Jane Austen jumped over the edge, to which I followed her, then Kitty and Jane jumped in as well.

The water was cold to the skin, yet it was marvelous! Every rule that we broke in doing so, every gasp that would be exhibited by our actions, and every rumor that would spread from our guests after this day to their friends elsewhere did not seem to matter.

We swam to Charlotte who remained at the boat's edge.

"And what had possessed you to follow after me?" Charlotte said, surprised.

"We could not see you ridiculed, now could we?" Jane Austen said. "For there is strength in numbers. The more of us who jumped in, the more likely you were to be less laughed upon by the rest of the ladies in the group."

"Thank you," Charlotte said.

"And what possessed you to jump in?" I asked.

"It will seem foolish to you," she whispered.

"It is too late to be afraid in looking foolish, don't you think?"

"Yes, you are right. I suppose that I simply wanted to do something brave, for once. No matter how it made me look. And my, do I feel brave now. Foolish and in error, but brave."

"Well then," Kitty said, "be brave enough for competition."

"Kitty and Elizabeth!" Colonel Fitzwilliam cried from above.

"And Jane and Miss Austen!" Darcy cried. "We are lowering ropes so that you may come back aboard."

"Forgive us," Kitty said, "for we cannot yet, my love. When we were children, there was a pond that we all often loved to swim in, and this moment brings back such memories."

"I shall prove to be the fastest one, I believe," I said.

"You shall not!" Charlotte replied.

"Wait there!" Benwick cried, standing up. "Are you all planning to race to us?"

"Yes, we are."

"Oh," Jane whispered, "I was always too slow to win. Oh well..."

"Well then," Benwick said, "I shall place my bet on the courageous Mrs. Collins."

"I find that I cannot choose," Harvill said. "There are too many in the group who look like good swimmers."

"Place your bets!" Jane Austen said to the people on the boat far above. I looked up on the deck and saw Darcy look down at me with wonder, yet I was happy to see that it was not a look of wrath. Then again, Darcy never discouraged acts of tenacity as long as they showed nerve and daring that was harmless.

"Are you ready?" Harvill cried from the rock.

"Ready!" We all shouted.

"3,2,1!"

We all pushed against the boat and began to swim as swift as our petticoats allowed us! I enjoyed the sport of it very much as Kitty swam to my left and Charlotte was on my right.

Eventually we reached the rock, and I was not very disappointed when I saw that I was not the victor. I was surprised however when it turned out to be Jane, my sister!

"You said you were slow!" Jane Austen said as Harvill and Benwick helped us climb on the large collection of rocks.

"I lied!" Jane replied. "I may be the slowest runner, but I actually am quite the swift one on sea!"

"You bluffed?" Charlotte laughed.

"Yes, I did. I have been learning how to do that from my students at Pemberley."

"Well, upon my honor," I said. "I never thought that they would give you an education of that kind."

We all sat on the rocks, and we looked ahead at all our party, who gaped at us on the ship. Amongst those faces were Darcy's and the Colonel's.

However, nearby, Maria was there, feeling very antsy.

"Well, if they get to do it," she began.

"I'm coming as well," Miriam said, taking her hand. "We used to do this often in the river in Philadelphia!"

"Wait!" Miss Elton cried, "I'm coming as well."

"Ariella!" Mr. Russell cried.

"Oh, Edward! Wouldn't you like your fiancée to have one brave action to her name?"

"Then I am coming as well!" Miss Crawford agreed and the four of them also jumped overboard, splashing into the water. When they were lined up, Harvill also gave them a countdown and then they swam toward us as well.

"Darn our petticoats!" Kitty noted how the gowns had become balloons in the water. "Look how they are slowing them down. It slowed us down as well!"

The next set of women reached us, and Miss Crawford reached her hand out to Benwick pleadingly as she neared the rocks. I looked between her and the captain. Rather than bearing her any ill will from the ball, he reached down to her immediately and helped her up, smiling fondly on her.

Of that set, to our surprise, Miss Elton proved to be the fastest. She looked up at the people on the ship and while her parents looked at her in anger, Mr. Russell did not. On the contrary, he was clearly dazzled.

಄

"It is all so upside down," Miss Crawford said as she sat next to Benwick. "Now the rock has more of our company on it than the ship!"

We all sat there and laughed, and then I waved to my husband. His face was like stone, yet I did not know if it was anger or him growing decisive. Then he stood back and took off his hat and began to remove his jacket. Seeing his resignation to join me, I smiled fetchingly at him.

Seeing his cousin giving in, Colonel Fitzwilliam and Bingley began to follow suit.

"Wait!" Captain Wentworth said, then he came forward and removed his hat and jacket. "I think I ought to join you. In case you drown, I might be able to save you."

"Oh, shut it!" The men groaned, their pride stirred as they made sure to rid themselves of any loose belongings and then they dove in the water!

"They can dive?" I cried. "I had no idea Fitzwilliam knew how to dive."

Indeed, watching him do so was so...sensual. My emotions were quite affected, and I was taken greatly unaware.

Harvill then counted down to one and the men were off. With great speed, they swam, and it was most marvelous to behold. Yet I was even more so surprised when my Mr. Darcy had won!

My surprise was not that of being non-supporting, but practicality. Darcy never enjoyed moving swiftly and he was opposed by a soldier and a Captain who was a sailor! Naturally, I would have thought his efforts were honorable, but never did I expect him to triumph over Captain Wentworth!

When they reached the rock, I moved down to the edge and offered Darcy my hand. He looked up at me and grinned wickedly.

"What are you planning?" I asked.

"This!" He grabbed my hand and pulled me into the water.

When I fell in once more, Darcy swam underneath, kissed me quickly, out of everyone's view, and then we rose to the surface.

"Was that you punishing me for jumping into the water?" I pushed my hair from my eyes. "For that is a delightful reprimand I dare say."

"No that was me punishing you for not winning your race, for I bet on you."

"You lost your shilling? Oh, good heavens. Whatever shall you do? For you must have lost a fortune," I said in jest. "But you, how are you so fast?"

"Oh, the small lake on the edge of Pemberley," he said. "Very often Richard and I would swim in it. And I would do laps in it by myself quite often.

"Oh, so you are a gifted swimmer."

"As you are a gifted walker."

"Thank you for not being angry, Fitzwilliam."

"I was at first, but then I realized that it was the same impulse to walk those miles to Aginfield that drove you to jump into the water. How could I hold you in disdain when that was the very part of you that I fell in love with?"

"Indeed, you had better not be capable of such hypocrisy," I said, resting my head on his shoulder. I looked along the rock and I considered all our partners in mischief as they sat there. Miriam and Mr. Bingley held hands, Kitty and the Colonel embraced, Miss Elton, Charlotte, Jane, Maria, and Jane Austen huddled near Captain Harvill and Captain Wentworth as they honored them on their excellent swimming. Yet what was the most curious thing were Captain Benwick and Miss Crawford. From what I had seen, they were both looking fondly at each other, not tearing their eyes from one another at all. The look exchanged seemed to be one of passion —or at the very least compassion, and I wondered at it. Then Miss Crawford tore her attention from him and waved at her parents on the ship and Mr. Nelson as well, who looked flabbergasted.

Perhaps I had seen something where there was nothing, but I could not help thinking there was something hidden there, something of which we did not know.

⚜

Although, the time shortly came when we had to swim back to the ship as the rope ladders were thrust over the railing. Therefore, we left the rocks, swam back to the ship's bottom, and made our way to the rope ladders.

One by one we climbed up them and while Mr. Darcy and I were the last to climb one ladder, Captain Benwick and Miss Crawford were the last to climb the other one. As he held the ladder down for her to begin climbing, I saw that they held each other's hands underwater briefly before she began her ascension back on deck.

That simple gesture was a severe break in decorum and my thoughts dwelt on it more, yet I told myself that I was being paranoid. Perhaps Miss Crawford had only been remorseful of her treatment of Benwick at the ball and was doing everything to show that she truly was repentant.

And though their holding hands was not permissible, it would and could be a natural gesture of two people who had come to some form of reconciliation.

When we all were back on board, blankets were brought from below deck and we all took them with all speed. Mr. Russell placed it around Miss Elton affectionately, yet further down I could see Miss Crawford's parents having some short words with her while Mr. Nelson stood nearby, flexing his hands as he looked at Miss Crawford. It became quite clear that her parents had set their sights on Mr. Nelson being a suitable partner to their daughter and were now furtively vexed at her for doing anything to dampen his affection for her. Yet if I was to be inquired on the subject, I would think any man who would question my daughter's delicacy for her simply swimming in the open sea as being quite without nerve and lacking in spunk and sense of humor. Yet on such matters, my views would be very much in the minority.

As the ship set out, Captain Benwick moved to Charlotte's side and spoke with her all the while as we commenced on our journey. However, what Charlotte may not have seen was that never was Captain Wentworth far from them. For he may have stood there, acting as if he was looking at something behind them. Yet he eyed them all the while, paying close attention to their interaction.

⚜

Our ship made berth and Lady Russell ordered the carriages immediately so that we could return to Cumberland and change into warm and dry attire.

Our company told her that we ought to return to our inn, so that we may have access to our rooms and clothing, for we were not staying at Cumberland and nor was our luggage. Seeing the sense of this plan, they drove those of us who were wet to The Queen's Hand, dropped us there and the rest proceeded to Cumberland.

When we had gone to our individual rooms, the fire was made by a server and Lucy tried to see to me, but I said that she could return to William and Caiden, for her services were not needed. She left while Mr. Darcy entered, joining me.

"Are you certain that you shall not need Lucy to tend to you?" he asked.

"Not at all. I do require assistance, but her company is not the help that I need," I said, eying him slyly.

"And," he grinned, "what does that look mean?"

"It means that I desire you, Fitzwilliam."

"Ah, do you?"

"When I saw you remove your jacket and boots, then dive into the water in such a masterful manner, I thought that I never saw anything so incredible to behold before. You are beautiful, Fitzwilliam, this is undeniable, yet I cannot explain how...but that action showed your masculinity to be of the highest renown. You were glorious."

"Oh Lizzy..."

I rushed to him, and we kissed. Our clothing was still very wet, so it was hard in pulling it off, yet we succeeded in doing it eventually, then we jumped onto the bed and kissed passionately.

As he ran his hands and lips over my breasts, stomach and in between my thighs, I felt our lovemaking all new somehow, as if our latest experience had altered us in some kind.

Back and forth he stroked my most intimate of places while his hand worked most vigorously in between my thighs, and he kissed my breasts with a voracious appetite. I then rolled on top of him and kissed him. Afterwards I moved my hands down his chest and my lips followed suit.

I had never kissed his chest before and I found myself curious as to explore all of him that instance, therefore I moved my lips along his chest and stomach, hearing his breathing heavy and raspy from passion. Out of instinct, I moved further and further down, kissing the inside of his thighs.

"Oh, Lizzy!" he whispered hoarsely. "Please do not cease! Continue on, please!"

I kissed him more and more while he grew stiffer and then I felt the pleasure in his body rose, yet before he reached his pinnacle, I raised my head, placed my legs around his hips and he entered me. We rocked against one another until we had both reached a climatic feel together. Our bodies stiffened most potently before we released simultaneously and our bodies relaxed, with I lying on top of him.

"Good heavens," he rasped. He kissed my forehead and ran his hands along my bottom gently and also stroked me in between my thighs as well, for he knew that I could never get enough of that intimate action.

"Yes," I whispered.

"How did you know to do that to me?"

"I did not know. It was an impulse, and for some reason, I desperately wished to taste you in full."

"And now you have. And I enjoyed it greatly. You must do so to me more often."

"I shall, as long as we are always intimate often. I live for these moments between us."

"As do I. Yet what truly prompted this moment of passion for you? Who do I have to thank for this?"

"I suppose we must, surprisingly, be grateful to Charlotte, for today we felt wild and free, and Mr. Darcy, at your most wild and free moment, with liberty in your eyes as it flashes like lightning out of a clear blue sky, is a great force to behold."

"You really love me," he said with a wicked smile.

"Yes, I do."

"Good, for I am happy to know that I married a woman who is not a simpleton...and who realizes that I am pure perfection."

"Oh, you self-adsorbed devil!" I cried, pinching his chest.

"Oh, you know you believe that!" he declared boldly.

I rolled on top of him and continued to pinch him wherever I could.

# 29

# CALM WATERS

That evening we returned to Cumberland for a dinner and when we all met, there was a great deal of comfort around the company, for our daily excursion had torn down some polite apprehension we had all possessed before. However, there were some individuals amongst us who clearly censured our previous actions, yet I could not be bothered to care for them.

We all sat down to dinner and afterwards card tables were brought out as well as backgammon. I sat down to the backgammon with Admiral Croft while Mr. Darcy stood at the fireplace and watched me over Admiral Croft's shoulder, every now and again giving me clandestine and charming looks.

Darcy had never been much for playing board games or cards either, and never found much joy in them, therefore as the rest of the company was at cards, he was the only one to remain in a solitary state.

Near our table of backgammon, Captain Wentworth sat at a table with the Bingleys, Mrs. Croft, Georgiana, and Jason, while to our right was the table with Charlotte, Maria, Captain Harvill and Jane Austen.

Amid our game, Admiral Croft turned to Captain Wentworth.

"Frederick, I forgot to tell you something earlier."

"What was it, Croft?" Wentworth said, still looking at his cards.

"It was about Lady Applegate. Oh, pardon me Mrs. Darcy, but a few months ago, Wentworth and I were in Lisbon and our ships were stationed at the docks. An acquaintance of ours needed to book passage on one of our vessels." He then turned back to Wentworth. "If you had been a week later at Lisbon, instead of leaving when you did, Frederick, you would have been asked to give a passage to Lady Sofia Applegate and her daughters."

"Should I?" He huffed. "I am glad I was not a week later then."

"A very ungallant reply, Frederick."

"And impolitic too," Georgiana said. "Would you not give so much to a woman?"

"I do not ever mean to offend the fairer sex, Miss Darcy. But if I know myself, this is from no want of gallantry to women by any means. It is rather from feeling how impossible it is, with all one's efforts, and all one's sacrifices, to make the accommodations on board suitable for women and up to a high standard. There can be no want of gallantry, Admiral, in rating the claims of women to every personal comfort—and this is what I do. I hate to hear a woman on board, or to see them on board. And no ship, under my command, shall ever convey a family of ladies anywhere, if I can help it."

"Oh Frederick!" Mrs. Croft cried. "You can be so thick and hard-headed, brother."

"You have called me that often, so what reason do you have for casting aspersions on me this time?"

"Because I cannot believe it of you. And the idle refinement that your words wreak of. Women may be as comfortable on board as they would be in the best house in England. I believe I have lived on board ships as much as any other Captain's wife, and I found myself quite at ease."

"Yes, but you were living with your husband, and you were the only woman on those ships."

"But," Harvill said, "Frederick, do you forget the service you rendered me? You brought my sister, Mrs. Grierson, her cousins and her three children, round from Portsmouth to Plymouth just so that they could see me."

"Oh," I said, "if that is the case, then where was that superfine, extraordinary sort of gallantry of yours, then?"

"All merged in my friendship, Mrs. Darcy. I would always assist any brother's wife that I could, and I would bring anything of Harvill's from the world's end, if he asked it of me."

"Oh, Frederick," Harvill laughed. "You sound quite soft on me. Should I come over and kiss you?"

"Oh, don't be cheeky—and don't kiss me!" He laughed. "However yes I transported your family, but do not imagine that I did not feel it an evil in itself."

"But I am sure they were comfortable," Harvill said.

"And," Mrs. Croft added, "pray what would occur if all men on ships thought as you do? What would become of us poor sailors' wives? We would be forsaken for long periods of time when we would prefer to travel with our husbands."

"I still feel resolute."

"Then by all means, this is a resolution that you should re-think. For I hate to hear you talking so, like a fine gentleman and as if women were all fine ladies, instead of rational creatures. We none of us expect to be in smooth water all our days."

"As has just been proven today," Charlotte said suddenly, from her table to which Captain Wentworth's head became erect, his attention focusing on her, and his expression startled by her direct address. "As you have just seen today when it was nerve that prompted a race of free spirits."

Captain Wentworth's eyes turned keener.

"Is that what you call what happened today, Mrs. Collins?" he asked.

"Yes, should I call it otherwise?" Charlotte replied while looking at her cards. "Would you prefer me to call it offensive and vulgar?"

"No, I do not, for there was nothing offensive or vulgar about it. I simply am surprised that you call it nerve, instead of calling it *your nerve*, for that was where the heart of today's actions lay."

"Whether I was the perpetrator or not is of little matter."

"Is it?"

"Yes, for it was not my identity that was of import, but that I was not a *fine lady*, but just a woman who felt no need to remain shackled down and therefore be a bore. That I was simply one who saw a wild and reckless act for what it was: a pure one and not something to be feared. Nothing about my actions was that of calm waters, or still ones. Deep and turbulent my decision would become, but I could not regret doing it. For over time, one's instincts will always be to find liberty. To not labor under the restraints of convention and break free of it all. This is a human instinct, and not one that only belongs in the realm of man, but woman as well. Therefore, it can be said that if we every now and again have the impulse to break through the many layers of elegance and find the sordid truths of reality, as you do, how are we too delicate to live on a ship? No, I want to believe that we can endure much."

"You wish to sway me, Mrs. Collins?" Captain Wentworth said, eying her intensely.

"I do not think so. I just simply wished to speak. For that is within my control, yet your mind is not. You shall make up your mind however way that you like."

"Many ladies of high rank would argue and complain if they were on a ship."

"You are right, they might. I know some ladies who are very much like that. Yet here's a to-do in regard to the point I wish to make: we women change. Or at least have the power to. We can learn to adapt to a situation, to overcome our own false beliefs. There is always that powerful thing: hope. Hope that we shall evolve, in mind and body. Hope that we shall develop into the person that we wish to be as opposed to the person that everyone sees when they behold us."

"And what is the sort of soul that a lady wants to possess? What sort of person do you all wish to be?"

"I cannot speak for all women. I can only speak for myself."

"Then what say you of yourself? What do you wish to be?"

"Someone who learns from her mistakes. Someone who also desires to undergo an adventure, in truth. And someone who I wish to believe...could live on a ship and see the interesting journey of it."

Charlotte then looked up from her cards for the first time and beheld Frederick.

"Oh, do not worry, Mrs. Collins," the Admiral said. "One day, our good captain here shall eat the very words that he has put much energy into."

"And how so?" Wentworth exclaimed.

"For when you have got a wife, you will sing a different tune." Admiral Croft turned to me and smirked. "When he is married, if we have the good luck to live through another war, we shall see him do as Harvill and I, and a great many of other Captains have done. We shall have him very thankful to anybody that will bring him his wife."

"Aye, that we shall," Lady Croft said, to which Frederick responded by throwing down his cards in mock-anger.

"Now I have done," he stated boldly. "When once married people begin to attack me with 'Oh! You will think very differently when you are married', I can only say 'No, I shall not', and then they say again 'Yes you will' and there's an end to it!"

⚜

That was the last interaction that Charlotte and Captain Wentworth had, for Charlotte found herself often being accosted by Captain Benwick, who was desirous of her company.

It was nice to see them together, and my ever-active mind began to wonder at them, thinking them possibly with the chance of being an adorable couple, but I chose not to confront Charlotte on the subject. We women think flirtation is the first step toward a more serious attachment, when in truth it is simply that a woman and man feel comfortable around each other enough to be in each other's path constantly.

However, when I drew near to Charlotte that evening, I looked down at her.

"Were you attempting to be brave there?" I whispered.

"Why Lizzy," she grinned, "I have no idea what you are speaking of."

"Oh, yes you do. You spoke to him without any fear of being despised or mistreated. Why? What has changed?"

She sighed. "Nothing much. I just realized something."

"And what is that?"

"That I believe I have gone through the worst already, and I have survived them, therefore I predict that I shall be undergoing calm waters now. Yes, I feel it in my bones."

## ❦ 30 ❦

# A WHIRLWIND AT CUMBERLAND

Over the next couple of days, Captain Benwick had remained close to Charlotte whenever we were a part of the main company, from walking along the seashore to looking at the ships. It escaped no one's notice that at a picnic we had, he sat with her, and they spoke mostly to each other. While I worried that it would be too soon after the death of Mr. Collins, for while Benwick was a nice man, Charlotte's preference for him might have been marred from blindness. After Mr. Collins, any man who offered her pleasing attentions and seemed to have a calm, steady and sensible manner would be regarded as a blessing, and she might be persuaded to believe herself in love.

However, Charlotte was full grown and older than I even, therefore she could take care of herself, I determined.

As we sat at the picnic, I overheard them talking about poetry with Darcy and Richard speaking next to me.

"What are your interests besides being a captain on a ship, Captain Benwick?" Charlotte asked as she ate some ham.

"I love to read."

"Do you?"

"Yes."

"And what do you prefer to read? What are your tastes?"

"I enjoy a great deal of poetry."

"Oh, indeed you are wise. For we are living in richness of the present age; there are many first-rate poets in our time period."

"You read it as well?"

"Yes, I do sometimes. I greatly enjoyed *Marmion* and *The Lady of the Lake*."

"Do you have a preference between them?"

"I must say that I prefer *Lady of the Lake*."

"And I prefer *Marmion*. I also love *The Bride of Abydos*."

"And I love the *Giaour*."

"Oh, yes that is quite good writing."

"Yes, some of the best."

"However, what makes it so exemplary is how the poet uses words to accurately depict the image of a broken heart, or a mind destroyed by wretchedness."

"You speak as a man who has suffered disappointment."

"I have."

Charlotte looked on him with sympathy.

"So have I."

"Have you? How so? Oh, yes, your late husband. I am sorry for your loss, truly."

"Thank you, Captain, yet it is not only that, but other trials and experiences."

"Such as?"

"I have made mistakes."

"We all make those, and the world comes down hard upon us after we do."

"And sometimes the world comes down on you for wishing to do the right thing, advising you against it because of propriety, honor, and family duty, so it encourages you to not follow your heart."

"Oh, yes! Love can make things complicated, yes, but the complications are often more worth it than not. In true love, there is always vexation, grief, and sometimes no wealth, but it is very much worth it. And for the world to deny us that," he said, looking passionate, "is monstrous often...the woman that I loved was not allowed to wed me."

"Was she not?"

"Yes."

"Why so? You are an honorable man."

"Thank you, but I am one of profession. Her family made it very clear that with her being a gentleman's daughter, and I still having to make my way in the world, we were not allowed to wed, and now she is lost to me."

"Oh, poor Captain," Charlotte whispered. "I am indeed very sorry. Yet take comfort, there is always hope."

"Is there?"

"Yes, I have seen it."

"I confess that I cannot be so generous in my outlook."

"You must. Did she love you?"

Captain Benwick looked at Charlotte with firm certainty.

"I know that she did."

"Then let that knowledge fuel you. Poetry may be the food of heartbreak and agony, yet it is also the food for hope in other views. This woman loves you, therefore take heart, and allow it to make you stronger."

"Thank you, Mrs. Collins," he said warmly, eying her with fondness.

"You are very welcome. Now, just to offer a change in your reading selection, I think you will find it beneficial to also read a great deal of prose as well. For too much poetry can poison the heart, just as too little may leave it starved."

"You are very kind."

"Thank you."

We all continued to eat on, and I thought of what I had overheard.

Benwick had been in love with another woman, and it seemed to be a recent loss, therefore his desire for Charlotte's company could very well have been friendly at best, with him just seeing a kindred spirit in her. However, their manners and tempers were so much alike that it left more to be considered. For Charlotte's condolences were so profuse and wanted that her pity for him could always lead to his wishing more from Charlotte. Therefore, I could determine nothing—for anything was possible.

The next day, we were spending the morning at *The Queen's Right Hand* and I was sitting in my room with Caiden and William, while also Jane, my sister, and Charlotte were sitting with me. Jane held William while I crawled on the floor with Caiden walking beside me and Charlotte was reading a letter.

"Upon my word!" she exclaimed as she read.

"What is it?" Jane asked, looking up from William.

"It is my brother, Samuel. He was away in London when we left Hampshire."

"Yes."

"And now he has gone to America."

"What?!" Jane and I gasped.

"Yes, he has written to Lucas Lodge to say that he has gone to America."

"But why? And where in America?"

"To Philadelphia. He said that there was something he had to do, as a form of penance and that he hopes he shall be home in two months' time at the most."

"Not just something he had to do," I said, "but someone he had to see."

"Then you think..." Jane began.

"Yes. I believe he has gone to see Deborah Darcy."

"Who?" Charlotte replied. "Is that one of Mr. Darcy's cousins?"

"Yes, and she is a woman who your brother was in love with."

"What?!"

"Yes. When Samuel had gone to America, he had met Miss Deborah Darcy and they fell in love."

"But...how come I have never heard of her?"

"He did not speak of it to you ever, I believe. The reason we knew of it was because we met Miss Deborah Darcy and she told us of it."

"Then, my brother is going to America to woo her?"

"That may be difficult," Jane said, "For she is a nun."

"A nun?"

"Yes. And she is named Sister Mary Ignatius."

"Then why would he go to see her? Oh, never mind that was a foolish question. If he was in love with her, he perhaps is curious simply to see her again. Yet I am angry that he never told me, for I am his sister, and I had the right to be in his confidence."

"Charlotte, not all sisters are in their brother's confidence. As a frank matter, not even all sisters are in each other's confidence either, therefore do not take offense to it. And he perhaps did not wish to speak of it at first because he did not offer her anything, thinking their worlds too different."

I sat, amazed. "And now he might have gone just to see her. Is that not something amazing?"

"Indeed, it is wonderful."

"Yes, yes, it is."

Indeed, I would not have believed it if Charlotte had not read it, but it was all so fantastical! Samuel Lucas had risked all just to see Deborah one last time, and it was truly heart-warming. However, I did not see how it could end well, for either outcome would send him home bitter. Either he would go, they would not get along and he would think he had wasted his time and money, or they would get along splendidly, and Samuel would return to England with heartache and angry with himself for not having married her when he had the chance.

Indeed, the outcome in whichever style would look exceedingly bleak.

"Well, come what may," Charlotte said, "besides, if Samuel does do this, I confess that he has more nerve than I ever gave him credit for. I just hope that he is safe."

"Samuel always seemed too lucky than to lose his life on the ocean. I believe he shall make it to America well enough. It is only what is awaiting him there that is the most undetermined."

"Do you recall, Lizzy?" Jane asked, "how Cousin Emilia was happy in knowing that someone was once in love with Deborah?"

"Oh yes. I therefore wonder what shall happen when she meets Mr. Lucas, because he will stop off at Canterbury."

"I know. His appearance there might put many things in motion and cause an avalanche."

Our conversation was interrupted because we heard raised voices in the hall. Charlotte stood up to open the door, but it was opened suddenly by Kitty and Maria, who was followed by Lucy.

"Lizzy, Jane and Charlotte have you heard the news!"

"What news?"

"It is most alarming!"

"For heaven's sake, what is it?"

"It is Miss Crawford," Lucy said, "There is a whirlwind at Cumberland, for she has left Cumberland and has eloped with Captain Benwick!"

## ✌ 31 ✌

# SAVED BY FOOLISHNESS

"**W**hat!" we all cried, startled.

"Yes," Lucy continued, "I have received the report of it only not so long ago."

"But..." Jane gasped. "How could this...it is nonsense."

"I know her personal maid," Lucy began, "named Ana, and she has just been down to tell me that all of Cumberland is in an uproar, for when her mother went to her daughter's room to wake her, she found Miss Crawford missing and the lump in the bed were pillows, and she also found a rope of sheets hanging from the window, meaning that Miss Crawford had climbed down them. She also left a note on her desk for her mother, but Ana, unable to withstand her curiosity, opened the letter and read it. It said that she could not deny her affections for the captain any longer. And that while they had forced her to refuse him before due to his lack of wealth, their seeing each other once more here had rekindled their still existing desires."

"But..." Charlotte gasped. "That makes no sense, for she hadn't even cared to dance with him at the ball."

"And that was also explained in the letter. She said that they had concealed their affection to a great degree, and she did the best she could to persuade her mother of how she was indifferent to him, in hopes of them not seeing her plans."

"It was all a ruse," Maria cried. "She was paying attention to Mr. Nelson just to make her parents believe that she had forgotten Captain Benwick."

"Then, Miss Crawford was the woman who he was in love with but had not been allowed to marry."

"What?"

"Oh, it was something he had told me. Now I see it."

"And I had not been in error, as I thought I had been," I said. "I was correct in that there was an attraction between them, for there were the furtive glances and them holding hands. I had argued with myself to deny it, but I had been accurate all the while. A part of me wondered if I should have voiced my suspicions, yet I had no proof, and this was an intimate act that was no business of mine. Indeed, it was distressing, and I did not know what to think."

"I am sorry, Charlotte," Maria said suddenly.

"What?" Charlotte said. "Why should you feel sorry for me? What has this to do with my person?"

"Well, it was clear that you were beginning to fall in love with him."

"What!"

"Yes," Kitty added. "It appeared the two of you were becoming fond of each other."

Charlotte turned to us all, looking over our faces, her cheeks quite flushed.

"What? I never liked Captain Benwick in that way."

"What?" Jane replied.

"Indeed," Charlotte continued. "And I had never known that I had even given that impression. Oh dear, I was truly not aware. He never liked me, nor did I like him at all. We simply were amiable to one another, and nothing more."

"Then...you never were in love with him?" Maria asked.

"No, Maria, I never was."

"Oh."

Charlotte looked around us once more.

"Indeed, I feel very foolish now, for I was so concerned with my own comforts that I did not see how I was making myself appear, and now it has exposed me to some very impertinent remarks and observations."

"Do not worry over the matter, Charlotte," I said. "People will always speculate. It is simply our nature, and you have not committed any acts of vulgarity of manner or impropriety."

"Nothing more than give people the wrong impression," she said, looking saddened, "and now I wonder who else thought I was giving my heart away to him."

I did not speak it, but I was certain she was thinking of Captain Wentworth.

❦

We eventually met the rest of our company and told them of the situation. There was much surprise and alarm felt by all. Yet it was a quiet shock, for none in our company were directly related to the couple who had taken their plight. Therefore, we did not feel anything more than amazement. There was no judgment on Benwick and Miss Crawford's part, because we did not view them as villains for this extreme action and as such, when we all sat there, there was nothing else to do but wonder if they would make it successfully to Gretna Green, or would the happy and hasty couple be found, discovered and punished for their actions.

"And to think," Darcy whispered beside me, "I worried that our scandalous dip in the sea was going to cause much rumor and notorious reports for our family. Yet now that this elopement has occurred, it will be quite forgot, and this will be the true scandal."

"Yes, indeed it does go to show how whenever one worries of the repercussions of one's actions," I sighed, "there will always be something else to come along and make an avalanche over your miniscule wave."

"My dear, were we saved from censure by the folly of others?"

"Yes, we were."

"Ah, saved by foolishness. Indeed, it always seems the way."

## ❧ 32 ❧

# A CONFESSION

Charlotte remained alone inside her room, pacing back and forth, anxious.

*How foolish I have been!* She thought savagely. *Yes, I have been a great one indeed!*

She believed herself at the age where one did not expose oneself to the world for being a flirt, and how she had proven to her mind that she was no more or less mature than she had been at one and twenty.

The rest of the company had gone to Cumberland to offer their condolences to Mrs. Crawford and to be there for the Russells. But Charlotte asked to remain behind, afraid to face everyone knowing what they must have thought of her—especially Wentworth. And it was a great shame, for she felt that they had finally gained an equal footing with one another and had come to an understanding, but she had blinded herself to her own folly.

Pacing back and forth in her own meanderings, she was startled when the door to her room opened and the serving girl entered, followed by Captain Wentworth!

"If you please ma'am," the servant woman said, bowing, "Captain Wentworth is come."

"Oh!" Charlotte said, surprised. "Captain Wentworth!"

The servant woman left, closing the door behind her. As Charlotte and the Captain looked on one another, they realized that this was the first time ever that they were all alone.

Charlotte felt her pulse race. "Captain, it is a pleasure to see you."

"Forgive me," he said, equally nervous. "I did not mean to invade your privacy, yet I came as soon as I could."

"As soon as you could?"

"Yes, I knew that I must come. Charlotte, though he is not present, and I am not him... I must apologize for the actions of Captain Benwick. Indeed, I was as surprised as anyone, for he has always been an honorable man until now, yet what offends me most is that he has committed a grave offense on you. You deserved better, Charlotte. And his actions wound me deeply because they effect more than himself. Indeed, you did deserve better, and I can assure you that time shall heal your wound."

"My wound? My..." Charlotte closed her eyes. "Indeed, you are mistaken sir, but I can assure you that it is not your fault, for I am now shown that my actions rendered me ridiculous—for they were not what I was feeling. Captain, let me put your mind at rest. There may have been many times, where due to my lack of observation and reflection, that I allowed Captain Benwick and me to appear as if we both were fond of each other. Yet it was never the case at all. I never felt anything more than camaraderie for him, nor did he for me. There was no deep affection, just a casual acquaintance. And therefore, he has neither injured me nor imposed upon me."

"But...then this is true?"

"Yes. I never liked Captain Benwick in that way. I rejoice in him choosing another, and only feel sorry for his having to resort to this extreme action to pursue his love."

"Yes, that is unfortunate," he whispered. At a loss of what else to say, he walked over to the fireplace and looked down upon it, quiet from reflection.

"And to think," he said finally, "that I had come here to comfort you."

Charlotte gazed at his broad back as he stared into the fire. "Your actions are admirable and indeed I feel the compliment of them. However, you need not fear. I am well, whole, and completely unaffected by this outcome. I only feel shame of how I allowed myself to look as if Captain Benwick and I were otherwise than what we were."

He turned and looked at her. "It is not your fault, for he was bent on using you as a distraction from his real intentions. And now he is a most fortunate man!"

"You sound as if you envied him."

"He got what he wanted at the great expense of others. And he was able to change his fortune to gaining what he desired. In one way, I envy him very much."

Charlotte looked on him with wonder, trying to find the hint of his meaning, and hoping she was hearing something that she never thought he would say.

"You will not ask me more on this?" he asked.

"I do wish to ask you more on this," Charlotte replied.

"I..." Captain Wentworth began, but then he grew disturbed and began to pace. When that was not enough for him, he leaned against a desk. "Yet perhaps I should not...now that I come to it, I do not know if...Charlotte?"

"Yes?"

"I... I have a confession. I regret that—"

There was a general commotion outside of the inn and there were many shouts along the street. Distracted, and welcoming the distraction, Captain Wentworth went to the window and looked down to hear cries.

"It has begun!"

"It is most tragic!"

"I hoped it would not come to this!"

"Good heavens," Charlotte said, "What is the matter?"

Captain Wentworth looked at her.

"I shall see."

He rushed out of the room and Charlotte followed him. Together they went down the steps as the innkeeper and his wife were sitting in the tavern of the inn, serving their customers amid the commotion.

"What is it?" Captain Wentworth said, mindful of Charlotte being still beside him. "What has occurred?"

"We are now just getting the news," the innkeeper said, "and the town-criers are shouting it all over Lyme. War has finally been declared."

"War?" Charlotte cried. "Between Britain and America?"

"Yes, we have just received the news."

"Indeed," a person sitting at a table said, mid-bite. "The Second War between us has begun."

Charlotte and Captain Wentworth looked upon each other.

"Good heavens," she whispered, "it has finally come to this."


The End


෨෪෩


Don't miss out on your next favorite book!

Join the Satin Romance mailing list
www.satinromance.com/mail.html

## THANK YOU FOR READING

Did you enjoy this book?

We invite you to leave a review at your favorite book site, such as Goodreads, Amazon, Barnes & Noble, etc.

## DID YOU KNOW THAT LEAVING A REVIEW...

- Helps other readers find books they may enjoy.
- Gives you a chance to let your voice be heard.
- Gives authors recognition for their hard work.
- Doesn't have to be long. A sentence or two about why you liked the book will do.

# ABOUT THE AUTHOR

Ney Mitch has been a long-standing Jane Austen enthusiast, having written forty novels that were inspired by her various works. Since stumbling on Miss Austen's books after graduating from college, she has always dabbled in Austen inspired literature, ranging from writing works for teens to adults. Originally, her desire was to adapt Jane Austen's writing in a way to help young adults connect with her, however over time, she has spread her aims to other genres and styles. Having received her BA Degree at Desales University, she is a writer, both literary and dramatic, as well as being a Historic Reenactor.

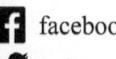 facebook.com/courtney.mitchell.589

 twitter.com/CMMitchelPsyche

 pinterest.com/shebaanna

# ALSO BY NEY MITCH
## WITH SATIN ROMANCE

### *The Memory Series*

Moments of Moments Past

Moments of Moments Present

Moments of Moments Future

Moments of Moments Infinite

### *Pride & Prejudice Reimaginings*

Rapture & Rebellion

Fortune & Misfortune

Desire & Destiny

Pride & Peace

Resolve & Revelations

Hope & Hopelessness

### *Chances Series*

Chances Are

Chances Come

Chances Fade

Chances End

### *Novels*

The Tale of Mr. & Mrs. Bennet: A Pride & Prejudice Christmas Tale

www.ingramcontent.com/pod-product-compliance
Lightning Source LLC
Chambersburg PA
CBHW022030260626
47156CB00017B/1144